A SNOWFLAKE CHRISTMAS

VICKEY WOLLAN

This is a work of fiction. Names, characters, places and incidents either are the product of the author's imagination or are used fictitiously. Any resemblance to actual persons, living or dead, events or locals is entirely coincidental.

To the extent that the image or images on the cover of this book depict a person or persons, such person or persons are merely models, and are not intended to portray any character or characters featured in the book.

Learn more about Vickey Wollan at:

https://vickeywollan.wordpress.com

vickeywollanauthor@yahoo.com

ISBN: 978-1-7355340-1-5

❀ Created with Vellum

To Paul...

Your support, encouragement, and belief in me have made my dream of being a published author come true. You are an extraordinary human being and the best partner on every level possible.

ACKNOWLEDGMENTS

Since this is my first published novel, there are so many people to thank. Let's start at the beginning. My first single-copy book was created as part of Mrs. Connelly's class in elementary school. Being able to hold the paper and cardboard version of a book that contained my story inspired me. In high school my creative writing teacher was Mr. Sulfsted, and my high grades for creativity gave me courage.

Romance Writers of America and the local chapters Central Florida Romance Writers, Volusia County Romance Writers and First Coast Romance Writers provided more knowledge and support than I can begin to describe. The members of these organizations are nurturing and generous beyond words.

Please forgive me if I forget someone. The following published authors have been instrumental to the publication of this book (whether they realize it or not): Ruth Owen, Barbara Whitaker, Connie Mann, Debra Jess, Marie Long, Miriam Carter, Jennifer Santiago, Zena Gardner, Abigail, Sharpe, Alyssa Day, C.L. Thomas, Debby, Grahl, P.K. Brent, Melody Johnson, Leah Miles, Karen Renee, Lia

Davis, Gloria Ferguson, Maggie Fitzroy, Sara Walker, Wynter Daniels, and Catherine Kean.

A special thank you goes to author and Editor Charlee Allden.

I can't begin to thank Abigail Owen of Authors on a Dime for creating a cover that is gorgeous and properly represents the *A Snowflake Christmas* series.

Stacey Johnson Photography did a wonderful job of capturing my playful and carefree self.

Most importantly my family and friends provided unwavering support and encouragement starting with Diane, Bonnie, Dee, Erica, Jill and Kathy B. Thank you to my parents and sister for helping me to believe that if I put my mind to it, I could accomplish anything. The biggest gratitude goes to my husband. He allowed me to follow my dream and gave me a boost every time I needed one. Your love is the greatest gift I've ever been given. Again, thank you so much to one and all.

CHAPTER 1

SNOWFLAKE, MONTANA, WHITEFISH MOUNTAINS

"Achoo."

Rachel Welch twitched when her nephew unleashed a mammoth sneeze directly into the doctor's face. "Oh, Parrot! You didn't."

The doctor turned away quickly and pushed back. Rachel wanted to wave a wand to undo the five-year-old's innocent faux pas but melted into a slouch instead. Not the best way to create a good first impression with the doctor she hoped would become her new boss.

The one-physician clinic had been shut down for months after the unexpected exit of the previous doctor. When the city couldn't afford to pay their salaries, the office manager took a job at the hospital and Rachel, the clinic's only nurse, went back to running the café she had inherited.

Rachel managed to string several words into a coherent sequence as she quelled the need to swallow. "Jacob, sneeze into your shoulder or cover your mouth, please." The request resembled a nursing instructor reprimanding first-year students. Not what she intended. A big pile of regret muddled her mind. Her nurturing side always offered to help even if it made carrying her mammoth load of responsibilities almost impossible.

"I'm sorry," Jacob whispered as he deflated into a blob on the examining table.

His too timid voice and the way the tilt of his face slid toward the floor, kicked her nursing skills into overdrive. Wanting to take back her overzealous response, she scooted closer and smiled. Well, she tried to smile, but her lips didn't seem to receive the message.

Gathering her inner calm, she found the comforting bedside manner her patients had come to appreciate. "The doctor will have you feeling better in no time. Hang in there, sweetie."

This recon mission had her out of sorts. Dr. Alan Garcia might not know she worked as a nurse for the previous doctor. Her main goal was to assist her pregnant sister-in-law. The fact that she could meet the medical office's latest tenant while incognito was an added benefit.

Rat-a-tat-tat-crackle, squeak. The sound of small metal wheels crossing a tile floor stole Rachel's attention. Dr. Garcia glided his low-slung, four-legged stool over to the tiny porcelain sink. She stared at the back of his head, noticing his dark military-cut hairstyle, and braced herself for the range of reactions he might unleash. As he washed his hands, an awkward hush fell over the closet-sized, bare-walled room. The only adornment was a one-foot-tall Christmas tree with about five white lights that didn't blink. But this forlorn pine still did its best to represent the spirit of the season.

For a second Rachel allowed herself an inward grin, but then her stomach did a backflip as she watched. His back still to them, the doctor's long, graceful fingers grabbed a baby wipe and swiped it across his hidden face. Rachel crossed her legs, her foot tapping to an unheard beat, and then she uncrossed them again.

Dr. Garcia laughed, tossing the thin cloth at the trash can and missing it by a mile. His laugh continued, growing louder by the second. A full-body, deep-from-the-belly chuckle rolled out of him like a carnival ride. Her shrinking, tense posture began to relax and regain a dignified position. *Click!* The vault called, *I don't have time for romance in my life,* around her heart unlocked. If not for the ruckus coming from the doctor, Rachel was certain they all would have heard it. Warmth emanated from her very core, oozing up into her chest and settling in for a long stay.

She glanced at the squirming boy, but her focus was pulled to the physician drying his hands. *Hmmm, what wide shoulders you have. Correction,* muscular *wide shoulders.* She shut her eyes briefly and then peered once again at her nephew. He shrugged at her and managed a lopsided smirk. Rachel gave her mouth, currently pressed into a thin line, permission to climb a fraction of an inch on each side as she gave her nephew a gentle pat on the knee.

After one more snicker, the doctor rolled back to her nephew. "Ah, little man, I needed that laugh." Turning to Rachel, he added, "No worries. Not the first time. Won't be the last." She hoped her cheeks remained their already-too-ruddy hue, but she feared the pink grew into red. She wanted to run out the door. Instead, Rachel gave a speedy affirmative head bob, raised the corners of her lips further, and hoped her smile didn't appear falsely manufactured. *Speaking of lips, good gracious his are a pleasant vision.*

As he began to examine Jacob, she mentally shook herself. *He's a doctor and you made a promise to yourself to never date medical men ever again. No amount of good looking can make you break that vow.*

Determined to find fault with Dr. Captivating, Rachel scrutinized every action and method he used to make a diagnosis. She had to admit that he was very thorough. At least Jacob would receive appropriate care.

Putting his stethoscope on his patient's chest Dr. Garcia asked, "Jacob, can you please take a deep breath for me?"

Her nephew inhaled, then sat up straighter than a steel rod, and slapped both palms to his mouth.

She sighed. "Parrot, turn your head." Rachel remained calm, but her words were a cross between a plea for help and a beginner violinist. "Let's not have a repeat performance, please."

Jacob twisted away from Dr. Garcia and barked a loud cough, causing the physician to skate backward on his stool a full foot. "Okay, then. That's going to need a script." Standing, he stepped to a drawer and unlocked it, then pulled out a prescription pad.

With a rustling of the protective tissue paper, Jacob popped off the padded table and crawled into her lap.

Rachel didn't quite know what to think about the lock and key, but it drew her eye and reminded her of the gift she had placed on the counter. "Oh, the bag is for you. That's a loaf of my café's holiday cranberry bread. Welcome to Snowflake." She liked working in the restaurant her parents had built, but nursing was her passion. She just needed to convince the new doctor to hire her since this was the only nursing job for miles.

Dr. Garcia opened the foil and breathed in a deep whiff of the baked good. "How thoughtful. Smells delicious, makes my taste buds water." Surprise flashed across his face, but as he spoke a warmth eased into his words. He stepped toward her. "I guess we'll be seeing a lot of each other, neighbor. Your gift means a lot to me." He started to shake her hand, but Jacob launched into a coughing fit that held him in place.

"Ah, Parrot, sorry you're not feeling well," cooed Rachel while she stroked the small of his back.

As he reached into a glass jar of candy he added, "This might help." The doctor exuded compassion as he redirected his attention to the cuddling boy. Rachel snuck a longer peek at his face, flecks of green and gold sparkled in his hazel eyes. *He's a healer, not a male model—don't gawk.* The scent of cherry, a welcome distraction, tickled her nose. "Can I give your son a lollipop?"

Seeing Jacob's eyes widen, Rachel couldn't help herself. "He's not my son." *Oops, that was a little blunt.* "I mean, I get your confusion since we have the same last name, but he's my nephew." The doctor continued to stare, stone-faced.

"I'm available, you know." She had been fidgeting with the cuff of her sweater, but then her head ricocheted back. She wanted to become the smallest item in the room. Rachel cleared her throat. "Scratch that; I'm single." She flinched, drawing her eyebrows together. "You didn't need to know that either." At first, he pulled back slightly, but then a grin tugged at the corners of his lips until he looked away.

"What I meant to say was, yes, you can give my brother's son the lollipop. His mother is expecting. I'm helping to care for him in case he might be contagious." Rachel reminded herself that this visit allowed her a sneak peek at the new doctor before deciding if she wanted to work for the out-of-towner. Too many local men knew her family name and wanted to cash in on her assumed wealth. Looking down and away, she clamped her mouth together to keep herself from spewing more unnecessary words. *Get a handle on the over-sharing.*

Dr. Garcia handed her nephew the candy. Within a nanosecond, Jacob ripped off the wrapper and began enjoying the sweet treat. With the cutest tussle of Jacob's hair, the doctor asked, "I guess I picked a flavor you like?"

Her chest tightened as she waited, but Parrot didn't speak so she extended her elbow and gave Jacob a nudge. "What do you say?"

"Why that's a grand thing to give a young man," replied the boy.

The doctor's gaze ping-ponged from Rachel to Jacob. His expression conveyed his confusion. Rachel tried to speak but couldn't find the right words.

"Come on, Doc. Don't you wanna play?" Jacob stuck the sucker back in his mouth.

"Um, let me try to explain." She paused and paused some more. "You see, Jacob got his nickname, Parrot, because he does a very good job of repeating the phrases he hears from the adults at our restaurant." She scratched her head and nervously giggled. "His game is for you to figure out who he's imitating." Putting his candy wrapper in her pocket she continued, "Honey, Dr. Garcia hasn't met the folks who hang-out at the café yet."

"But games are my thing. So give me some time, and I'll join in the fun." Revealing his pearly whites, Dr. Garcia relaxed and Rachel began to see his jovial nature. The doctor held out the prescription, by the very corner of the paper, like he didn't want to allow their hands to touch.

Jacob is the one who may be contagious, not me. She mimicked his action as a joke by pinching the opposite corner. His alert but relaxed body language told her the non-contact hand-off pleased him. *What the heck was that? I don't have cooties. Based on his sneeze to the face reaction, he's not a germaphobe.*

"Thank you, Dr. Garcia. Jacob, say thank you to the nice doctor."

But before her nephew could form the words, the white coat was almost out the door. Dr. Garcia turned back, "Welcome. Feel better soon, Jacob. Thanks for the bread." And then he closed the door behind him.

Rachel exhaled with a whoosh, and her eyelids flickered shut.

"What's wrong?" Jacob mumbled around the lollipop.

"Oh, I don't know." Rachel tried to clear the pleasant haze in her mind.

"It's okay, you'll see him soon. He's gotta come to the café so he can play my game."

DR. ALAN GARCIA opened the patient file, placing the electronic tablet on the elbow-high platform just outside the exam room. Staring at the software's preformatted screen, feeling the smooth surface under his hand, he urged his fingers to type the notes he needed. His face tilted down and his forehead touched the wall.

Propped against the side of the hallway like an out-of-place mannequin, his thoughts overpowered him and he whispered aloud. "I hope all my neighbors are as nice as she is." *What a beautiful lady inside and out.*

Family meant everything to Alan and seeing that quality in his neighbor gave him hope he would like his new home. While running a business and caring for her nephew, she still made a point to bring him a gift. Old-fashioned manners and family values. Just the type of woman he hoped would be his bride someday. But not now. He needed to get the medical clinic functioning smoothly again.

Instead of concentrating on his work, a snapshot flashed across his mind. That hair. *I want to get lost in those long, soft waves.* Her dark hair flowed down the back of her five-foot, seven-inch frame. The curve of her hips had caught his attention until his need to remain professional made him look away. What was that sweet smell, he wondered? Note to self—investigate the cause of her intoxicating aroma. Shampoo, or maybe soap?

The sounds of high heels and heavy boots on the tile floor barreling toward him pulled him from his daydreaming, dislodging his pose.

"Yoo-hoo! Dr. Garcia. We won't take much of your time."

He straightened to attention, struggling to suppress a salute. He'd recognized the voice in an instant. His everything's-fine smile glided onto his face.

"Mrs. Jameson! Oh, and Mrs. Wilson too. How nice to see you ladies. Please thank Mayor Jameson and Sheriff Wilson for giving you time out of their offices to come see me." Alan drew on every spare ounce of self-control to sound calm.

If these two town matriarchs walked shoulder-to-shoulder, their energetic presence could block out the sun. But he could see his office manager, also known as his mother, tip-toeing over so she could be seen between his unexpected guests as they marched forward. Teresa silently mouthed, "Sorry."

Mrs. Wilson was dressed in a brown uniform as if she were one of the city's police officers, but with no official markings, and Mrs. Jameson looked more like a plus-size fashion model for the Park Avenue boutiques most folks couldn't afford. *What an unlikely pair to be best friends.*

"Howdy," chortled Mrs. Wilson, giving Alan a hearty slap on the back.

Alan, not expecting the enthusiastic greeting, came off his heels, launching forward until his face came less than an inch from the green cellophane wrapping on the basket carried by Mrs. Jameson. *I appreciate a strong woman, but geez what a way to say hello.* Righting himself, Alan gestured down the corridor. "Ladies, please step into my office."

Just then, he saw Rachel and Jacob exit the exam room. Alan felt his feet fix themselves in place. "Thanks again for the bread. I'm looking forward to meeting your sister-in-law and the rest of the

Welch family." Alan knew his unexpected guests had influence in this tiny town but building a relationship with all of his neighbors was also important. Rachel glanced in his direction and his heart rate rose. The three women greeted each other with great affection. *I want that. Maybe Rachel can help me find that?*

Mrs. Wilson released Rachel from a bear hug allowing her feet to touch the floor again. "Good to see you've met Rachel. She'll be a big help in getting you aquatinted with Snowflake. Mark my words."

"I won't keep you ladies from your mission." Rachel took Jacob by the hand and turned toward the lobby.

Alan wanted to follow her, one leg stepped toward her, but he remembered his workspace was full of Christmas decorations. He had left them overflowing like they were trying to escape from their boxes when his first patient had arrived early. Alan couldn't let his important guests see he had left a chore unfinished. He preferred to handle his responsibilities on his own. Relying on handouts to get by during his childhood had left him with a festering wound. Alan waved goodbye to Rachel while she could still see him, then scurried ahead of his critical callers.

Business first. She's your neighbor, bound to see her again soon. He led the ladies into the room, then to follow privacy protocol, he closed his office door. He did his best to reposition the Christmas trimmings back in their storage bins, or at least onto his cot, as Mrs. Jameson and Mrs. Wilson placed two baskets on his desk.

Alan recognized that the green basket covering was paired with an orange one. "What a thoughtful gesture, you remembered I'm a University of Miami alum," offered Alan, taking a seat at his second-hand pressboard desk. Each woman pulled up a worn plastic patio chair facing the lone piece of office furniture and sat down.

"Oh, dear. Is that paint I smell?" asked Mrs. Jameson, fanning her silk scarf under her primly turned-up nose.

"Look, Heidi, it's pale yellow!" Mrs. Wilson bellowed like she was talking to recruits, and Alan almost jumped to attention.

"Yes Irene, my vision is just fine, thank you," scoffed Mrs. Jameson, rolling her eyes. "Did you get written permission to paint?" She waved her scarf with escalating speed.

"Yes, ma'am. Directly from the mayor himself, and he approved the color, too." Alan fidgeted in his folding chair and added, "I thought I'd bring some sunshine from my home state since the Montana winters are so long and dreary. Eggshell white felt too sterile and institutional."

Mrs. Jameson threw her scarf back over her shoulder, shaking her head from side to side, and bit out, "Don't let the city hall PR staff hear you talking like that."

Alan froze, jaw dropped. *Did I just accidentally put my foot in my mouth?*

Pushing the orange basket forward, Mrs. Wilson laughed out loud. "The city hall staff is just us. Heidi, who are you kidding? What was the last census count—population 532?" Turning her attention back to the desk, she added, "These gifts are compliments of the Snowflake City Council. The orange basket is filled with winter survival supplies. Our town is small, and this clinic is the only medical care for 100 square miles. You'll be busier than you know, with no time to prepare for our harsh winters."

Interrupting, Mrs. Jameson joined in, "And the green one is overflowing with non-perishable food you can eat at the office while treating the heavy flow of patients. The 90-day probationary period to retain this job will just fly by. But, don't worry; I'm sure you'll manage to pass...somehow."

Jumping up, Mrs. Wilson swatted her dark tan cowboy hat across her thigh. "Come on, Heidi, get a move on. We've taken up enough of the busy doctor's time." Thrusting out her right hand, she waited for his perfunctory shake.

Standing with grace, Mrs. Jameson sauntered to the door, then called back, "He needs his fingers to work—don't break them with your arm-wrestling grip."

The lower portion of Alan's body came to parade-rest, and he was about to allow his palm to touch hers, but stopped, eyebrows rising. Mrs. Wilson adjusted her offering to a fist bump, and Alan obliged with an inward sigh when his fear of losing his ability to work, eased. "Please thank the council members for me," shouted Alan before the town's most prominent women got out of earshot. *Don't worry about the 90-day probation? Well, I wasn't, but I am now.*

As he left to treat his next patient, Alan took a moment to internalize the latest messages received. Writing down his goals always helped him prioritize. With a fresh batch of anxiety levied upon him, his list commenced:

1. *Pass the 90-day new hire probationary period.*
2. *Keep mom safe.*
3. *Find a way to keep my expenses from growing beyond my control.*
4. *Ask Rachel Welch on a date.*

Tossing the pen on the desk, he folded his arms across his chest. Then picking the pen up again, he drew a circle around goal number four. Romance shouldn't be on his mind, but something about Rachel kept bringing his thoughts back to wanting to see her again. *How can I make our first date memorable? Will she even say yes?*

Then he stuffed the list into the shredding machine adjacent to his desk with a zrr, zrr, zrr…

CHAPTER 2

Rachel sat with core muscles tense in Mrs. Wilson's SUV as they raced out of town.

"Thanks again for doing this. I didn't know what else to do," said Mrs. Wilson, pushing the gas pedal down a bit more.

"No problem, always glad to help. The café was slow tonight." A couple of days had passed since Rachel had met Alan and now she was going to be providing medical care as part of the town's volunteer fire and rescue squad. He was sure to hear about it. First thing tomorrow morning, she planned on walking across the street to tell Dr. Garcia about her BS-RN degree. She would tell him she hadn't wanted to seem like she was questioning his capabilities with Jacob, so she'd respectfully withheld that fact. *He'd understand her intentions, wouldn't he?*

Irene's car resembled the SUVs used by the sheriff's department, except without the sirens and flashing lights. The big red holiday bow that flapped in the wind on the front grill was also a dead giveaway that this vehicle was not a real police car. Rachel had to look out the side window to hide her chuckling reaction to the flowing ribbons' flight.

The distraction she needed from her latest batch of budget revisions was offered by the Montana big sky just as the orange hues of dusk appeared. No towering buildings marred the expansive blue that made her feel at home. She could zone out on clouds all day but on an emergency call was not the time.

Rachel made her medical training the focus of her mind, while she monitored the horizon. She pulled off her hairnet and replaced it with her favorite knit cap. "What type of injuries should I be prepared for?"

"I'm so sorry, not sure." Mrs. Wilson slapped her palm to her forehead and then returned it to the wheel. "I just wanted to help and didn't ask."

Patting her frantic companion's shoulder, Rachel replied, "Like you said, the doc is already out on a call and all of the deputies too. Full moon, small town, minimal staff, we do what we can." She checked her backpack's first aid kit to confirm what tools she'd have to provide care. Looking out the windshield, she could see smoke billowing toward the darkening sky ahead. *You got this*. While sitting motionless, eyes closed for a quick stress management exercise, Rachel gathered her thoughts until the car lurched to a stop.

"The caller told me to look for the campfire by the lake. This must be it," commented Irene her voice steady and low. "The lady said they were by the pavilion."

Before Rachel could ask any more questions, Irene swung the door open wide and started running. Following close behind her, Rachel blinked often due to the burning in her eyes caused by the smoke as she scanned the scene looking for victims. At least the smell was of wood, not plastic or any other man-made materials.

A no-frills Jeep stood alone on the far side of the partially enclosed wooden structure. The walls that were designed to keep out the cold wind also blocked her view. Crackling came from the roaring fire positioned between the cement slab and the water's edge. Rounding the building to the open side that faced the lake, Rachel stumbled into Irene, who had stopped without warning.

"Oh, that's my ride. Gotta go, toodles." Mrs. Jameson stood from a picnic table, waving at Mrs. Wilson. She had been speaking to a man, not ten feet away from where Mrs. Wilson had halted.

"What the..." Regaining her balance, Rachel looked to see if Heidi was in distress. Mrs. Jameson seemed to be her usual picture of health. Staring at one matriarch and then the other, she anticipated their explanation. Silence.

Irene did a military about-face, giving Rachel a sideways nudge as she returned from whence she'd come. Heidi picked up her pace, doing her best to match her footsteps with Irene's.

"Hey, where are you going? What about the..." Rachel's fists found her hips and she kept herself from letting out a heavy sigh. Before she could utter another word, Rachel realized she was not the only person being left behind. A man with his back to her wearing a red, white and blue ski jacket also rose from his heavy wooden seat. A basket rested atop the worn surface of the table. "What are you doing?" Rachel called out to the backs of the two meddling friends. *Setting me up for a blind date, again.* "Why?" *Don't you think I'm able to pick my dates?*

Without another word, the ladies climbed into the still idling SUV and drove off into the brisk night. Rachel ran after them a few steps then yanked her hat off in utter frustration before trudging back to the non-rescue scene. *Whose cousin just moved to town this time?* Resigned to her fate, Rachel allowed the sparkle of the emerging stars to improve her mood. She prepared to introduce herself, but the faux-date was not just another random man. Her breathing stopped, thoughts ceased, eyes stared.

"What just happened?" asked Dr. Garcia. He had a smile on his face, but his body language was all kinds of rigid.

"Well, um...you've met our city's managerial women, right?" Rachel, without knowing, switched on her good-manners autopilot. She tugged to straighten her woolen scarf, jammed her hat in her pocket and tucked her hair behind her ears. The last move with her hair always betrayed her poker face to those who knew her. "They mean well, but they have a habit of interjecting their own will for the good of townsfolk." She grinned at the ground but wanted to see his eyes—his beautiful, heavily-lashed eyes with their dancing flecks of hazel. Instead, she turned and walked toward the fire, needing to sneak a respite from her reaction to the man who had starred in last night's dreams.

Rachel knew the locals held grudges when an outsider didn't understand the unspoken be a good neighbor code, and she figured helping the doctor would get her back to working as a nurse sooner. *Act like last night's dream didn't happen.*

"Here's a crash course on the tiny piece of the world called Snowflake. Not sure if you heard. One of our largest employers, the mill, in the Lodgepole Valley shut down a couple of weeks back. That'll have wide-reaching effects on everyone for miles." Rachel shuffled a bit closer to the flickering flames. "Um, folks here have always used an alternative payment method..."

She paused distracted by the glimmer of a new star as the darkness of evening fell around them. "Well, let's just call it Snowflake currency. We pay for things with equivalent services or good deeds. You know bartering. I expect that's gonna happen a lot until the mill re-opens."

She could hear his footsteps grow louder as he joined her.

"I thought my meeting with Mrs. Jameson had something to do with my 90-day probation?" Alan's voice faltered. "She called me saying we needed to talk."

Rachel could see him making the air quotations. She glanced further over her shoulder and the concern on his face made her heart sink. *Is this a romantic set-up or a nursing interview?*

She raised her palms toward the comforting warmth. "I have no idea." She made a point of allowing him to view her expression. Rachel wanted him to see the honesty conveyed on her face. "I've never heard that the city council could run a doctor out of town. The probation concept is the mayor's latest procedural change of many." She shrugged. "I think that's Mrs. Jameson's odd, but helpful tactic to get you quickly acclimated to Snowflake. Has anyone offered to pay you in free-range eggs?" Rachel moved to the stone bench close to the blaze and propped her feet on the loose rocks used to enclose the fire pit.

"Wow, never. But I'll adapt. I have too." He tipped his face up to the twilight sky and sat in silence for a moment. "So, this probation thing, do you think I'm overreacting?" Alan burrowed his fist into his coat. "I've always gotten high marks on my medical care, I think probation for a doctor is overkill." He extended his legs pushing his feet next to hers. "I was going to ask each council member for guidance via email." He shifted his weight. "Too much? It's just so important to me, to us—Mom and I." His head dropped, as did his volume when he mentioned his mother.

Alan took a beat before he spoke again. His voice grew louder his confidence seeming to rebound, and then he pointed past the pavilion enclosure. "My Jeep's here. I can take you home. No need for you to be dragged into my office politics."

"I've dealt with the mayor enough to expect his maneuvering. I'm already embroiled in his politics. You didn't drag me anywhere." Rachel found herself enjoying his company and wanted to extend the conversation. "Okay, next question. When you handed me Jacob's script, your fingers barely had a hold of the paper. Why?" She anticipated this explanation with a grin.

Alan let loose one of his full belly laughs that drew Rachel closer. "My overreaction to bedside manner training."

She didn't want to be mesmerized by him, but she could feel herself falling for his self-deprecating comedy act. "Need more details please."

"I try to get people to look at my smile and not freak-out about the medication." He flashed a view of his toothy grin, and a hint of mischief crossed his face. "Oh, and I got poor marks during a role play because my thumb covered the name of the drug." An energetic sparkle danced into his eyes. "Found out later that my pseudo-patient had the hots for me. I had no idea." He zipped up his coat until the collar reached his chin. "Hopefully my being too fastidious hasn't had a different negative effect."

She shrugged and gave him a wry grin. "Too funny," Rachel giggled. It felt so comfortable to talk with Alan. "New subject." She made a point to not look in his direction. "How much do you know about why Snowflake needed to hire a new doctor?"

Rachel felt his heat when he settled closer to her side. An inch of space kept his clothing from touching hers. "The mayor said he was drawn back to the big city to be closer to family." With a move that looked more relaxed than she guessed he was feeling, Alan opened his arms to spread them across the back of the bench. "Do you know what they didn't tell me?"

"I do." Rachel picked up a stray pebble while gathering her thoughts. *Just be honest. Tell him what he needs to know.* "I guess I should have told you the day we met." She let the dance of the fire inspire her next words. "I'm going to be straight with you because I respect you." *And I think you're handsome as hell.* "I worked for our last physician, Dr. Remington, as his nurse. I'm an RN."

Without stopping, before she lost her courage, she charged on. "He left because of me." Rachel paused to let her confession sink in. Not that she could see the inner working of his mind, but she knew he had to be processing her revelation. Alan carried himself in a way that made his intellect take center stage. Sexy. That was the only way she could describe it.

"Oh, good to know."

Rachel heard a bit of surprise and what she hoped was gladness in his well-guarded response, but she didn't want to let her yearning to be working as a nurse cloud her interpretation of his words.

Rachel reminded herself that Miami had a higher concentration of nurses than Snowflake. *He doesn't realize I'm the only nurse in town.* "You did a great job with Parrot. Thanks again."

"My pleasure." His chest puffed out just a bit as he sat taller, but then he rubbed his end of day whisker stubble. "Are you at liberty to tell me why Dr. Remington left?" Rachel suspected his anticipation got the better of him as she watched his heels bounced in and out of the snow. "Did you witness malpractice?" Still waiting, he leaned in toward her. Rachel caught a waft of his musky cologne. *Nice.*

"Oh, nothing like that. In fact, just the opposite." Rachel leaned back and allowed the worn granite seat to carry all of her weight. Her free-flowing hair touched the sleeve of his padded coat. "This is going to sound like I'm conceited, but I'm not." His head tilted her way with a blank stare. "No really, I'm not." She sighed. "In these parts, I'm one of a very few eligible women my age. I grew up here, so I'm not going to bolt after a harsh winter. I'm educated and financially stable. That's why men ask me to marry them all the time."

Alan stiffened and snapped his arms to his side. "Huh?!"

She snickered her way through the rest of her answer. "It's hard to explain. You know that saying, always a bridesmaid, never a bride. Well, I'm always asked, but still never a bride. A girl has the right to hold out for love, right?"

Rachel hesitated, watching Alan tighten the scarf around his neck before she ventured on. "Seriously." She nudged his shoulder with her own, trying to make her next sentence the punch line of a twisted joke. "The prior doc..." Rachel went silent for a beat to make certain Alan understood she was about to answer his original question. "He asked me to elope, having never dated me, not so much as a kiss. When I said, no—he closed up shop and left town."

Alan blinked. "His loss, he should have tried harder."

"What?" Rachel's head popped up and her eyes widened.

"I get it. You're smart, attractive. He needed to have his head examined for not getting to know you and then compounded his mistake by giving up too soon."

"You think I'm good looking?" Rachel completed a hair toss maneuver that landed a large chunk of it over the back of the bench. *What are you doing? That's so not you.* She cleared her throat. "I mean, right. His loss. He found out about my family history and tried to cash in." *Oops, now I've got to explain that too.*

She saw the stiffness soften in his posture. With an unintentional look up, her eyes found his and locked in place. "Has anyone ever told you you're easy to talk to?"

Without releasing the strength of his piercing stare, his head moved side to side. Rachel's confidence wavered. Having the Welch name had caused her to lose more than one possible suitor. *Wait a minute. You want to work for this guy, not date him. Remember? Besides he doesn't need to know you're paying your parents' medical bills.* She needed to find an escape route fast. "Have you looked inside the picnic basket," she asked with a playful lilt in her voice. "Our hostesses may be a bit conniving, but they know their way around a kitchen." *Saved by the food.*

Alan leaped off the rocky surface and then tried to not look eager as he peered at the pavilion. "No." He licked his lips. "I'm glad you're okay to stay." As he made a mad dash to the table he called back, "I didn't have time for lunch, so I'm starving." Genuine joy beamed from his face as he threw open the basket. "On the menu tonight, we have… Wait, everything is in separate containers." His face contorted, and he took a double-take.

She busted out laughing. "Say what?"She attempted to get control over her cackling. "You see, I have this thing and the ladies of city hall have known me all my life." Rachel also peered into the basket and hauled out plates with compartments. "I prefer that my foods don't touch each other." Her face warmed and she knew it had to be displaying several shades of pink and rose, but she didn't care. Having an unexpected night off and eating dinner with a sophisticated big city man under a glorious sky was not a bad consolation prize for being the victim of the buttinski duo, after all.

Then Rachel saw a fresh-cut piece of mistletoe among the food. *Oh, dear. Can't let him see that.* She shoved it to the bottom of the basket and covered it with a napkin. "I'll set up supper. Can you please tend the fire? Did you build it?"

Alan moved to the bonfire pit again. "I know how to build a fire, but I followed Heidi's exacting specifications. I thought this was some kind of test." Rachel kept catching herself stealing looks while Alan built up the burning embers. The flutter of the flames only enhanced his fetching silhouette.

"Oh my! Irene really wants us to have fun. Look what I found." Rachel held up an unopened bottle of 12-year-old Irish whiskey. "Yes! And fixings for s'mores too." Rachel acted like she didn't hear Alan's stomach growl when he climbed onto the wooden bench. "Whether he knew it or not, the sheriff played his part in this charade, too." She presented his dinner. "Fresh caught bluegill, no doubt Chuck's handiwork. Mrs. Wilson makes the best-baked lemon pepper fish." *The sheriff has a bad heart, but I'll let him tell you that.*

Stillness settled over them as they devoured the props used to get them together under false pretenses. Eating outdoors was one of Rachel's favorite things, so thoughts of how she'd gotten to be doing it faded away. Rachel gawked at the moonbeams bouncing off the lake, snuck as many views in Alan's direction as she dared. *I wonder when he's going to hire his nurse.*

Having eaten his last bite of food, Alan lowered his fork, asking without warning,

"What?" He leaned toward her. "I can almost see the question rolling around in your head."

Rachel shifted her gaze without moving her head. *Is he reading my mind?*

He hesitated, just a second, and made a funny face. "I'm a straight shooter." Alan pulled on his belt imitating a gun holster and pronounced his words with a cowboy twang.

Rachel couldn't contain her giggling as she moved to stand by the base of a fallen tree adjacent to the campfire. "Was that supposed to be John Wayne? What'd you do, watch westerns before you moved here?" She took this jovial moment to open the alcohol and give him one finger in a rocks glass. To her pleasant surprise, he sipped it without choking or coughing. Not all city men could drink whiskey straight-up.

Smiling, seeming uninsulted, he responded, "Nah. Been a Wayne fan since I was a boy." Flashing another brilliant smile and grabbing the bag of marshmallows, he wandered over to the fire. "What's the question?" In the distance, a car drove by with Christmas music playing so loud they could hear an entire verse of *Oh Holy Night* as it passed. Rachel gave Alan a sideways glance and mouthed the words in an overly dramatic pantomime. They both laughed.

She picked up the chocolate and graham crackers and planted herself on the stump next to the rock bench where he sat. "This is none of my business, so you don't have to answer." Skewering several marshmallows, she lowered her head. "I don't mean to pry, but why did you move here? I heard your interview answer, but you uprooted your medical practice from Florida to Montana. Why?" She saw a fleeting moment of emotion she couldn't ascertain. Then 'the veil' fell over his expression. *Oh, no. Doc, I've seen that move before. You're turning on your inner calm. Busted.*

He took a sip of his drink. "You were at the interview?"

"Of course. Me and most of the business owners on Main Street." She paused, hoping he wouldn't clam up now. "You were hired over the other candidates because you had additional education and experience with emergency medicine and obstetrics than most general practice physicians. Doctors without Borders, impressive." Rachel built herself a s'more. "Councilman Bodaway Crow, being his proactive self, advised us that most doctors get investigated during their careers, and no charges or penalties meant you were innocent." She took a long slow inhale allowing Alan to confirm or deny her assumption.

"Correct." He pointed at her like a game show host congratulating a contestant.

She wondered why she hadn't noticed before that along with his alluring hazel eyes, Alan possessed a strong, square jawline. He was her type. Not that she wanted to have a type, but his face had something unique and fetching about it. She became a giddy schoolgirl inside, her heart raced and her palms sweaty. *Hold it together. He's a medical man.*

"Been waiting for someone to call me out on that obvious detail." He popped a cold marshmallow in his mouth. Rachel froze, trying not to stare, but something about seeing the motion of his lips sucked her in.

She saw his long eyelashes blink, and it became clear to her that he was waiting for her to say something. "Continue." *Remember, you're not interested in dating him or anyone right now.* She swallowed and looked away, all the way away. "Please continue."

"The long version is the only way it makes sense, so settle in." He poured her another shot and proceeded. "Back in August, a hurricane blew through Miami. Widespread power outages, gas shortages, gang looting. They broke in and stole my prescription pads." He shook his head and Rachel thought the veil would break, but it didn't.

"The FDA traced black market opioid scripts back to me. I'd seen what addiction could do to a person and their families, so I forwarded the security tapes from my office. The camera's back-up battery had lasted longer than any of us expected." He tossed another marshmallow into his beautiful mouth and took a taste of whiskey. The veil slipped ever so slightly. "I'm off the hook with the FDA. Still paying off the lawyers' fees for my defense. But, then the gang started retaliating when some of their members got caught in a law enforcement sting."

Wow, that must have been scary. When he starred at the ground for a long moment, it gave her time to process the magnitude of the events that had changed the course of his life and brought him to Snowflake. He had opened up to her. That was a good start. Maybe if she gave him space, he would feel comfortable telling her a bit more. Rachel offered him a warm s'more and made one for herself.

They sat in companionable silence. She held his gaze and hoped he would see her understanding in her face. Clouds cleared away, allowing the moon's light to brighten the solemn mood. "We've got our fair share of ruffians here, but no gangs." She hoped her comment would encourage him to keep going. To her surprise, when their fingers connected during the s'more handoff, the veil fell away.

He hesitated, lifted his chin and then started talking. "They targeted my mom to make me pay. The prank calls came first. Then a virus via email." His voice began to shake. "Next a brick through her living room window." Rachel couldn't help herself. She covered his hand with her own and squeezed. He sandwiched her hand between his and returned the supportive gesture. "My full name was in the news often and my patients stopped making appointments, the insurance companies investigated me, and my office manager quit out of frustration and fear."

He cleared his throat. "The bills started piling up from attorneys, private investigators and security staff." He finished off the glass she had poured him. Rachel offered the bottle, but he shrugged it off. "I became a doctor to make my late *padre* proud, but my patients were too scared to enter my office." His shoulders slumped and his voice trailed off.

Alan got up and scooched over to share her stump with her. She welcomed his warmth. "I was more nervous about my mother's safety when I first came here. The inquisition I endured from the city council was nothing." He raised his feet onto the stone fire barrier to warm them, but then his gaze shifted to her face and his voice softened to a whisper. "Okay, I just bared my darkest secret. Your turn."

The companionship he provided sitting next to her was intoxicating, more so than the whiskey. She hesitated, thinking.

"Sorry, I had no right to ask. I'll take you home." Alan got up as if to leave.

"No! I mean, no, I want to tell you." Rachel captured his hand for the briefest moment and tugged him back. His new position on the stump was even closer than before. Her breath hitched, but she fought to continue. "I mean, I asked you first, so it's only fair that I tell you about my family too." Alan held a batch of marshmallows out for roasting and waited.

"The Welch family helped found the town of Snowflake. I come from generations of cattle ranchers. People here assume if your name is Welch, then you're loaded." Rachel felt herself lean away while waiting for his reaction. *Here's where people either latch-on or think I'm spoiled*. Most men, in particular, misunderstood her attempt to explain money didn't drive her.

"Ah, that's what you meant by—cash in." Alan went to give her a one-armed hug but stopped. "Sorry, my problems are on the other end of the spectrum." He allowed the cap of his shoulder to nudge hers like a teasing big brother. My *madre* worked long hours, but we still lived in subsidized housing." His normal confidence drained from his body as he expressed his truth.

"I had scholarships for college and med school, but at thirty when I opened my private practice I had no idea one hurricane and tangle with the DEA could put my finances into a red ink spiral." He sighed. "I was barely making payroll let alone the rent and trying to help my mom pay down her credit cards before the storm." Alan stopped talking his gaze locked onto the dance of the flames.

As if he had shut a door to his past, Alan turned to face her. His expression went from serious to curious. "I doubt I'd be able to understand your circumstances. But like you, I'm not motivated by money." He shifted on the rock and blew his warm exhale into his cupped ungloved hands. "Being wealthy is a problem?"

Rachel took a big bite of the freshly smashed s'more he'd made for her, leaving a chocolate smear on her cheek. "It can be." She had spoken with her mouth full so she quickly chomped down again, but then swallowed without further chewing to explain. "Some folks get all weird. They act differently when they find out, try to take advantage."

"I won't." Alan twisted to bring his face closer to hers, bridging the distance she had put between them. "I'm guessing lots of people say that. Time will prove my words are true."

The next bit of silence became uncomfortable. Even the crackle of the fire didn't help. He was right. She'd heard that pledge too many times to count. Rachel choked on her fear and the sugary dessert couldn't fix it.

"See if this is a little bit similar? Maybe I can relate another way."

Rachel didn't hold out much hope, but she had to give him props for trying. "I'm listening."

Alan wolfed down his food this time. "I don't know what it is about being a doctor."

She didn't move a muscle. *He's trying. Give him a chance.*

Alan assumed a position that resembled the Thinker statue. "I didn't date much. Books became my companions. But when my med school acceptance news spread, women chased after me." He stared at his empty glass. "Made no sense. I hadn't changed. But I think that in a smaller fashion it's like the shift you feel from people?"

Rachel mirrored his pose. "Maybe." She wouldn't let herself be swayed by his offer of compassion. But the step was in a favorable direction.

"I bet if we worked side by side my not-a-gold-digger status would be made clearer faster." There was a genuine smile on his face, but then he waited not breathing as if to make certain she caught his meaning.

Her eyebrows shot up. She had been waiting so long to work as a nurse again. "Are you offering me a nursing position at the clinic?"

CHAPTER 3

Just as Alan was about to step into another exam room, he felt a tug on his lab coat and turned. His mother grabbed his wrist and led him toward his office. Since this was not her usual behavior and she had grown a bit pale in the last hour, he followed her even though he could see the waiting room was uncomfortably crowded.

"I need to ask you something," said Teresa as she closed the door behind them. She pointed at his desk. "You eat, I'll talk."

Alan's digital watch showed three in the afternoon and his breakfast was devoured before six so his hunger outvoted his empathy for his new patients. "What's up?"

Teresa strode toward the window facing Main Street and then rounded to begin her stride heading for the opposite wall. Alan ripped the wrapper off an energy bar and took a big bite to keep himself from grinning. He held a napkin up in front of his face, so his mom didn't see him talking with his mouth full, "You're pacing. That means you're worried." A worried mother he could deal with but a scared *madre*, like in Miami, that had pushed his composure to his limit.

She stopped at the dilapidated plastic chair. "I expected a backlog of appointments to be rescheduled, but people are standing in line out in the cold." The energy from her feet found its way to her hands and then she rubbed one atop the other. "This woman showed up. She said she's a nurse, saw the line and came over to volunteer her services."

Alan tried to breathe through his food but choked. "Does she have beautiful hair?" He coughed and gulped down some water. "Is her hair dark and long?" He swallowed hard. "Is her name Rachel?'

Teresa's head flinched back and then she frowned. "How did you know that?"

"I offered her the nursing job last night."

"You what?" She threw her hands in the air and let them fall limp to her side.

"She's lived here her whole life and worked for the prior doctor." Alan dumped some peanuts straight from the jar into his mouth.

"Didn't we agree to wait until we could see what the normal patient volume would be before we hired anyone?" His mother's back was to him as she started the path to the window again, her arms hugging herself.

"Correct. I didn't give her a date of hire, haven't discussed salary. She used the word volunteer, right?" Alan chugged the last of the water and scooped up a handful of butter mints.

"She did. But do you know the depth of her skills? Trust her?"

Alan stopped to hug his mom. With his mouth full again he managed to say, "Yep."

"I just want you to be cautious, but I do respect your intuition when it comes to the staff you hire." Both of Teresa's thumbs flipped up and she smiled.

Then he flung open the door and put his stride in double-time to get a glimpse of the woman who had fascinated him the prior evening. Today's view did not disappoint.

He caught sight of her before she realized he had joined the crowd. Dressed in all white, including her shoes and the bow in her hair, Rachel held a clipboard and was signing in patients. Alan took a moment to watch the good people of Snowflake's reaction to having her back in service. Everyone knew her name and the warmth between her and each person confirmed his suspicions. His soon to be nurse was beloved by her neighbors and a natural caregiver.

The thud of Alan's heart perplexed him and, with breathlessness in his voice that he didn't comprehend, he called out to her. "Thank you, Rachel. Welcome. I'll be in the exam rooms or my office if you need anything."

Her acknowledgment of his presence glued him to the floor. It took all his will to get his body to move from her sight. As the day wore on, minor miracles came to life as he worked with her. Although their paths rarely crossed and they said only work-related words to each other, the fact that she was in his office, assisting in the treatment of his patients, made him happy. He hadn't felt this self-assured since before the storm in Miami. If his fate was to move to Montana so he could meet her, work with her and get to know her better, then he could make peace with the events that steered him to her.

As Alan escorted his last patient to the exit, he couldn't help from beaming when he saw his mother and Rachel sitting behind the reception desk together. Camaraderie had grown between them more than he experienced with any other coworker. All tension left his body. He could work the long hours, do without the creature comforts as long as these two women were safe and happy. Before Alan could join them, a cold rush of air had their heads turning.

A monster-sized man entered. The hood of his coat scraped the top of the door frame. He surveyed his surroundings before speaking. "Rach, Sophie told me you were here. I'm bringing you those Welch Holdings, Inc. financial documents as promised." A warmth flowed in his voice, but his scruffy longish hair and beard reminded Alan of Sasquatch and put him on edge. Rachel stood with a smile and Alan's trepidations began to melt.

"This is my brother Brett." She took the envelope he offered. "Brett this is Dr. Garcia and his mother Teresa."

The Paul Bunyan doppelganger waved hello, but then hitched his thumb over his shoulder. "I need to explain a few things, so you'll be prepared. Can we chat at the café?"

"Sure. I think we're done for today."

And in the briefest of moments, she was gone. The coolness in the office grew, not because of the evening air, but because Alan's confidence seemed to thrive when she was around. He hoped she would be able to volunteer again tomorrow.

THE CALL from the mayor had come just after Rachel and Brett had left the night before. Alan was to arrive for a 9:15 AM meeting to review the status of his 90-day probation. The tone in the man's voice had him worried. Alan had given up the rest of his evening to pull together the updated stats he used to negotiate reimbursement with insurance companies. He was confident the town would be pleased with their return on investment based on the first week of operations, but he didn't appreciate having to reschedule his early morning appointments. The day's load was heavy as ever. Well, at least his mother could say the command performance requested by the city council had caused his unexpected absence.

A sucker punch hit Alan's gut when he walked into the designated room. Everyone else must have arrived at nine o'clock because they were all in place and all business. Tripping over a chair, Alan looked at his watch.

"You're on time, Dr. Garcia. Please have a seat," requested the mayor, his voice booming with authority.

The city officials all sat on one side of a row of tables, looking out toward the entryway. The sheriff and his wife, seemingly spectators, sat with their backs against the wall, and two lone empty chairs faced the inquiry panel. Alan felt a bead of sweat roll down his back in the otherwise austere and chilly room. Placing his briefcase on the floor by one of the inquisition seats, he pulled out copies of the reports he'd created.

"Let it show for the record that Sheriff Charles Wilson is here as a witness, and Irene Wilson will be today's scribe." The mayor cleared his throat. "Let's have the council members reintroduce themselves to our good doctor. I'll start. Mayor William Jameson." He pointed to one end of the table.

Alan did his best to focus and relax, but his foot wanted to tap the floor, and he circled his pen between his fingers. *These are kind folks,* he reminded himself. Alan didn't understand the stuffy protocol until he saw a camera positioned over the mayor's head. The recording equipment had him and the spare chair in its crosshairs. *Great. Let's interrogate a doctor, caught on tape.*

At least the friendliest face started. "Bodaway Crow, owner, Trading Post."

"Rene Brown, manager, Main Street Savings and Loan."

"Jackson Lively, owner, Lively Veterinarian Clinic."

"Brenda Ito, attorney at law."

Cracking open his bottled water, Alan took a sip and stifled his need to cough. "Nice to see you all again, ladies and gentlemen. I brought a repo—"

"Let me get to the point," interrupted the mayor. "We'll review your report later. Today's fact-gathering session has two primary agenda items." He paused until Alan put down the papers he was holding. "Finding funding to join the co-op established to reopen the mill and deciding if the city needs to subsidize your practice so you can hire a nurse. You see, one expenditure influences the other."

Alan did his best to keep his jaw from hitting the floor. "Um. And what does the council want from me?"

Councilman Crow rescued him. "We hear good things about your ability to give quality medical care, but more services can be given if you hired a nurse. Based on your budget projections, when will that occur?"

The mayor refused to be upstaged. "We want you to hire someone as quickly as possible and we'll pay that employee's salary to make it happen."

Alan didn't know what to feel. *Okay, I'm not being fired, but they think I'm bleeding red ink all over my balance sheet in my first week?* He wanted to scratch his head but remembered the camera. "I planned to hire an RN just after the New Year. Is that not soon enough?"

The town vet must have felt his pain because he jumped into the fray. "Dr. Garcia, the council understands the economic impact the mill's closing has had on many of our citizens' ability to pay for your treatment. Our obligation is to our constituents to use the city's resources to provide the services we feel they most need. Medical care tops that list."

The mayor interrupted again. "For the sake of brevity. You can't pay your student loans and home mortgage with the farm fresh eggs and venison our town's people will want to offer you as compensation. Until the mill re-opens, the city will subsidize your practice's cash flow."

Every nerve in Alan vibrated and he bit his tongue. *I can handle my budget. I'm my own man and need help from no one.* This thought echoed in his head. The words from his mouth were different. "Prudence dictates that I should consider the city's offer. I'll run some numbers. What's my deadline to get back to the council?"

The banker's voice rose above the rest. "I propose we earmark a $50,000 subsidy to the medical clinic and divert all other Snowflake capital to the mill."

Before Alan could blink, someone seconded the motion and it passed unanimously. Part of him sighed in relief—no late fees for the student loan. But most of him was angry, astonished and frustrated. He forced himself to ease open his fist before he broke the pen and got ink all over his best suit jacket. What kind of place pokes their nose so deep into a doctor's business?

Glancing out of the corner of his eye, Alan noticed Mrs. Wilson stand and walk to the door. "The council will see you now," she said to someone outside the room.

Huh, am I dismissed? What's next in this circus act? Out of curiosity, Alan looked over his shoulder and was gob-smacked to see Rachel enter.

CHAPTER 4

Having been asked to these types of meetings on prior occasions, Rachel was familiar with the camera and room set-up. She had, however, expected more people to be in attendance. Seeing one empty chair for her and only one other non-council participant had the hair on the back of her neck standing straight up. She then looked closer at the occupied audience chair. *A white lab coat—please tell me it isn't Alan.*

Alan's unmistakable hazel eyes stared at her with flashes of disbelief and confusion. *Why is he here? Can he afford to contribute to the mill reopening fund?* She gave Irene a panicked and questioning look, but Mrs. Wilson just motioned for her to have a seat. Standing in what felt like shoes made of cement blocks, she held her position, saying, "The summons sent to Brett and I said this session was about the mill. Where are the other business owners of Snowflake?"

"Oh, that's the next item on the agenda, but we have something else we wanted to discuss first, dear," remarked Mayor Jameson.

Ugh, this can't be good. The mayor is using his pompous 'I'm in charge, do as you're told' voice. Wanting to get through what she knew would be an exasperating meeting as quickly as possible, she complied by dropping into the seat. The Welch financial documents slapped the floor with a thwack. They were in reach, but she didn't dare retrieve them. Rachel gave Alan a sideways look, trying to convey to him that she did not know why she had been coerced into participating in this pre-meeting meeting.

"Let the record show that Rachel Welch has joined this discussion," pontificated Mayor Jameson. "As we were saying, Dr. Garcia, the city of Snowflake will infuse funds into the clinic so that an RN can be hired with the utmost speed."

Phew, good thing I told him I was a nurse.

The mayor continued every word a dagger to her heart. "The council is pleased the recipient of the Snowflake medical scholarship, Ms. Rachel Welch, RN, will again fill the position we are sponsoring at the clinic."

"What?" Alan shouted as he stood. "Don't I have a say in who gets hired?"

Rachel wanted to crawl under a table and hide—she wished she was invisible. Why did the council think they could force her on to Dr. Garcia's staff? She wanted to work there, but Alan should make that decision.

To her surprise, Rachel was pleased to see Alan's veil drop and the uber professional doctor emerge. With a fabulous mix of casual and calm, the man on the hot seat turned to face the council members, particularly focusing on Bodie and the veterinarian. "For the record, I have already offered Ms. Welch a nursing position." He turned and was about to place his hand atop her shoulder but waved it over the area instead. "The medical practices I've been associated with allowed the physicians to pick their staff. Wouldn't the business owners of the esteemed panel agree?"

Rachel kept her cool. Dr. Garcia handled himself so well. He championed her professional dignity and fought for his rights with such grace. The amount of respect and caring she already held for this extraordinary newcomer grew tenfold. Her heart felt like it had grown to bursting proportions.

All of the people in the room started talking at once and Rachel couldn't decipher what any one person said. She was about to join

Alan, standing by his side to show her support, but the mayor clobbered the makeshift podium with a scarred wooden gavel. "Order, I'll have order this instant!"

The room quieted, but the mayor took his time, his authoritarian airs returning. "If the city provides the clinic's office space free of charge, paid for Rachel's education and will pay the salary, then the council has a right to strongly encourage this course of action."

A rush of concerns clouded Rachel's thought process—she had lived through the intrusive behavior of the mayor before. Knowing this was Alan's first taste of it made her want to touch his forearm and tell him, in a whisper that only he could hear, that everything would be okay. But the steady blink of the red light let her know the camera was live, and kept her still, like a doll sitting on a shelf, waiting for others to control her every move.

"Mayor Jameson," the female attorney's assured declaration rang out. "Might I remind you that Ms. Welch is under no obligation to the city for having been the scholarship winner. She serves on the volunteer rescue unit and administers flu shots at the school *pro bono,* thus showing the citizens of Snowflake her gratitude."

Finally, the voice of reason speaks. Rachel realized she had given her lip a gentle bite. A slow exhale escaped, and her eyes shot toward the supportive esquire. The vet and Bodie backed up Alan's claim that the city council had no grounds to interfere with who the clinic hired, but the mayor squelched their testimony.

He slammed down the gavel again. "We will table this discussion since we have more pressing matters." An uncomfortable version of silence filled space between the stark white walls. "An employee policy at the clinic must be changed." Mayor Jameson offered a stack of papers to the people on either side of him. "This updated employee handbook will go into effect immediately. No employee fraternization among medical staff will be tolerated. This council will not endure having another physician run off after a marriage proposal is rebuffed."

Rachel heard a gasp and wasn't sure if it had come from her

mouth, but after seeing Irene bring a hand to cover her lips, she understood the source.

The mayor bellowed on, "I know that Dr. Garcia and Nurse Welch were recently brought together at the lake under false pretenses. That is forbidden. If any clinic employee shows the slightest hint of romantic inclination toward another staffer that will be grounds for immediate dismissal of them both." He stared at Alan and Rachel then pointed up at the camera. "Is that understood?"

Rachel was astounded by the speed with which her head bobbed up and down. The sight of Alan doing the same caused her to slump in her chair. A quiver started up on her chin and she was pleased the intrusion of the blinking light could not capture that portion of her face.

This new declaration sent the room into chaos again. A tunnel of focus surrounded Rachel—all she could think about was how Alan would react to that bombshell. He didn't move. No acknowledgment he'd heard a word. *Will he fight harder to hire someone else? I guess he wasn't attracted to me after all.* Then she thought of the big picture. She wanted to live in Snowflake. The only nursing job was at the clinic. Her career was more important to her than the beginnings of a romance.

Tears stung Rachel's eyes, not of sadness but from anger. She was about to give in to her fury for being objectified by the mayor's abuse of power when the thought of her mother came to mind. *How would Maria deal with this?* As if energized by lightning, Rachel sprang to her feet. "Hey, I run three businesses. I can't just abandon them all." The volume and commanding tone of her voice surprised even her. Traipsing up to the mayor, she tossed the envelope she'd brought with her on top of his gavel. "Sophie is going out on maternity leave soon. I can't step away like I did for Dr. Remington. No one in the Welch family will be on-premises."

As if she had been eavesdropping from the other side of the wall, Mrs. Jameson burst through the door. "Hello everyone, I have the solution to that. Tell them, dear."

The mayor stood, looking at his watch. "The council has an

appointment with possible investors for the mill. My wife, I mean, City Clerk Jameson, has taken it upon herself to gather candidates for the café to free up Ms. Welch to work at the clinic." The gavel found the top of the table its final time. "We are adjourned."

Before she knew it, Heidi had Rachel by the arm and was literally dragging her out of the meeting. She looked back, wanted to ask Alan for time to talk, but he hadn't moved. Everyone else was gathering their belongings, but Alan sat in the chair like a cardboard cutout. No emotion, no life. Rachel called out his name, but no audible sound was created.

Heidi wrenched her into the chamber across the hall, and she sucked in air when she stumbled over her boots. Yanking herself free, she was about to turn and run back to Alan, but two young women dressed for an interview gave her an eager greeting before she could take a step.

"I'm pleased to meet you, I've heard so much about you," cooed the redhead with freckles.

Grasping her resume, the most senior candidate offered a kind smile. "I wish I could have met you under more hospitable circumstances. I'm Tameka."

Knowing Mrs. Jameson was standing guard at the entrance, Rachel acquiesced and did her best to give these women her full attention. *Did she still want to work for Dr. Garcia? What if he rescinded his offer? It was only verbal with no details. The connection she thought they had because he was an outsider, was that all in her mind?* The conversation she knew she needed to have with Alan required much more time and even more privacy. City Hall would not provide either. That problem would have to wait on the back burner for now.

Rachel's annoyance at Mrs. Jameson began to wane as the ladies told their stories. Both had lost their jobs when the mill closed. Jackie, the receptionist, wanted to get married but had to postpone everything until her finances could be improved. She would do any kind of work to be able to start her married life. Tameka had an accounting and operations background and understood how to run a business, but just needed the opportunity to use her skills.

Rachel allowed herself to consider the possibility of letting these ladies fill in until Sophie returned. But then her dilemma hit her like a ton of bricks—she could follow her passion for being a nurse or continue to manage the family businesses she had inherited and take a romantic chance with the doctor she knew so little about. Such a big decision, how could she choose?

CHAPTER 5

ALAN LOCKED the lobby door and pulled on a pair of surgical gloves. Swabbing every surface any contagious patient might have touched, he grumbled, "Telling me who I can hire and probation for a doctor, in this small town, they've got some nerve." He yanked the trash bag from the can, straightened the lining that remained, and then surveyed the waiting room for any item out of place. With jerky movements, he closed the blinds to help keep out the cold. Alan counted in his mind when the three months would end. December had begun, so by St. Patrick's Day he could mark that task as complete. Alan paced around his office and waved his hand through the air like he was swatting away his negative thoughts.

"The town did give me use of this building rent-free, and the sheriff has been very supportive of my security needs." Realizing he was talking to himself out loud, he clenched his teeth and tightened the muscles of his face to keep his private thoughts from becoming sounds. He just relocated his mother and his career—not like he could do that again without an abundance of collateral damage on so many levels.

He hadn't been looking for romance. Why did it appear in his life now? Or had it? *Was she into me? I'm not a good judge of such things.* He hadn't felt so comfortable around an attractive eligible woman in his life. Just when he allowed himself to hope he might find someone to fall in love with, to be his partner in life, the overreaching rule dashed his dreams. He had to do what was best for his *madre*. The world spinning around him seemed to slow down. A piece of his heart and brain went dark. He withdrew into himself and thought of his late *padre* and his father's Special Forces buddies, who taught him to be a man. He would make his way in the world on his own and alone. He needed to make a list to keep himself on track.

But his grumbling belly drowned out his deliberations, redirecting his attention. With a somber face, he walked toward his office, where he could see his mother typing away with her tongue sticking out, pointing up at her nose, a sure tell that she was focused and oblivious to her surroundings.

Alan arrived at the threshold and stopped on a dime. Slamming a book shut, his mother thrust it onto the floor. "Mother Mary, how am I supposed to learn all this?" Teresa squawked then flopped back into the chair, her arms crossed over her chest.

"Everything okay, *Madre*?" Alan was third-generation American, but his Cuban upbringing and Spanglish oozed out of him when he was not in full control of his emotions, which wasn't often. Stepping around the boxes of Christmas decorations still waiting to be hung, Alan got a better view of the open book she held.

"These ICD-10 billing codes are driving me beyond batty." Wiping her hair from her face, her tone sharpened. "You know I can handle the accounting, all day long, but learning which sequence of numbers goes with each medical procedure is more than I bargained for." The light went out of her eyes and her shoulders slumped. "Sorry."

In three long strides, he dashed to his distressed mother, grabbing one arm and hauling her up into a giant bear hug. "But, you're safe here, no more looking over your shoulder. I'll help you with the invoicing. It's all going to be fine; you'll see." Squeezing her one more time, he added, "Forget about all this tonight, let me take you to dinner." Pulling back, he flashed her his best boyish grin, which he knew would melt her heart.

Her fists landed on her hips. "Can we afford that?"

Buzzkill. "Um, well, maybe not, but the provisions we brought from Miami are pretty much gone. I haven't seen a grocery store yet, have you?" He thought hard about the roads he'd driven the past couple of days—nope, he didn't recall seeing anything resembling a store that sold food. "We can go to the café across the street to eat and ask them where they buy their supplies."

Snatching his coat from the old-fashioned rack, he helped his mother into hers. As they ambled onto the sidewalk in front of the medical clinic, he stopped, looking both left and right. "Unbelievable."

"What?" asked his mom as she gathered her hood closer around her face.

Laughing, he crossed the street explaining, "This is about the center of town, but I can see the last building considered to be part of the historic downtown district in both directions. I guess that's what they mean by one-horse town."

Alan opened the door of the café for his mother and a whoosh of heat and the smell of homemade apple pie welcomed them both.

"Sit anywhere you'd like," called a voice from the kitchen.

He picked the booth furthest from the entrance, and his adoring mom, who had never seen snow, huddled deeper into her jacket as she sat down. A hint of sweetened apple aroma lingered, but the scent of tonight's special, beef stroganoff, put Alan's nose in a happy place.

The exterior of the restaurant looked western and fit in with the town's rural cowboy appeal, but the inside had begun to transform into a celebration of Christmas. Fresh sprigs of pine garland adorned the top of the walls where they met the ceilings. Rows of chasing lights had his eyes following them from one booth to another, and in the corner, the primary pieces of a nativity scene were gathered to create a festive display. He could tell other holiday decorations needed to be positioned, so he looked forward to his next visit.

"Today's specials are on the whiteboard, I'll be there to take your order in a minute," continued the invisible but cheery kitchen help.

Did he know that voice? Was Rachel in the kitchen? Alan rested his weight against the rustic, tree-like back of the booth, gliding his fingers across the smooth table, which seemed to have at least 100 coats of clear shiny varnish. *I could watch her at this job and no one could question my motives.*

Alan surveyed the menu, scrawled in large cursive letters, while giving a side glance to the woman carrying plates stacked up her arm, delivering meals to a nearby booth. His medical training kicked in. *Hmmm, that must be Jacob's mother. She's about five months into her pregnancy,* he figured. *Should she be doing this type of physically demanding work?*

The pregnant waitress addressed them while clearing the dirty dishes from a table across the way, then wiping down the surface, "Oh, Doc and Mrs. Garcia, so glad you joined us for supper. I'll tell Rachel you're here, and thanks so much for taking care of Parrot's cough. Sorry about the sneeze to the face. What'll you have?"

She knows who I am. How? Alan shuffled her staccato phrases around in his head more than once. *She said, Rachel. My Rachel?* Taking another peek at the board he, choked out, "I'll have the meatloaf special."

"Make that two," added his mother.

In a whirl of thoughts, the Welch family was connected to the café. Deciding to scan his surroundings to learn more about Rachel, he studied the posters, pennants and pictures decorating most of the free wall space. But he was too far away to tell if she was in any of the photos. A shelf about a foot from the ceiling, encircling the dining area, was filled with antique figurines and children's toys. On opposite sides of the restaurant area, were large doorways. Over one a sign read 'Squeaky Saddle Saloon' and the other 'Gift Shop & Post Office.' What an odd combination of businesses for one building, he pondered.

Thunk, thunk, thunk... "Daddy!"

Just as Alan realized that the commotion was Parrot running down a wooden flight of stairs in cowboy boots, the enormous father entered the room from the kitchen. Rachel's brother. *I wouldn't want to get on his bad side.*

Parrot leaped into burly arms of the potential Sasquatch and hugged him with all his little might until a coughing fit broke their reunion. Trying not to stare, Alan was about to ask his mother a question to be less conspicuous, but then their platters arrived.

"Sorry about the noise. I've told Parrot a thousand times, folks deserve a bit of peace when they're trying to eat," said the server as she slid the hot meals into place.

"Oh, miss," interrupted his mother. She motioned the expectant women closer to the table. In a whisper, she asked, "Where's the nearest place to buy groceries?"

The waitress took a second to compose herself, as she was trying to hold back a chuckle. Smiling wide, she answered, "The Trading Post." Blocking her mouth to hide a snicker, she added, "It's about two doors north of the medical clinic, same side of the street, can't miss it."

With a quick spin on her heels, she was off, picking up more plates from an empty booth, until suddenly she grabbed her lower abdomen and dropped to her knees with a gasp, the plates crashing to the floor and shattering into several pieces. She cried out in distress.

The Big Foot impersonator swiftly lowered Parrot to the ground and came running. "Sophie, honey. Are you okay?!" Looking back toward the kitchen, he yelled, "Rachel, get out here!"

Alan instinctively leaped into action. "Let me help." Kicking shards of plate out of the way, he knelt, easing his newest patient to the floor. "Where does it hurt? How bad's the pain?"

"Coming, Sophie!" A shout came from the kitchen.

Looking up, Alan felt his heart flutter in his chest. The natural beauty he'd begun to care about stood next to him. Even with her long, luscious locks hidden under a less-than-flattering hair net, she was beautiful beyond words. The view made it hard for him to think. He instinctively reached for his stethoscope around his neck but found himself grasping at air. *Left it on my desk.* Alan forced his focus back to Sophie.

In an instant, Rachel was crouching next to him, and continuing to lean closer to him. *Don't touch me, I can't get fired. I've got so much riding on this job.* Before he could pull away, her mouth brushed his cheek, warm breath drifting past his ear as she choked out, "After Jacob, she's had two miscarriages."

RACHEL WATCHED as Dr. Garcia stiffened at the news. But then, a very curious thing happened. Starting with his face, she saw every muscle in his body relax. She was beginning to like the usefulness of his veil. Rachel told herself she'd have to ask him where he'd learned that trick. She could think of so many ways in which that move could help her in her career and personal life. Projecting a gentle yet commanding presence, Dr. Garcia examined her beloved sister-in-law.

"That's it! You promised, Sophie," barked Brett just before he kissed her palm, pulling it to his heart. "You and Parrot will move in with Rachel so you can have complete bed rest. You hear me, COMPLETE bed rest."

The pounding in Rachel's chest began to subside. She was pleased the thorough Dr. G had asked all the right questions and confirmed or ruled out all of the possible symptoms. *He's got this. She'll be fine.*

"I already moved into the spare room, the master is all yours," chimed in Rachel with as much sunshine in her tone as she could gather.

She began to wonder why Alan was maintaining eye contact with her for so long, but she was relieved when he added, "I agree. Bed rest as a precaution. The spasms have subsided, right Sophie?"

Catching worried glances from the two men while still kneeling on the floor, Rachel sighed as Sophie's face softened, and her body relaxed. Her sister-in-law was doing her best to put on a brave face under the circumstances.

"Think so."

"I got this," interjected Brett.

Tapping Dr. G's shoulder, Rachel stepped back. A smile filled her face and soul. She knew just how much Brett loved his wife. He was capable of providing whatever she might need, including a lift up the stairs to her temporary lodging. The good doctor hesitated, but then following her lead, clearing the space around Sophie.

Feeling proud of her brother, Rachel was interested to see Alan's reaction to what she knew was about to happen. Brett scooped Sophie up as she wrapped her arms around his neck. He lifted her with ease and grace not often found in a big man. Brett strode through the kitchen to the stairs Parrot had just bounded down.

"Oh, right. Wouldn't expect you to know. I live upstairs." Rachel broadened her grin, motioning him to follow. "Come on up and give your patient her treatment instructions." *Not every day you invite your future boss into your bedroom.* Picking up Parrot for a piggyback ride, Rachel ascended the stairs, Dr. Garcia in tow.

"I'll get you a to-go box," called out Mrs. Garcia to her son before they rushed away and out of sight.

Easing Parrot to the floor, Rachel made a request of the doctor, "Wait here, let me get her settled in. I'll come get you when the coast is clear." She entered the bedroom and gave Brett a quick side hug, then lowered herself next to Sophie on the bed, kissing the top of her head as she went. "The résumé the mayor showed me for Dr. Garcia listed extra maternity training, and I trust him. I'll be here to care for you, too."

Rachel knew word about the prior day's council meeting had sped all over town. She assumed Brett and Sophie had heard. "I'll continue working at the café so you can rest. The mayor can't make me take the nursing job now. I'm sure Alan, I mean, Dr. Garcia will understand." The husband and wife shared a dumbfounded look but said nothing.

Raising her voice, Rachel said, "You can come in now, Dr. Garcia. Sophie's bun needs a little more time in the oven."

ALAN TIPTOED INTO THE ROOM. A real Christmas tree stood bare in its stand, waiting for loving decorative touches to find it. Then the three people that were part of the historic Welch family became all he would let himself see. *Just a house call, no big deal. Then why are my*

palms sweating? He knew this would be a high-profile case on many levels. He would be helping the Welch family bring another healthy baby into their world.

This was a whole different set of nerves he had to control. His 'I'm a competent physician' mask was well in place. Alan stretched his neck and rolled his shoulders enough to feel the release, but not draw attention, then gave Sophie all the high-risk obstetric patient protocols.

"I promise she'll be a compliant patient." Rachel's velvety voice dragged him out of his patient education speech. Sophie's vitals were back to what would be appropriate for an expectant woman. This crisis had been averted, but vigilance was paramount.

Patting Sophie's forearm, he said, "I'll...Well, we'll get you through this. Let me know if anything changes or if you have any questions." Alan offered a handshake to Brett but received a bear hug instead. "I'll make her a top priority patient," he whispered into the flannel-covered chest.

After Brett released him, he waved to Sophie and Rachel, then saw himself down the steps to rejoin his mother. Alan slid into the booth and smiled at his mother. His full plate remained untouched, cooling by the minute, but he didn't care. He was warming up to this town. Being a physician here was going to be fine. He could do some real good.

Shoveling in a lukewarm piece of meatloaf, he tried to remember Rachel's bedroom. At the time he'd tried not to notice, but Alan had felt comfortable being in her private space. Like her kindness to new neighbors and not being driven by money, this was more evidence she was his type of woman. He wanted to think of her as a romantic interest. Hiring her to be his nurse would make that impossible. *No dating between employees.*

But as Rachel said, a Welch needed to be onsite at the restaurant to manage the businesses. Maybe she wouldn't accept his offer? Maybe he would be allowed to ask her on a date?

CHAPTER 6

Rachel watched Olga in the kitchen via the pass through as she stuffed sugar packets into their rectangle holders, part of her daily prep work. Olga with her long blond braids and the happy grin was giving her new hires, Tameka and Jackie, the basics of the server station setup.

She'd hired Olga, a local gal who had just graduated college, several months back. She was a great addition, but she couldn't handle the holiday rush at the gift shop, saloon and eatery by herself.

Rachel didn't want to admit it, but Mrs. Jameson's café candidate-search ended up being a big help. With Sophie unexpectedly on bed rest, even if the nursing position didn't work out, they needed help to keep the restaurant running.

She kept an ear out for the ever-present CB radio as some of Snowflake's residents couldn't rely on having stable cell phone service. Something about the white noise of CB static and her rhythmic vegetable chopping allowed Rachel to indulge thoughts on her current dilemma.

She knew Dr. Garcia was working on her official job offer. Those details would work themselves out, she had faith. But this morning she felt a sense of loss. Rachel expected Alan to start using the stereotypical behaviors she usually received as a Welch woman, but he hadn't. This was a pleasant surprise. But now this well-mannered guy was romantic suicide.

Rachel would never put her career at risk for a good kisser. Well, she didn't know if he had skills in that area but his full lips promised that just one touch would send her over the edge. She picked up another white bermuda and told herself the tears rolling down her face had nothing to do with finding a soul mate and everything to do with the onion.

"Hi, this is Quinn." A tinny-sounding voice came over the CB radio. "Can anyone hear me? Um, what's the saying...oh yeah, mayday, mayday." That word got her attention. Dropping her knife, she made her way to the make-shift desk in the back corner of the kitchen, where the CB radio sat.

"Rachel, coming back. What's your twenty and your situation?" She knew where Quinn lived, and if he needed assistance, she would have to activate the full rescue team. That included Alan. Her heart started a pitter-patter, but it wasn't nerves. *Why am I so excited to work with him outside of the office?*

SPENDING a Saturday morning at the clinic treating overflow patients while his *madre* completed paperwork was not Alan's preferred way to start the weekend, but sacrifices had to be made to transition to his new life. Rachel's voice from the town-provided CB radio brightened his day. *I've got to learn that lingo if I want to fit in.*

"Miss Rachel is that you? You're Parrot's kin, right?" The young man's voice was calm, but a bit hyper.

"Roger that. What's up?"

Alan had to remind himself that this could be serious, but he allowed himself to enjoy listening to her CB chatter.

"Um, my dad needs stitches, can't come to you. We're at the tower hunting cabin. You know my dad. His nickname is Monkey." The radio cut out for a split second. "Fresh snow here. You copy?"

"Brett? Doc? You got your ears on?" Rachel's voice began to climb in volume.

As Alan made a mad dash to the radio, his mother got out of his way.

She looked at him and shrugged her shoulders. "I don't know how to use that thing."

Kissing her on the forehead, he picked up the microphone.

Before Alan could speak another voice responded. "Brett, coming back. Betsy and I will meet you on Main Street in five."

Alan figured more than one guy in this town could act like a parrot, so he gave speaking on the CB a try. He held the mic button down. "Dr. Garcia, coming back. I'll be ready. Quinn, how bad is it?"

"Um, not sure. But dad says he's had stitches before and he's certain he needs them now."

"Brett, floor it!" commanded Rachel. And then her reassuring voice returned, "Stay calm Quinn, we'll be there in a flash."

Alan grabbed his coat and medical bag but stopped to see what it contained. This was the prior doctor's emergency case, so he wanted to confirm its contents. "Well, at least we just saw our last patient for the day. Don't hold lunch," he shouted as he ran out the clinic's front door.

Rachel was already on the sidewalk on his side of the street. He noticed she was carrying the same backpack from the other day at the lake. "You coming too? We work these calls together?" he asked.

"Well, yeah. You're not getting to the hunting cabin without me." She stepped out onto the street to see if her brother was in view. "It's time for your emergency medicine skills to shine. Have you ever had to place sutures in freezing weather?"

"Yes. And my skills at stitching are good enough for plastic surgery. I used to cross-stitch with my *madre* but don't tell anyone." If anyone else had asked about his qualifications, he wouldn't have minded, but having Rachel asking got under his skin. "Who's Betsy?"

"Wait'll you see her. Brett and Sophie were married before Betsy came along or Sophie would've been out of luck." Rachel made this statement with such a matter-of-fact tone that she had Alan all kinds of confused.

Looking in the same direction as Rachel, he could see a monster-sized something speeding toward them. Giving Rachel a questioning look, he waited.

"Oh, that's right, you're a beach boy. Betsy is the snowplow's nickname. She's the biggest, baddest baby on the road." She said it with such pride. He couldn't help but grin. *He'd let the beach boy comment slide for now.*

Climbing up an external ladder, Alan let Rachel guide the way into the elevated cab. The truck's interior was not ordinary—custom-built after-market gadgets lined the dash and back wall. The plush bucket seats in the front complimented an upholstered bench in the back with easy access from either side's door. Alan wanted to activate all hooks and levers on the dash but squelched his urge to touch. If this wasn't a medical run, he knew Brett would give him a tour. *Hmm, a chance to bond with Rachel's brother over a manly mechanical marvel. Wait a minute, can't ask her out. No need to impress the big man.* Alan's chest tightened and his anticipation to be in Rachel's presence floundered. *Just do your job, nothing more.*

The three-volunteer EMT crew first headed toward the lake, but then took a left and started gaining altitude up a winding mountain road. When he had passed these mountains previously, he had been driving. As a passenger, he could take in their beauty for the first time. Multiple peaks pierced the clouds. The white caps brilliance shown in vivid contrast to the azure sky. The exposed earth from where dynamite had been used to carve the road revealed layers of granite and sandstone at right angles to one another. Different types of trees emerged from the landscape. Laurels and oaks at the bottom and spruce, firs and pines the higher they traveled.

Alan expected Betsy's huge engine to be loud, and when she chugged away on the steeper incline the sound of the pistons firing faster was impressive. The elevated decibel levels drown out almost every other sound. Leaning forward from the backbench, Alan shouted, "Where's the tower cabin, and who's Monkey?"

Brett answered. "It's on the highest peak in these parts, and Monkey maintains the radio and cell towers. He looks like a monkey crawling around up there, so that's what we call him. Don't know his real name." Brett maneuvered Betsy off the road, and she pushed the snow to one side with ease, all the way to a tiny shack of rotten wood. It slanted to one side so much it looked like it could fall to the ground at any minute.

Before he knew what was happening, Rachel leaped from the plow and disappeared into the dilapidated shanty. He climbed down after her, stepping into a high snowdrift the frosty powder crunching under his feet. With a puff of smoke and the roar of an engine, she returned to his view, straddling a gleaming blue and white snowmobile and gunning the engine. She surveyed him head to toe, and shouted over the engine, "What…no boots, no hat, no gloves?"

Shrugging his shoulders, he frowned. "My gloves are on the counter in my office. I put them down to inventory the medical bag."

"Lucky I've got hand-warmers. You need dexterity for stitches. Put your surgical tools in my pockets." Rachel pointed to her neck, and Brett tossed a tattered scarf hitting him in his chest. He guessed the siblings' thoughts were on the same wavelength. Alan wasn't certain he'd heard her correctly over the rumble of the engine. *Hand warmers? Never needed them in Florida.* She gave him a helmet and donned one herself.

Rachel strapped his gear onto the back of the snowmobile, waved goodbye to Brett who had made a u-turn and pointed as she regained her seat. "Your paws in my pockets, now. Grab my waist." *I can't do that. What if someone sees us?* Reminding himself his patient was still waiting, Alan complied. He threw a leg over the snowmobile and plunged his hands into her warm coat, holding on tight. *How am I going to keep my attraction to her from showing? I need the job, still on probation, must pass.*

With a jolt, they were off. The fast movement had him squeezing her. He would adapt to the ways of this community and hope any onlookers understood what was required to save the patient. Alan couldn't see a road or trail, and he had no idea where she was going.

The sun was high, but it made the glare of the glistening snow almost painful. Even with the shield of the helmet, the blasts of cold air burned his nose, making it hard to breathe. Hearing the engine kick into a higher gear gave him cause for concern. And then they were airborne.

"Yee-haw!" If not for the need to cling to his driver for dear life, he might have enjoyed her exuberant holler.

"Almost there," she shouted over the noise. "Gonna get steep now."

If this wasn't already steep, he didn't know what was.

She leaned forward as if to help the machine, so he did too. A flash of reflecting light above the trees caught his attention, and he recognized it from Miami. Alan knew a cell tower when he saw one. They cleared a grouping of evergreens and he could see the log cabin, small but sturdy. Slowing the snowmobile to a halt, Rachel hung the helmet on the handlebar. As he lifted his visor, a swath of her hair glided past his nose. That wonderful, sweet smell he couldn't place tickled his nose again. But now was not the time to think of such things. They were off-limits now anyway.

Opening the door, he found Monkey, a lean lanky man in his mid-thirties, lying on the floor, pale and shivering. His son, Quinn, a toe headed boy of about eight was helping him press down firmly on his wound. Rachel slammed the well-worn wooden slab shut, closing out the frosty air. Racing to the sink, she removed her backpack. He thought to himself, *she does know her stuff.* But watching her in action, he couldn't help but appreciate how well she commanded the serious situation.

"Are you scrubbing in, Doc?" Her words pulled him back to the rescue activity.

"Right. Yes, of course." Trying to keep the patient calm he started a conversation. "So Monkey, what happened?"

"T-T-T-Trying to sharpen an ax." The man was growing weaker and closed his eyes.

Alan went to the sink and to his surprise Rachel came past him, having already snapped on surgical gloves.

"What?" she asked, looking at him with indignation.

"Sorry, I'm trying to guess what other supplies might be in your medical bag." Alan scrubbed his fingers, stomping his feet a couple of times trying to regain some circulation. Slip-on dress loafers were not designed for this type of work. Alan turned back to his patient and saw more standard procedures being completed. Rachel had laid out the tools he needed to place the stitches and was cutting open Monkey's pant leg for better access to the wound.

"You'll be assisting me?" Alan asked it as a question but meant it as a statement of fact.

Rachel crinkled her nose and made the strangest face. "Not my first rodeo. You gotta be prepared for everything in the mountains." Kneeling next to Monkey, Alan fully immersed himself into providing the best care possible. But before he made his first stitch, Rachel yanked off his shoes, wrapping his feet in a blanket. "No frostbite on my watch," she grumbled, peeling off her gloves and, grasping into her backpack for a new pair.

Alan patched up the patient while Quinn found his dad another pair of pants. He surveyed the humble cabin as he listened to Rachel's wellbeing related questions to confirm the naturalist duo had food and wood to last through the night. The interior was sparse and plain, but the father and son had everything they needed. Speaking to Quinn under his breath, Alan asked, "Will your mother be returning soon?"

"Nah, she's in the Navy, deployed to the Gulf. Dad's single again, but we get by. We're survivalist men, you know." The answer would have made him apprehensive if Quinn didn't seem like a well-adjusted, happy boy.

With stress levels subsiding, Alan took another look at the décor of the cabin. A three-foot fake Christmas tree stood on a round table draped with a green velvet cloth. The tiny multi-colored lights were built in and twinkled away. The tree supported five ornaments that he could see. "I guess you're still decorating your tree."

Quinn laughed for the first time since the rescue team had arrived. "Good ole Charlie Brown's got nothin' on us. What you see is all we got, but we love it just the same. Right, Dad?" Monkey gave an energetic two thumbs up from his resting position on his bed.

Feeling confident the boy could manage while his father recovered, Alan headed back to the snowmobile.

With several inches of snow crunching under her feet, Rachel passed him adding, "Tomorrow I'm taking you to see Bodie. We've got to get you winterized, Mr. Miami."

Well, at least he moved up from boy to mister. On their way back down the mountain, Alan used Rachel's pockets again. Holding onto her made him want more. He wanted to protect her and care for her like the duo they left in the cabin. He could be her champion without being her boyfriend, right?

CHAPTER 7

On the way back to the makeshift garage, Rachel stopped the snowmobile as a loud rumble in the distance froze her like a deer hearing a predator. Her whole body went numb. "Oh no! Rockslide! We've gotta get to a radio!"

She became dizzy and tried to tell herself the ground movement was the cause. *No flashbacks, not now.* Rachel looked for the puff of snow thrown back into the sky and listened for the crackle and pop of breaking trees. After she pinpointed the direction of the debris she knew a well-traveled road could be blocked. Taking proactive action was the only thing that would keep her from choking on her adrenaline.

Alan shifted behind her then handed his cell phone over her shoulder. She snatched it up looked at the number of bars and frowned. Rachel tossed it back, grumbling. "No signal. We'll use the snowmobile to get to the cafe. If I use the off-road trail, it will be faster than trying to catch Brett. I need a CB radio!"

Gunning the engine, she felt Alan's warmth slip away from her, but then return. Something about having him as a passenger made her relax. Many a man had sat on that seat behind her but having this outsider with her was different. He had a compassionate bedside manner, but another trait made working with him easier. While treating Monkey they worked together without having a debate. Their brain waves seemed to vibrate on the same frequency. She had never experienced that with anyone. Working with him would be a dream come true. But what about her other dream? She wanted to find someone who loved her for who she is, not just her last name? *He can't be in that dream, remember?* Her body slumped toward the handles and she stared into the distance. The snowmobile found its way to the backdoor of the diner all on its own.

Rachel jumped off, not looking back, and ran to the CB in the back corner of the café's kitchen. Nothing but static, no chatter about any accidents. She grabbed the mic and clicked the button on. "Sheriff's Department this is Rachel Welch. Just heard a rockslide on Highway 2 a bit north of the volunteer rendezvous point, copy?"

"Roger that. I'll send a car and let you know what we find. I appreciate the extra set of ears out there. Sheriff Wilson out."

"This rockslide that you heard. Do you think there'll be injuries? How can I help?" asked Alan.

Rachel gasped and dropped the mic, clutching her chest. "Sorry, didn't realize you came in after me. She felt the lightest touch of his hand on her shoulder for the briefest moment.

"Didn't mean to startle you. My bad. You seemed concerned. What can I do?"

Rachel took a quick glance around the café. Who might see him standing so close to her and start spreading romance rumors about them. When she heard most of the activity was in the Squeaky Saddle, she let that batch of nerves unwind just the tiniest bit.

Rachel sighed and rubbed her temples. "Won't know anything 'til the sheriff reports back. Hope no injuries. Not a hiking trail there but might be a car accident." With her last words, the heat drained from Rachel's body. She tucked her hair behind her ears with more force than needed. "I hate this. The waiting gets to me." She rubbed the back of her neck.

Alan pulled over a chair and placed it next to hers. "You can talk to me. Tell me what you need." She wanted him to hug her but couldn't take the risk of anyone seeing. A deepening chill grew where his hand had been. She shivered. Her gaze darted around the room to see what her staff and customers might witness. All the activity was in the main dining room.

A crackle came from the radio. Rachel jumped up, knocking over her chair, but Alan caught and righted it before it slammed to the floor.

"I got you. You're okay," he whispered.

Easing down at a turtle's pace her weight found the seat again. Rachel willed the now-silent machine to save her from her self-induced anxiety.

"Do you have a history with injuries from accidents?"

She snapped her head toward him and all her fear spewed out in her glare. Alan flinched but stayed steady preparing to endure what might come at him next.

"Who's been tellin' you tales?" Surprised by the low growl in her voice, she clamped her lips together in a thin line.

She lifted her gaze to meet his. Rachel expected to see annoyance or at the very least incredulity, but what she absorbed from him was steady comfort. Her heart rate slowed and the tension in every muscle began to ease. She opened her mouth to speak but couldn't find the words. This was more than gratitude enveloping her whenever he was around. If she could only carry the feeling with her, she knew she could survive and thrive.

"Sheriff Wilson, unit twenty-four on the scene. Rockslide on US 2 at mile marker 193. Some debris on the road, no accidents or injuries to report." A short band of static filled the air. "Brett, I can clean this up myself, you're off the hook."

"Roger, that. Enjoy the rest of the day everyone," Brett said as if he was speaking in code only to her.

Pressing the button down, pulling her face closer to the mic, Rachel added her two cents. "Thank you, gentlemen. Sorry if I overreacted. Rachel out."

The sheriff broke in as she uttered her sign off. "Nah, you got great instincts. If your worrying keeps even one accident from happening, you got my vote."

"My vote too, but don't run for mayor. That's my job. Great work everybody," said Mayor Jameson. The CB's audio meter went back to zero.

"You've got my vote, too," added Alan with a bit of a smirk, trying to keep the mood light. "I'm glad you're my nurse, neighbor and friend."

That last word stabbed at her heart. *Of course, just friends. Nothing more than friends.* Maybe as her employer, her private doctor, she could confide in him. Rachel stared in his direction and added a squint until she saw Alan's jaw tighten. "No really, who's been tellin' you tales?" If he was going to be her friend, then she deserved nothing but honesty.

"No one! Um, really. I don't have time for gossip, wouldn't listen if I did." The shock and confusion on Alan's face almost made her grin. But she kept her scowl in place. "The concern in your voice, the slight tremor in your stance, and the pallor of your skin were symptomatic."

"So, you were diagnosing me?" She crossed her arms over her chest. "Well?"

"Maybe." He shrugged and his veil melted away. "I'm here for you, only trying to help." Like the air leaving a balloon, Alan sunk deeper into the chair, looking at the floor, waiting.

Rachel's heart skipped a beat. *What is it about this man?* She couldn't keep her feigned anger flowing any longer.

"Oh, fine! You're right. I can't believe how riled up I get. It's been years." Her fear reached up and choked her. Her eyes filled with tears and she blinked them away, turning so he couldn't see her expression. "My parents nearly died in a car accident caused by an avalanche." Saying the words out loud was the release she needed. She felt better but, how would he react? Could he continue to be her rock, or would he think she was unstable?

"That must have been rough." Alan brushed her back with a delicate touch and let his palm rest there for a long moment.

"Yep." She got up, keeping her face from his view. "Left Mom a paraplegic and Dad with severe frostbite on his hands and feet. Couple years back, they moved to Scottsdale, gave Brett the ranch and me the businesses here in town. I miss them every day." Rachel began to walk away. This was where most guys found a way to escape. They wanted her money, but not her emotional pain. They might say a supportive couple of words, but they didn't truly mean them.

"You want to carry on their legacy and thank them for all they've done for you." She could practically feel his breath on her ear he was so close. He had chased after her, not run away. She turned toward him.

He opened his arms. She collapsed against him. Rachel felt him take on her weight, almost picking her up to help her carry her burden. *I want to stay here forever. I've not felt this safe since their accident.*

The sound of movement from the café had her pushing out of his embrace. But, he stood there in his same stance offering his support. She looked left and right, then she watched him do the same. She took one more step back. "I've pulled myself back together. I can't begin to thank you enough. Guys don't show me their genuine emotions. But you just did. Why?"

"I told you I would prove myself to be different. I'm not after your status or bank balance." With a slow casual gate, he walked past her toward the café's front door. But, the back of his hand brushed hers as he passed.

Did he do that on purpose?

CHAPTER 8

THE NEXT EVENING, Alan was sitting in his office, trying to finish his patient notes for the day. Rachel had said she'd come over before he went on his winter shopping excursion. His mind was playing a game of 'how to rob Peter to pay Paul.' Alan knew he needed cold-weather gear. He just wasn't sure he could afford it. Very few of his patient's cost-share bills had been paid. He didn't know what to think about that but knew he shouldn't spend money he didn't have.

With a knock on the door, his heart jumped into his throat. "Come in." Alan did his best to keep his smile from dimming when his mother walked in. With a great deal of gentle grace, Teresa placed two hundred-dollar bills on his desk.

"I think you'll need these tonight," she said, heading back out the entrance.

With lighting speed, Alan picked up the bills and offered them back to her. "*Madre,* I can't accept these. Where did this money come from?"

Sighing, she stopped and faced her son. "Consider it an interest-free loan."

"This is your money. You keep it and buy yourself more warm

clothes." Alan realized he had clenched his fist and did his best to reverse the reflex, but his pulse raced beyond his control.

Alan waited patiently as his mother made her way around his cluttered desk and hugged him. She whispered in his ear. "This is not charity. You have made your way in this world on your own. Please, my love, get what you need, and we'll settle this later." Pecking him on the cheek, she moved away and then left the room.

Alan shoved the cash into his pocket and paced behind his chair. His mother knew him so well. They had argued many times about this subject. Having grown up needing the assistance of others, Alan knew he had a chip on his shoulder relating to acts of generosity bestowed on him. He would give anyone his last dime but did everything he could to pay his own way. Always.

Just as painful childhood memories began to drag him down, he heard Rachel's voice. A sense of peace and comfort enveloped him. The presence of this woman made everything feel right in his world.

"Hey there, got a second to chat before we head over to the Trading Post?" Rachel was dressed in jeans and an oversized sweater in multiple shades of pink. Taking off her coat, she meandered into the room. When she gathered her lengths of loose hair and tossed them over her shoulder in her usual nonchalant way Alan's toes curled.

He forced himself to wipe the boyish grin off his face and sat down. "Are you sure you have time for this? Isn't the café busy this time of night?" He so wanted to spend this time with her. But he didn't want her to feel obligated to help him, just like he didn't want to use the money given to him by his mother.

She laughed, taking her time to look around the room and get comfortable in one of the patio chairs. "I like what you've done to the place. Feels like we're outside in summer." She crossed her leg, exposing the oddest pair of boots he'd ever seen. They were a cross between a grizzly bear replica and the bottom of a thick-tread tire. Not feminine at all, but she wore them well.

Alan realized Rachel was more comfortable in her skin than any other woman he had dated. That characteristic made her more appealing, sexy in her own way, no matter what she wore. *She'll be working for you soon. Can't think of your employee as sexy. Close the door to that subject forever.*

"Olga graduated college just as Sophie needed to move in with her aunt in Kalispell. Funny how life sometimes gives you what you need, when you need it. She can run the place by herself." He half-heard what she said, but the *forever* realization within his thought track drug him down. His mouth released words before his mind had a chance to sensor them.

"Oh, good. I don't want to impose." Alan heard himself speaking the line often when turning down acts of kindness from others. "Wait a minute. What did you say about Sophie?" He gave his head a quick shake to bring himself back to being present.

"Sorry, didn't mean to gloss over that. Sophie's move has nothing to do with your skills to care for her. She needed to be closer to the hospital. Not easy getting there in snowstorms. You understand, right?" Rachel leaned across the desk and reached for him but was a fraction too far away to touch his hand.

Alan allowed his hand to move forward until his fingertips brushed hers on his way to scratch the itch on his scalp that didn't exist.

"Sure. Totally. I still need to endure a Montana winter to fully understand the complications of life here." He forced himself to pull away, lean back. His walls to protect his ego flew to the ceiling. Well, he told himself it was his ego, but his heart had practically leaped out of his chest at the opportunity to be held by her extended hand.

"Snowdrifts we can prepare for, but the closing of the mill, now that's complicating things." Rachel shifted in her chair. "Folks here, especially now because of the mill, use a payment method..." She paused and he could see the wheels of her mind working. "Well, let's just call it Snowflake currency. It's a form of bartering. Bodie is the king of Snowflake currency. I wanted to give you a heads up before we met with him."

"Okay." Alan knew she was trying to tell him something. The main point had sped right past him because he was using all his spare gray matter to contain his yearning for her. A physical need already existed, but being with her had his desire creating a physical symphony of pangs and twinges. They threatened to overrun his thoughts. To cover his wayward phantasm, he asked a question. "Where are we meeting this Bodie?"

She smiled. "Uh, Bodaway Crow owns the Trading Post. Mrs. Jameson gave him the nickname, Bodie with a long 'O' and it stuck."

Coming to stiff attention in his seat, Alan interrupted, "Wait a minute. Mr. Crow, isn't he on the city council?"

Looking confused, Rachel answered in slow motion. "Right. And he's an elder of the local tribe. You know, Native Americans?" She waited for him to make the next move, a scowl easing its way onto her face.

Alan got up and starting walking in circles around his desk. Rachel followed his progress, even straining her neck when his path went behind her chair. In the middle of his second lap, he asked, "Is my shopping trip connected to my 90-day probation?"

"What?" Rachel choked out the question. "Um, NO. Where did you get that idea? Bodie is unique, and I wanted you to know how he rolls before we meet with him. That's all." She continued her contortions to follow his movements until he found his chair again.

Alan knew he needed to get past his anxiety concerning that subject. Trying to hide the embarrassing blush he could feel, he looked at the floor. He then drew from his new self-playing music and visualized the gaps of his confidence being filled. "Sorry, I do appreciate your help and your understanding of how to do well in business in this town." He raised his chin and sat up straighter. "Please continue."

"Right, no problem." Rachel leaned forward, using the front legs of the patio chair to tilt toward his desk. "Bodie has this knack for knowing people's sizes. He's amazing at getting people what they need. It may not be exactly what they want, but it is, more than they may know, what they need." She stood, yanking down her sweater. "So, just let him do his thing, okay?"

Forcing himself to stop fidgeting with his pen, Alan tossed it on his desk and helped Rachel into her coat before retrieving his own. Once outside, they started the short walk to the Trading Post. He couldn't help but notice she chose to walk a couple of feet further away from him than she needed.

Halfway there, Alan stopped her mid-stride. "Can I ask you a question?" He sensed her apprehension. She didn't move. He took that as a yes. "I noticed these historic buildings all have ramps for people with disabilities. Were they installed for your mother? Sorry if that's too personal of a question." He waited for her to give him grief for asking, or just not answer.

To his surprise, a glow bloomed on her complexion and the tension left her body. "Now you're catching on! Yes, they're for my parents. Not that anyone in my family asked. Isn't it amazing?" She threw her arms open wide and spun in a circle. Alan could see the steam from her exhale as she continued to talk and moved toward the store again.

"Each business owner, in their own way, made their place wheelchair accessible. No one owned up to who did the work or how the expenses were paid." She giggled like a schoolgirl. "Not even Mrs. Jameson. Nope, ramps just kept appearing mysteriously built overnight." She opened and held the door for him, adding, "That's the beauty of Snowflake. We take care of our own."

They entered the store, which was full of holiday shoppers busy finding deals. The shelving and merchandise cases were made of natural materials, like the expansive log cabin's exterior. Garland wrapped around the wooden railings and a mechanical Santa sleigh and reindeer hung from the ceiling. The counter, which created an aisle, was full of red or green boxes that offered a variety of holiday-style chocolates, and glittering 'on sale' signs were everywhere. But the display that made Alan's head swivel was in the center of the room.

Cordoned off so no one could reach it was a male mannequin in Crow Indian ceremonial garb, complete with a headdress. Alan's feet took him to see more before his brain had a say in the action. The length of the feathers was impressive, with white closer to the base of the shafts and black on the tips. The bright colors of the beads on the leather that held it all together kept Alan's eyes entertained until Rachel commented, "This time of year, Bodie decorates the store for the rest of us, but shows off his elder finery for his fellow tribe members."

Alan saw the man he knew as Mr. Crow walking across the store. Even though his stature had begun to contract with age his commanding presence remained. The festive lighting shone the brilliance of his silver hair reaching to his mid-back. Before he could offer a greeting, Bodie gave him a hearty slap on the back. "Dr. G, right this way. I have several things picked out for you." The owner gestured toward the back of the over-sized log cabin. "You wear an 11 shoe, right?"

Alan shot a sideways look at Rachel, who gave him a quick wink. On his way to the rear, he surveyed the shop. Everything a person might need to make a go at surviving a Montana winter could be found in this store. The displays were well organized, every inch an efficient use of space. Alan couldn't see much in the way of advertising, but the people who shopped here didn't really have a choice. With a town this remote, competing stores weren't a problem.

As Alan approached a spread of outer winter apparel, he was amazed. Everything from a long heavy coat to wool socks and the very same style of boot Rachel was wearing was laid out. Every item he tried fit him to perfection. He picked out the bare essentials and began to add up the price tags to see how many additional articles he could afford.

As he was making his calculations, Rachel stepped off to talk to another shopper. He wondered if she didn't want to be seen spending too much time with him in public. A five-second commercial of the mayor reciting the no-employee-can-consort-romantically policy played in his head. Alan was glad to have a bit of privacy with his host as he prepared to negotiate. But Bodie jumped in first. "Are you willing to give up the ski jacket in trade?"

"Huh? Of course, there's not a lot of coat choices in Miami. Between you and me, I got this at a Goodwill Store. It's not my style, but the price was right."

Bodie's smile brightened. "I have a young skier who could grow into that coat nicely."

Alan put on each item he wanted and surveyed himself in the full-length mirror. Not an outfit that would make the cover of Vogue, but comfort and warmth were more important. He clunked around in the furry boots a bit.

"Those are handmade by a local artisan, faux fur, waterproof and environmentally friendly."

Alan chuckled at the pitch but had to give the trader credit for giving him everything he needed.

Bodie seemed to want to close the deal. "As a member of our volunteer EMT squad, you get a discount and with the ski jacket in trade, you can have everything you're wearing for $99.00."

"What?" Alan started removing the garments one by one. "I pay my way in this world. I don't want some made-up discount." He yanked the boots off, and they hit the floor with a thunk. Bodie's head rocked back as if he had taken a sucker punch to his face. Alan grabbed for his red, white and blue coat and readied himself to leave. Returning from her side conversation, Rachel halted him in his tracks with a touch on his forearm and an exaggerated smile.

She and Bodie shared a look that must have spoken volumes through silence. "I get the volunteer fire and rescue discount, too." She picked up the discarded articles and offered them back to him. "We talked about this. Snowflake currency."

"The ski jacket will make a certain young man very happy," added Bodie.

With great reluctance, Alan gathered the goods. Swallowing his pride nearly made him choke, but he presented one of the hundred dollar bills to Bodie. "Pleasure doing business with you. I look forward to offering my medical services whenever they're needed." Alan donned his camouflage cloak, which included a smile this time. "Please, keep the change."

Wearing his new coat and boots, Alan opened the door for Rachel as they left the Trading Post. He allowed himself to enjoy the short stroll with Rachel. She again made a point to keep an obvious distance between them. But, when she stopped to take in the blinking red and green lights of the neighboring businesses, he snuck a peek at her joy. Her beauty accentuated by the holiday ambiance helped him shut off his annoyance at accepting charity from the city councilman. He concentrated on how he might find a way to spend more time with his beguiling companion. A strictly platonic activity. "Can I ask you a favor, please?"

"Of course."

"From one business owner to another, could you please give me a tour of the historic landmarks of Snowflake? Consider it a chamber of commerce civic duty. I need to learn more about what and who was important throughout the years in Snowflake."

Rachel started across the street, heading toward the café. "Sure thing Doc, just tell me where and when."

Alan wanted to reply—*It's a date*—but didn't dare. Instead, he ended the night by thanking Rachel for the heads up about Bodie and the reminder about Snowflake currency. He watched her walk away for longer than he needed to, even after Rachel entered the restaurant and was out of sight.

CHAPTER 9

RACHEL WENT to Alan's office in the middle of December and was so glad she had shown him her old contract with Dr. Remington to save them both time. He replaced Remington with Garcia, they both signed it and then he emailed it to the mayor. She was officially on staff and bound by the new version of the employee handbook. Today, when they worked in tandem, it elevated the level of patient care. She told herself that patient satisfaction would sustain her happiness. Olga, Tameka and Jackie had her businesses running smoothly even during the peak holiday season. All should be right with her world. Except it wasn't.

A nagging feeling kept poking her throughout the day. That she had to lock away the romantic part of her nature, hurt. It almost made her ill. Maybe if she showed Alan her tomboy and over-achiever side, he would stop giving her those knowing looks. From the first patient until the last, she had watched him begin to say something or do something but stop himself. Then the *look* would arrive as if to say, it's against the rules for me to do that now. The worst of it was she had mirrored his performance and offered the same sad expression too often to count.

She pulled her truck up to his office backdoor. Rachel wanted as few people as possible seeing Alan riding with her. This evening's meeting would require her professionalism, no problem. The ranch hands were jealous of the vehicle, but other men, the gold diggers, encouraged her to trade it in for an SUV, more fitting for a lady. *How will Alan react?* The diesel engine made its usual noise, like a kitten's purr to her. The jacked up and reinforced suspension saved her on many of her emergency volunteer duties. Ice and snow were no match for this monster. Rachel was pleased that Alan had accepted her offer to drive the winding mountain roads at night. The man was smart on many levels.

Rachel bit her lip as Alan stepped out and saw his transport for the evening. Seeing his reaction would tell her so much more than his words. She did her best not to blink as he came from the building. He had to have his veil on or put on a poker face. *No shocked look.* He grasped the latch, and then took the three steps up into the passenger seat. *If he is like the local men of Snowflake here comes some snide comment. Hopefully, he'll be different.*

"Nice! This bad boy must get the job done. Right?" Alan hoisted his palm for a high-five. Rachel met his offer with more of a tap than a slap. Everything about his words and demeanor was honest, truly meant to be a compliment. "Good call on you driving. You know the roads, and I can Google the hospital to find their local accomplishments then mention them during our conversation to impress medical director by having done my homework."

She turned to check behind her just as he pivoted to fasten his seatbelt. His coat fell open, and she saw his dark business suit with a University of Miami tie. *He's your boss, just a normal guy.* He had shaved for a second time today and donned cologne. Just enough to tickle her nose. *Damn.* The woodsy scent matched the acres of forest in his new home state. "Sure thing. I'll throw in some commentary on the landmarks for free." She chuckled a bit, but then glued her eyes on the road.

He asked all kinds of intelligent questions as they drove. Then he went silent in awe of his first view of the neighboring town, Lodgepole Valley with its natural lake sparkling in the hue of an orange moon, she heard his breath hitch. She could make an outdoorsman of him, she knew it. Not that it was her place.

The dutiful nurse helping her doctor earn admitting privileges at the only nearby hospital was her goal tonight. The last time they strolled together she had shown Alan the historical markers around Snowflake. *Maybe these after-hours tour-guide duties should stop?* She needed to focus on showcasing her medical qualifications.

"Is it always like this? Where is everybody?" Alan looked out every window of the cab, his jaw went slack as they pulled into the center of town.

Rachel's grip on the wheel tightened. "Mismanagement of the mill caused this. No. This city is usually much busier than Snowflake." Zero cars were parked in the customer lots of stores and restaurants. Many buildings were dark and empty of furnishings. The occasional decoration didn't nearly bring out the holiday cheer. Christmas must have forgotten this street.

"Oh, my. No wonder payments from the patients aren't coming in. This place makes my money problems seem tame." His teeth slam together, and he abruptly looked away. "I didn't mean to make light of how people treat the Welch family, sorry. Do they assume you don't empathize with their situation?"

"No offense taken." She fumbled with her keys and tried to find the words to convey her sorrow for her neighbors. "I agreed on a plan Brett created for Welch Holdings to offer a loan of sorts. The sooner the mill re-opens the better." She flipped down her visor and used the lighted mirror to put on lipstick. She only wore it when she needed to hob-knob with hospital executives. Rachel saw no movement from Alan's side of the truck. Needing to color within the lines of her mouth, she didn't dare use her peripheral vision to catch him staring. But she knew he had to be. "Let's impress a medical director."

"Right. On it. With you by my side, I can do anything." The cold air that hit her when he opened his door was just what she needed. *I wish he hadn't said that. Focus, focus, focus.*

Because the medical director asked, Alan agreed to meet him Wednesday at six in the evening at a location halfway between the both of them. Alan, assuming he was the doctor, gave a firm squeeze to the hand of the only customer in the steakhouse. "Thank you for taking the time to hear me tell my story, sir." He knew he would have to sell his version of events that led to the numerous investigations from the FDA, health insurers and hospitals in Florida.

The impeccably dressed man had stood when he saw Rachel enter the room. Alan caught admiration in the way the executive looked at Rachel. That caused his inner warning whistles to blare. Alan wasn't certain if it was because she was a Welch, a good nurse or a beauty inside and out. He hoped she hadn't put on lipstick because this guy was one of her former suitors. *Can't think about the men in her past or her luscious mouth.*

"Please, say no more. Thank you for making the drive to meet me here." Richard Andrews, MD waved his arm toward the oversized wooden table and chairs. "I wanted to put my expense account to good use. Help infuse a few dollars into this economy. Terrible thing, the mill closure." He straightened his tie and tugged on his shirt cuffs before he approached their white-linen covered table.

"Ms. Welch, always a pleasure." She gave him a polite nod as he pulled the chair out for her. "The Welch beef is sold far and wide, so this is just a blip on your bottom line, I'm guessing?"

He had said it in a joking manner, but Alan wanted to give the man a piece of his mind. Now was not the time, so he took out his anger on the linen napkin, opening it with a thwack before he laid it on his lap.

"Oh, Dr. Andrews, always a kind word. But we're not here to talk about me tonight." Rachel smiled and presented herself with such poise. Her example doused the fire that had ignited in Alan's belly on her behalf. He fed off her manners and regained his composure.

The medical director gave a signal to the server who hurried over with three menus. "Please order whatever you'd like." He leaned back in his seat and steepled his index fingers. "This isn't just a formality. I am following the protocol of legal counsel. In case your actions at my hospital cause the need for me to defend you in court, Dr. Garcia, I want to have first-hand knowledge of your qualifications and the tarnish on your reputation. I've completed my due diligence." He nudged Alan's forearm. "Being investigated by the FDA is a royal pain, am I right?"

The acid in Alan's stomach roiled. He expected the interrogation but enduring it was going to be more of a challenge than his self-confidence could bear. Would Rachel still respect him? "If I had to do it all over again, I'd take the same action. Except now I lock up my prescription pad every night, no exception." One side of his mouth tried to lift into a smile, but the other side drooped. He scooched his chair closer to the table and fidgeted with his silverware.

"I didn't lock up my pads until I reviewed your case. You taught me something new. I agree with your exoneration or I wouldn't be here. Relax." Dr. Andrews opened his menu which blocked Alan's view of his face, but the tone of his voice sounded like a vote of confidence.

Alan took in the deepest breath he had taken all day. "Thank you, sir. That means a great deal to me." He looked over at Rachel and she was beaming. He took a snapshot of her to keep in his mind. He would remember how she looked this night when he was not where he could see her.

With the business out of the way, Alan enjoyed getting to know Dr. Andrews. He was a down to earth guy who did a good job of playing his stuffy board member part. The executive had insisted they order dessert but had his boxed to go. He paid the bill and left Alan and Rachel to finish the meal alone.

After the formal farewells were complete, and Dr. Andrew had cleared the door, Rachel leaned over and gave Alan a seated sideways hug. "Congratulations! I knew he would approve you."

"Thank you. One more box on my list I can check off." Alan allowed a bit of silliness to flow through his movements as he acted out the motion.

He sat with Rachel in a restaurant that felt like he rented it out so he could dine without prying eyes. The residents of Lodgepole Valley didn't know about the new rule. So, no one might catch him in an action that would get him fired. Should he dare allow himself to act like this was a date?

He took one look at Rachel in the dim lighting and rustic surroundings and decided he could allow himself to celebrate. This type of happiness needed to be shared with someone who understood how much he gave of himself to become a doctor. Only Rachel or his *madre* could fill that seat. Even if this was a one-time delight, he would let his dream of dating Rachel be real tonight.

The waitress brought their dessert. "You can have some of mine if I can have a bite of yours." Rachel had a twinkle in her eye that danced with mischief and delight. As her fork stabbed into his plate, she threw her head back and laughed. Her glorious thick hair fell away from her shoulders. He wanted so badly to touch it. So, he did. Rachel was busy bringing the creamy cheesecake to her lips. She had no idea he had run his fingers through her long locks. Before he picked up his fork, he waved that hand under his nose. The sweet flowery smell of her shampoo was strong enough to still linger. Alan was in heaven.

He moved his plate and chair closer to the table's corner, and she did the same. Their forks did a crisscross like the figure skaters of an ice show. Then she held up a bite of her chocolate delight for him to eat. With great care and at a snail's pace he allowed her to feed him. His mouth slid over smooth metal, but he let himself think of it as his lips touching hers. He wanted her to do it over and over again. They could have been on another planet. No one else saw his flirtation.

"I like the way you celebrate Dr. Garcia." The words she said hadn't been meant to deflate their revelry, but she hadn't called him Alan. It sucked the air out of his lungs. He was her boss. He was just kidding himself. How could he put her job in jeopardy? He leaned away and only ate from his plate from that point forward.

Rachel offered to tell him about the businesses that were still open. He needed a walk in the cold to clear his head. This time he made a point of keeping a gaping distance between them. Physically, he was near her, but emotionally he had built an impenetrable wall. He had let her get too close. Why had he done that, to torture himself? Seeing her in the office knowing he could not date her would be harder than ever. He needed to find a way to keep his most favored nurse and date her, too. But was that realistic? Would he give up his job if it came to it?

CHAPTER 10

RACHEL LOOKED FORWARD to her day of giving flu shots to the children at the school. This was one of her volunteer nursing duties that she cherished. It helped that the school principal was one of her classmates from high school. They always had a bit of girlish fun, while still managing to complete their responsibilities. This year's flu outbreak was unusually bad, making Rachel's civic duty that much more important to her.

"What's going on with you?" asked her best friend Principal Hayes, when Rachel walked into the school cafeteria. She patted her ebony face. "I'm glowing because I'm expecting. What's your excuse?"

"Long story. I'm not at liberty to discuss it." Trying to redirect the conversation, she threw open her coat. "Look at these scrubs! Is this Christmas or what? Should help distract the kids from the needles." She'd found the scrubs online—the very busy green and red outfit was full of every holiday reference a person could imagine. Gift boxes, ornaments, Christmas trees and several versions of Santa dotted the fabric.

Her childhood friend hesitated but didn't push to learn more. "Check out this spread of Christmas cookies." The scent of the sweet-smelling confections hit Rachel's nose once her friend brought them to her attention.

"Mrs. Wilson outdid herself. How such a tomboy can be such a good cook boggles the mind." Joining Patsy in a good laugh, Rachel set up for the day and enjoyed viewing the homemade holiday decorations adorning the cafeteria's glass walls. They were displayed by grade, and Rachel didn't know what was cuter—the kindergarteners' depictions of Santa delivering toys or the eighth graders' construction paper ornaments.

Once everything was ready for the day's vaccines, Rachel began her usual twenty questions routine to catch up on Patsy's life. "So, how's the morning sickness?" Rachel asked. She took a bite of a tree-shaped cookie. Cinnamon, her favorite holiday flavor, danced across her taste buds.

Patsy rubbed her belly. "Can't complain. Had my first visit with Dr. Garcia the other day. Why didn't you warn me he's such a hottie?"

Rachel hadn't thought of other women in town realizing that the good doctor was good looking. She needed to think about the ramifications of his attractiveness. Her thoughts began to spin like a merry-go-round. She didn't want to date him, then she did. She didn't want to work with him, then she did. But, if she worked with him, would she be willing to give up dating him? Would he even consider dating her? *Oh, right. Not allowed to date anyway.* He had seemed to distance himself from her when they had strolled the empty streets of Lodgepole Valley. He just changed jobs. His mother switched professions and now worked in the clinic too.

Teresa Garcia had given up her job and moved several states to escape the gang's retaliation tactics. Alan would not put her at risk for a few dates. She sighed. The carousel kept spinning faster and faster. She went to take another bite, but her cookie broke off in her fingers and landed on the floor.

"Earth to Rachel. Surely, you've met this guy, right? Doesn't the town expect you to work for him?" Patsy had one fist on her hip, the other grabbing for a sweet treat that kept her friend's mouth from spewing more questions, for which Rachel was grateful.

"Um, yes I've met him. Anyone with eyes can see he's professional and well-mannered. He did offer me the nursing job." Rachel fidgeted with a row of band-aids. "Before the city council practically required it." Taking a break from the conversation by picking out a new cookie, Rachel worried that someone as close to her as Patsy could tell she was attracted to Alan.

"Get back here, you rascal." Zeb, the silver-haired school janitor, was standing by the cafeteria door, waiting for a child to exit.

A glimpse of white fur flashed past Rachel's feet and gobbled up the crumbs of the cookie that lay broken on the ground. "What an adorable dog. Who's this?"

Zeb rushed over to grab the collar of the fluffy visitor. He smiled and tried to conceal his angst by looking at the floor. "Mr. Cuddles ran away from the fifth graders who were supposed to be caring for him today." Picking up the escapee, he turned to Principal Hayes. "I'm so sorry. I know he can't be in the cafeteria. It won't happen again."

Patsy laughed and pet the bundle of energy. "Accidents happen, and no one from the state saw the crime. Besides, who can resist this sweet little guy?" She kissed his head while his tail continued its wild wagging.

With the hasty exit of the janitor and his K-9 companion, Patsy explained, "Mr. Cuddles is Zeb's rescue dog. He brings him in on occasion to help the kids learn responsibility, or to provide a distraction for children who are dealing with a family crisis, like the closing of the mill."

Getting back to business, Patsy picked up the sign-in clipboard and prepared to bring in the children to receive their shots. "Oh, I was about to say, Dr. Garcia is coming here today. I'll congratulate him for hiring you."

Rachel choked on her second attempt to eat a cookie. "Huh, what?" Beckoning her friend to come sit next to her, she chugged from a child-sized bottle of chocolate milk, which washed down the errant crumbs. Patsy motioned for the school kids to wait a minute and complied with Rachel's request.

Swallowing, waving her cookie in front of her face, and swallowing some more, Rachel managed to ask, "He's coming here, today? When?" She knew her friend well enough to know that Patsy could see she was hiding something, so Rachel decided to fess up. "The mayor instituted a new rule in the office. No fraternizing among staff." She paused for effect. "Any hint of romance is grounds for immediate termination. So, if I act weird or standoffish, around him, you'll know why." She topped off her performance with an award-winning Cheshire Cat grin.

Patsy looked at her watch. "He's due here any minute. What exactly are you trying to say?"

Before she could answer, she looked through the cafeteria's glass walls and saw Alan walking towards them. "We don't want to trigger gossip if folks see us together outside of the office." Making a dash for it, Rachel darted toward the cafeteria's kitchen. She looked over her shoulder and saw a perplexed look on Patsy's face. "Just play along for now, please." After making a narrow escape, she placed her back against the wall near the entrance so she could hear, but not be seen. Rachel dropped her chin to her chest, arms hanging at her sides, and felt her heart pounding. *Don't find out I'm here.*

"Mrs. Hayes, so nice to see you again. How are you feeling?" asked Alan, coming closer to the flu shot section of tables.

Rachel could hear Patsy picking up the cookie platter. "I'm good, thanks for asking. Have a cookie?"

"Don't mind if I do." Rachel wanted Alan to pick his treat quickly, for Patsy to put the tray down, and for them both to leave. The clap-clop of Patsy's high heels came closer to the wall she was hiding behind and she cringed.

"Thank you for coming here to discuss improving the nutrition of the school's lunches." Rachel willed Patsy to lead Alan away, but her thoughts weren't strong enough. "We'll be meeting in my office, but I wanted you to see we're giving the children flu shots today, as we do every year."

Rachel rolled her eyes. *Get on with it.*

"Rachel stepped away to the ladies' room, but if you're lucky you might be able to meet her later." She wanted to run away and hide but didn't dare move as that might cause a sound that would reveal her hiding place. "Speaking of Rachel, you know she and I go way back. Great choice. I feel more comfortable knowing she'll be part of the staff, this being my first pregnancy and all." *Oh Patsy, you smooth talker.*

"Nurse Welch is amazing. Glad you approve." Rachel caught a glimpse of Alan's reflection off the glass as he sang her praises. She wasn't sure if he had said it because that was what the mayor would want him to say. Rachel didn't have a good view of his expression. Was she an amazing nurse or an amazing woman?

"The city council made it very clear the office manager and I couldn't run the clinic on our own." Alan's voice began to trail off as Patsy led him to her office. But Rachel caught his last phrase. "She's a co-worker, nothing more."

Rachel slid down the wall until her bottom hit the floor. *Was he creating a smokescreen or was that the way he felt about her?* Had the swift departure of Dr. Remington messed with her self-esteem that much? Rachel felt like she had fallen into a well, with a giant splash.

CHAPTER 11

ALAN WAS protective of Rachel's staff knowing she had stepped away from running the café to be his nurse. Extra sounds of activity came from across the street all day. His curiosity was nagging at him, but Alan didn't have time to snatch a look. Fresh snow also called him to go outside and enjoy his new surroundings, but the higher than average cases of flu kept him shuffling in and out of patient exam rooms or on his tablet making notes all day. He only saw Rachel for a split second here or there all day. She was hustling as much as he was which made him admire her more. The day wore on, no lunch, no casual conversation breaks of any kind. He even felt guilty when he took a few-minutes respite to use the bathroom.

After the last patient left, Rachel went to work at her bar. Alan sent his mother home to enjoy a relaxing bubble bath and a chick flick, he began to unwind. With no sign of Miami gang activity in Snowflake, Alan had allowed his concerns about her security to subside. No hint of his former life had followed him to Montana. Alan was too busy to miss home. His best chance of happiness was to fit into the lives of the people of Snowflake. How would Rachel fit in his new normal?

He took a break to stretch his neck and think about what tasks needed to be completed before tomorrow's office hours. As usual,

Alan planned to work a half-day on Saturday, but the need for care was so high he expected another packed waiting room. Stomach growling, Alan searched the welcome basket for a couple of nutrition bars. At this rate, no way that supply would last the winter. He put them back and sighed. Rubbing his forehead, he opened another patient file for review, but then the rumble of a big engine piqued his curiosity.

Alan sauntered to the nearest window, and the scene outdoors caught him by surprise. The Squeaky Saddle Saloon had come to life. Every light in the place was on, including the flashing neon beer signs in the windows—even the life-size red saddle made of lights was aglow. He'd never seen so many four-by-four vehicles gathered in one place since his arrival. No way was he going to miss this. Putting his office closing activities into overdrive, Alan made his way to his favorite watering hole. Well, it was the only bar in town, but chances were good that he could strike up casual banter with Rachel while she worked.

A blast of frigid air hit him as he locked the clinic, and it felt more like Christmas to him than his hometown's warmth. Today's commotion, he realized, had been caused by several of the businesses on Main Street putting up their holiday decorations, including Rachel's establishments.

Thick strands of pine garland hung in half circles across the front of the gift shop all the way to the saloon, with old-fashioned green and red Christmas lights crossing the gutters and outlining every window. The colored lights danced in the snow, welcoming him as the wind helped blow him across the street.

Instead of using the café's front entrance, Alan made his way to the bar's side door. The sound of the jukebox blasting out a Garth Brooks tune hit him before his hand even found the doorknob. Shouts and laughter blended into the din as the smell of peanuts and beer-filled his nose. His stomach growled again. Alan was pleased to recognize Monkey and one of Brett's coworkers sitting at the bar. Taking a seat at the end, closest to the doorway, he chuckled to himself as he noted that the tops of the barstools were actual saddles.

Alan swore he heard his squeak as he settled into a comfortable position.

Monkey raised a heavy glass mug filled with beer in his direction. "Hey Doc, glad to see they let you out of the infirmary. The bartender went downstairs to tap another keg. She'll be back soon."

Alan told himself he was coming to the Squeaky Saddle to unwind, but a rush of butterflies filled his belly once he saw the woman tending bar was Rachel. A heap of shyness hit him, and he found himself staring at the wood-grain counter, brushing his fingertips back and forth, feeling the smoothness of the decades-old surface. *Keep it strictly business.*

"Hey, Doc. Nice to see you. What'll you have?" asked Rachel. He had hoped she'd be around, but she was working. He was exhausted. She had worked the same number of hours and was still working. Alan felt like he should help her bus tables or something. She was truly amazing.

Searching deep within himself, Alan found his inner confidence and did everything in his power to present a facade of casual calm. "What've you got on tap? Something local maybe?" he replied with a grin that made his cheeks hurt. "Do you serve food in the saloon? Oh, and how many children got flu shots?"

Grabbing a mug from a freezer, Rachel opened the tap and filled it to overflowing, bringing it to him with foam still sliding down the side. "Snowflake IPA, as local as you get in these parts. See what you think. And not enough, this season looks to be worse than most." Before he could continue the conversation, she was off tending to other customers. Alan took a slow sip, tasting hops and barley and feeling the frazzle of his hectic day beginning to ease.

He scoped out his surroundings. Everywhere he looked was old dark wood. Mostly men filled each booth. They were rugged, weather-worn guys in overworked clothes, but they seemed to be having a rowdy good time. As he scanned the walls, he saw the familiar chalk-written menu. All of the items were crossed off except lasagna and a buffalo burger and fries.

Monkey had given him venison to pay for stitching up his leg. Alan wanted to gift the deer meat to someone who would enjoy it but expected it would stay in his freezer for some time. He thought of trying buffalo meat for the first time since it was prepared by Rachel. *No way. Not happening. Not today, way too tired. I'll put that adventure back on my 'to do' list.*

Ready to order, Alan looked for Rachel. He spotted her in a corner, participating in an animated conversation. Eventually, she broke free and made another round through the room. He heard folks shout out requests as she passed so he decided to join in. "Lasagna for me, please."

"Coming right up," shouted Rachel to no one and everyone over the music and the ongoing chatter.

Alan recognized Olga, the new girl, as she came out of the café and placed the steaming square of lasagna in front of him. She vanished so quickly that his attempt to thank her merged into the sounds around him, virtually unheard. As Alan sat shoveling his dinner into his mouth, he began to realize just how much effort Rachel expended keeping her businesses running. This physically demanding job was in addition to her nursing duties. Yes, she had employees, but she tended the bar all by herself. At least thirty-five hungry and continuously thirsty people filled the place.

While Alan was counting people, the ratio of women to men became more obvious. Going back to each woman, he found that every one of them was wearing a wedding ring. Even Olga seemed to be wearing some sort of promise ring. He couldn't help but notice that Monkey was watching Olga's every move. She made no attempt to hide her extra-attentive level of service for Monkey, but he didn't know them to be an item.

Alan had so much in his own life to sort out, he had no business thinking about other people's love lives, but those thoughts were a nice distraction, if only for a brief moment. He circled his thoughts back to the fact that Rachel was the only single woman in the saloon. He didn't consider himself a jealous man, but he decided to see which guys might be flirting with her. He wanted to know who his competition would be even knowing he could never ask her out.

One thing was clear, Rachel knew every customer by name. She was dashing from one task to the next, but she smiled all the while and laughed easily. He wasn't sure if she was working hard or hardly working. The old adage came to his mind, "if you love what you do for a living, it doesn't feel like work." Alan surveyed four or maybe five booths all filled with men who seemed to be connected somehow since Rachel spent a great deal of time serving them.

As Alan's mind processed his potential hurdles to romancing Rachel, a chill reached him. He turned and saw the side door open and Brett walking in. His scowl looked more like an angry grizzly bear than a loving sibling. Alan moved his fork with less speed, trying to go unnoticed, but Brett took up a rigid stance right next to him. As Rachel passed them to enter the restaurant, Brett grumbled, "I thought we talked about this. Why is the saloon open? And why are THEY here?" The protective older brother pointed to the loud-mouthed, motley crew of men.

Still carrying several dirty plates, Rachel halted. "Geez bro, relax. Nate called me—you know, the mill foreman. It's an informal attempt to help people find jobs." Olga came up and took the used plates from Rachel and made a quick escape to the kitchen. "We've got bills to pay!" She pointed to herself and her brother. "Oh, and they're also trying to figure out how to find the capital to get the mill re-opened. It'd be nice if you could at least hear what they have to say."

Brett looked over at the gathering of testosterone, and his head dropped in defeat. "Fine! But did you hear the forecast? Betsy and I are going to be out most of the night trying to keep ahead of the drifting snow."

"You can spare five minutes." Rachel took Brett by the arm and turned him toward Alan. "Besides, Doc is here, so I'm well protected." Her shoulder brushed his as she moved. He caught her wink with his peripheral vision. In a blur, she was back to serving customers, leaving him to pick up the conversation. The smell of her shampoo and the wink had him dazed. *Did anyone else catch that wink? What might people think?*

Brett's commanding presence became his most pressing concern.

Alan hauled up his mug. "The Snowflake IPA is good, huh?" He hadn't been trying to eavesdrop, but he had heard every word. Now he felt it best to act like he hadn't.

"That bunch has a history of getting a bit too rambunctious. Feel free to call the sheriff." Retrieving his phone, Brett added, "In fact, I'm going to give him a heads-up text." His thumbs flew across his keyboard, then Brett picked up an empty chair, turned it backward against a booth filled with mill workers, and joined the ruckus.

Just as Alan finished his meal, another cool breeze at his back let him know someone new had entered the bar.

"There you are. I've been looking for you all over."

Alan heard the words but tried to ignore them. *What could Mrs. Jameson possibly want with me at this hour?*

"Yoo-hoo, Dr. Garcia. I'm talking to you." And in an instant, she was in his face. "Hi there. I've been trying to stop by your office for days, but there's been a line out the door every time." She thrust a flyer at him with lots of red and green. "Snowflake's annual kick-off to the Twelve Days of Christmas is soon upon us." The always well-dressed woman threw her scarf back over her shoulder. "As the town's doctor, you are expected to be on our team."

The word "expected" burned in Alan's ear. "What kind of team?"

"The list of events is on the flyer." She cackled at a volume above the noise in the saloon. "The competing cities ride down Main Street on horseback and gather at the community center for a staged Wild West shootout. Oh, it's so much fun! Gotta go, more people to see. Ta-ta."

Before he could ask his questions, she was gone, another frozen breeze in her wake. Alan read the flyer and read it again. The competition included activities like ax throwing, barrel racing, cow roping and rifle marksmanship. The only event he might have a hope of being able to complete in was the trivia challenge. The comforting feeling of being around Rachel for the evening vanished into utter dread. Still dumbfounded by the bombshell news Heidi had dropped on him, Alan took another sip of his beer. The clatter of a table being bussed drew his attention.

"Ready for a refill, Alan?" Rachel's sweet voice brought him out of his misery. "The guys from the mill are picking up your tab for fixing up Monkey. So, what'll you have?"

"What? NO! I mean, they don't have to do that." No amount of frosty wind from the exit could extinguish the anger related heat rising in Alan. Just as he opened his mouth to protest further, he could see the expressions of Monkey and every patron sitting at the bar and reeled himself back. "Wow, that's so nice of them. I'll be sure to thank them before they leave." He held up his empty mug. "I'll have another, thanks." He offered a sheepish smile to Rachel, and the heart-warming grin she gave him back took his breath away.

After making a point of graciously thanking his benefactors, Alan spent the next hour nursing his beer, fidgeting with the flyer and keeping track of the more boisterous men from the mill. His worries must have been transparent to at least one other customer.

"Hey Doc, the sheriff has a stable full of horses. I'm sure he'll let you borrow one." Monkey tossed some cash onto the bar and left.

THE NEXT DAY, after an exhausting stream of patients, Alan mustered all of his willpower to get himself to the sheriff's stables. The aging man with his belly protruding over his belt and the ends of his mustache flowing well past the corners of his mouth stood atop a railing of a horse's stall."Thanks so much for being willing to let me use one of your horses, and more importantly, to teach me to ride." Alan had found himself choking on his pride all day. His father's Army Ranger buddies had taught him many things, but how to ride a horse was not one of them. The only thing that made this situation bearable was he knew Rachel would be a member of Snowflake's team.

"No problem, I'll teach you to ride and you can teach me how to use this darn phone," replied Sheriff Wilson. "What's wrong with using the radio? And this texting stuff, I'm a terrible typist and the abbreviations, I haven't got a clue."

Alan gave his newfound friend the basics to help him become proficient with his phone and then spent several hours trying to get the horse the sheriff had chosen for him to respond to his commands. At the end of the session, Mrs. Wilson met the men in the barn to assist with brushing down the horses. The two men reviewed which gang had tried to harm Alan's mother, and Alan confirmed the dates she would be in Miami for the holidays.

Sheriff Wilson called the Miami authorities to get their support for her protection. Alan appreciated that he had even given him names of reputable bodyguards. Accepting this generosity ruffled his feathers, but he managed to cage his insecurities for the benefit of his mother's safety.

As soon as he left Mrs. Wilson, without Alan's knowledge, called Mrs. Jameson.

"You'll never guess what I just learned about Dr. Garcia and his mother."

"Oh my, do tell," replied Mrs. Jameson.

CHAPTER 12

THE ENTRANCE BELL rang in the gift shop just as the lunch rush began to thin out. "Be right there, just gotta wash up," called out Rachel from the café's kitchen. *Glad to help people shop, but I don't have time for this today.* Olga needed time off, so Rachel was working both jobs spending a few hours where she felt she was most needed. She was thankful Alan was an understanding boss.

Drying her hands, she made a mad dash behind the customer service counter. "Mrs. Garcia, how nice to see you. How can I help?" Rachel's stomach jumped into her throat. Annoyed with her body for its response, she reminded herself that Teresa was one of the nicest ladies she knew. But being with Alan's mother outside of the clinic made her nervous. She felt the need to impress.

"Hi Rachel, how's it going? This is the post office, right?" Mrs. Garcia looked around, with fast glances in all directions. Rachel wasn't certain who was more jittery, herself or her visitor.

Laughing, Rachel replied, "I know it doesn't look like much, but I assure you I can ship any size package. This is a certified postal outpost."

Putting a large box on the counter, Teresa asked, "Can you send this to Miami? I need to be able to make a fast break when I arrive there tomorrow."

Oh, I wonder if she is scared to go back to where the gang had been harassing her. "Sure thing, no problem."

Mrs. Garcia stepped back and relaxed at Rachel's answer. "Oh good. I'm trying to keep a low profile." No sooner than she'd said it, Teresa clapped her lips together and tightened the muscles in her cheeks. Trying to ignore the unintentional release of details, Rachel busied herself with the steps she needed to complete for an outbound package. But she kept an eye on what had grabbed Teresa's attention.

"See anything in the gift shop that'll make a great Christmas gift? All of the items are handmade by local folks."

Mrs. Garcia gravitated to the display of quilts, passing her palm over the fabric. "This one is so manly and has colors that would remind Alan of the University of Miami." She stepped away, dropping her gaze. "But we decided not to exchange gifts this year."

Rachel had managed to get her stomach out of her throat, but now something was squeezing her heart. It ached for this strong, proud woman who had endured so much. The thought that she and Alan would be forgoing a family Christmas tradition created a rock in her stomach and her chest tighten even more. To break the awkwardness that had settled in the shop, Rachel told Teresa the cost of the postage. The distraction of getting out her credit card seemed to help lighten the mood.

With the transaction complete, Teresa moved toward the exit, but she stopped at the pile of comforters again. "Do you accept Snowflake currency?" The question came out just above a whisper.

Joining Mrs. Garcia in front of the quilt, Rachel was pleased to answer, "Absolutely! Most of the sales in this shop are made that way. What do you craft?"

A sparkle danced into Teresa's eyes. "I make silk flower arrangements."

Clapping, Rachel did a little jig. "You don't say! We've never had anything like that in here before. I could sell the mess out of them!"

"Really, you're not just being polite?" The doctor's mother gave Rachel a wary look.

"For real!" She crossed her heart and held up the scout's honor gesture. "The people who've lived here for a while already have the stuff the rest of us can make. Having something different would be appreciated, no joking." Rachel took down the display quilt, folding it and placing it on the bottom of the stack. "Let's just hide this one so it'll be here when you can bring in the flowers."

Mrs. Garcia must have realized how badly Alan needed the item. Before Rachel knew it, Teresa was hugging her. She dove deep into the uplifting feeling she got when she helped someone. When the embrace was over, Rachel noticed growing confidence in her newest customer. "Do you carry the soap I keep hearing the women talk about?"

Leading her shopper to the product in question, "Ah, you must mean the huckleberry shampoo and soaps?"

Rushing after her, Mrs. Garcia picked up a bar and smelled it through the wrapper. "Mmmm, this is it. And it moisturizes too?" She waved the bar under her nose and moaned.

"Yep, Mrs. Wilson makes it. Very secret recipe." Both women laughed. But Teresa put the soap back on the shelf. This made Rachel pause and ponder. Then an idea flashed into her mind. "Can the clinic spare you for another fifteen minutes?"

Teresa raised an eyebrow. "I think I could make that happen. Why?"

Rachel looked out into the diner, then back at Mrs. Garcia, her eyes finally landing on the soap. "You'd be doing me a huge favor. With the flu going around, I'm slammed with take-out orders for dinner. I'm short-staffed to boot." She gave Teresa a bottle of shampoo and two bars of soap. "I'll make you a deal. If you bus the tables in the café and then swab them down, I'll give you these huckleberry soaps."

"What?" Mrs. Garcia juggled the bottle and bars while she spoke. "The value of these items doesn't match the work, fifteen minutes for all this?"

Rachel laid her upper body on her counter and then labored to raise herself up on her elbows. "Honestly, working two jobs is catching up to me. I truly need help, please!" Reaching behind the counter she snatched a gift shop bag. Placing the huckleberry soap in it, Rachel took Teresa by the arm and led her into the kitchen. "Here's the gear, gloves and a mask if you want them, please!"

Just then, the phone rang, and Tameka stopped washing dishes to answer it. "To go order? Sure, let me get a pen."

Rachel grasped Teresa's hand in a shake. "Deal?"

"Deal." Mrs. Garcia hugged Rachel again. Donning the gloves, she headed into the restaurant.

Busy stirring a mammoth batch of chicken noodle soap, Rachel only glanced up as Teresa replaced the cleaning supplies. But it stopped her cold to see the new bounce in the woman's step when she snatched up the spoils of her labor and glided her way to the door with a wave. "Pleasure doing business with you."

ALAN SAT IN HIS OFFICE, trying to keep up with the crush of ongoing paperwork while he waited for Bodie to arrive. He was a bit stiff from his riding lesson, but something told him tomorrow the discomfort would be worse. Bodie had asked for the last appointment but wanted to meet in Alan's office, not an exam room. This had Alan puzzled, but he was certain all would be revealed soon enough. Alan had texted Bodie as requested since both men understood that the clinic often fell behind schedule as the day wore on.

When Teresa escorted Bodie into the room, Alan thought he picked up a bit of flirtation coming from the man toward his mom. He had seen this scenario before and thought he might need to give his potential pal some friendly advice. Alan believed his mother would never date. She had lost her beloved husband during an active duty incident when she was pregnant with Alan. Many men had tried to woo her, but his dedicated and loyal *madre* never gave any of them a second thought.

Bodie looked around at the updated office décor, giving two

thumbs up. But Alan recognized that having a cot in the room gave him pause. "Yes, I sleep here sometimes." *How do I say this without sounding like a workaholic, or needy*? "The cold is a bigger issue than keeping up with paperwork." Bodie's expression didn't change. "I bought the Russo place and gave my mom the master bedroom, so I'm staying in the oldest section of the homestead."

Alan laughed a bit but stopped when it sounded forced even to his ears. "I need my rest and the drafty room isn't conducive for sleep." The next few seconds of silence were almost painful. Alan knew Bodie was a man of few words, so he changed the subject. "Is that package for me?"

Bodie placed the box on Alan's desk with a file on top, then he sat in one of the outdoor plastic chairs, dwarfing it. "Thanks for accommodating my request. The Trading Post is in peak season, but this is very important to me."

Alan instinctively picked up the folder and assumed he would be reading Bodie's medical records, but they were for another man of similar age, Running Wolf. As he read on, the medical caregiver in him was intrigued—this man had a chronic illness but had refused treatment. "What's up with the box?" asked Alan as he turned another page.

Sitting up straighter in his chair, Bodie exuded a sense of peaceful pride. "That patient is a fellow tribal elder. All I'm asking is that you try to get him to take his meds. But you must go to him. He won't see any doctor. Indian remedies haven't helped him." He stood up, opened the door to see who might be nearby, then closed it and returned to his chair. "The box is Snowflake currency. Before you open it, please understand I see many things at the store. I see what people want. Maybe you can give that as a Christmas present?"

Alan had already grown to respect the man in his office, but this request just added to the warmth he felt for the aging patriarch. "Bodie, I'd help because that's who I am as a doctor. Not because you hold a seat on the city council, or were so generous with my winter supplies, but because I find my life's meaning and satisfaction when

I'm providing care." Alan started to give the box back to Bodie, but the man glared.

"I think you need to see what's in the box." The look on Bodie's face told Alan the man would not take no for an answer.

Against his better judgment, Alan peeled back the delicate tissue, revealing a multicolored scarf. The colors were his *madre*'s favorites. Alan hid behind the mask of detachment he used for patient care as he picked it up. The material was exceptionally soft.

"Cashmere," offered Bodie, breaking the long silence.

A lengthy list of questions swirled in Alan's mind. He replayed the many times he'd been outside with his mother since they'd moved to town. A vice grip took hold of his lungs when he realized she did not have a winter scarf.

Alan opened his mouth to speak but couldn't.

Bodie cleared his throat. "I don't pretend to understand women. Yes, I tried to sell your mother a less expensive scarf. I knew what she needed. My guess is she decided to wait until she could afford what she wanted." He scratched his five o'clock shadow and scowled.

Standing helped to put Alan in his doctor persona, removing all emotion and allowing rational thought to prevail. He straightened his tie and tugged at the lapels of his lab coat. "You and I both know how much my mother deserves to wear this scarf. If she wants it, I'll give it to her. We agreed to not exchange gifts, but I think she'll get over my broken promise."

Grinning widely, Bodie conveyed additional details about his closest friend and how Alan could go about making a house call to deliver the necessary medications. On his way out, he called back, "Oh, and the day you stitched up Monkey was the day you earned a passing grade from me. You know, that probation thing. Mrs. Jameson is making a bigger deal out of it than necessary."

Alan collapsed in his chair. His elation at making progress to earn a permanent job was squashed by his anguish about not noticing his mom had gone without warm clothing in this northern climate. *What kind of son would make his mother endure the frigid cold unprepared?*

❄

AFTER HEARING Mrs. Jameson describe the facts about Dr. Garcia and his mother differently to one of the deputy's wives who had come to city hall, Mrs. Wilson jumped in. "The details you left out changed the meaning of what I said and you know it."

"What details?" Mrs. Jameson got up from her desk and walked out the office door. "People hear what they want to anyway. I can't control if someone misinterprets the meaning of my words."

"But what you said was so different from the truth," said Mrs. Wilson to herself since her dear friend had succeeded in making a hasty exit.

CHAPTER 13

RACHEL CARRIED her trivia games to the back booth of the saloon where she had left Patsy propping up her feet to reduce the swelling in her ankles. “Hopefully people will leave us alone back here. Not many customers for the bar midweek. Thanks for helping me practice for the Twelve Days of Christmas games.”

“No worries. My husband is Christmas shopping, and I need something to distract me from my discomfort. My back aches and I can’t see my feet when I stand.” Patsy shuffled the flashcards as she tried to find a comfortable position on the wooden seat. “So, how is working for the new doctor going?”

Rachel tucked her hair behind her ears and thought twice about how to answer. “He’s a great physician, listens to my ideas on how to streamline the office procedures and his mother is so kind.” She tucked a pillow behind her friend. “There, better?”

“Yes. And don’t avoid my real question”

“What? I answered. Be more specific. What do you want to know?”

Patsy asked a few trivia questions and Rachel answered. Then she sprung what was on her mind. “You’re attracted to him, aren’t you?”

“What? Why would you think that?” Rachel did her best to hide the fact that Patsy had found her Achilles heel. “Being attracted to him and acknowledging he's attractive are two different things." She flipped over a card to see if her answer was correct even though she hadn't read the question on the front.

Patsy raised an eyebrow at her and waited. *Ugh, she knows me too well.* "No fraternization at work. Immediate dismissal. End of subject." Rachel's dexterity faltered and the games pieces she held spewed all over the table.

"Oh, you've got the hots for him that bad." Patsy scratched her forehead while she gave her noggin a shake meant to chastise. "Is he into you too?"

Rachel shot her confidante a knowing look. "I can't read his mind. Trying not to find out. I mean, I hope so. But that would be bad, very bad." She stared at the words of the trivia questions but couldn't make sense of their meaning. "Why are the doctors in that office such a problem for me?"

Patsy squeezed Rachel's hand. "Forget what he looks like and that he's off-limits. What makes him worthy of you?" Rachel sat dumbfounded. Silent. "This is me you're talking to, let it out."

"He doesn't want my money. His family means everything to him. He gives so much of himself to his patients. He's smart, honest and funny. I could go on and on." Rachel let out a small gasp and clutched her heart. "Oh, it felt so good to say that. I thought I had kept myself from falling for him, but I think I'm already there." She collapsed onto the back of the booth. Her whole body went limp. "Off-limits. I can't put his job at risk." Tears welled up inside her, but she stamped them down. She slammed shut the cage doors around her heart and buried the key in a cavern of sadness.

Patsy made her way to Rachel's side of the booth to hug her. "Rules are meant to be broken. If this thing between the two of you doesn't interfere with patient care, then maybe no one will care."

"Don't give me hope. I can't go there, can't be the cause of the clinic closing again. It would hurt his mother too. Oh God, this is awful." Rachel leaned into Patsy and let her friend help bear the weight of the burden. "Forget we ever had this conversation. Promise me!"

"I promise." Patsy stroked her hair and held her close. "Let's practice trivia to move your mind to less stressful topics."

ALAN LOOKED at the cold spaghetti his *madre* had packed for his lunch. He'd worked through the noontime meal again today. The clinic had a microwave, but he didn't have the energy to use it. Cold pasta for dinner at the office was better than an energy bar, Alan told himself. Another forkful found his mouth. At least his mother had made it safely to her Miami destination without incident. The extra security precautions seemed to be keeping her out of harm's way. That worry could be put in cold storage for today.

The care of his patients was moving in a positive direction. Alan recognized the credit for this accomplishment belonged to Rachel for agreeing to be his nurse. She knew how to get things done in Montana. Folks had a different thought process here, but Rachel worked her magic and the patients benefited. Alan went through his goals checklist: safe mother, stable career and improving medical reputation were all marked off. The entry for romance had an empty box. The lack of a check there made him feel incomplete. *Immediate termination.* That had been made abundantly clear. *Maybe he should try to meet someone new?*

Before he could shake off that notion, he and his dinner moved to the window. Rachel lived across the street, but Snowflake only had a few places people might be at this time of the evening. Alan scraped the bottom of his dish, all gone. Still hungry. He could let himself be seen and let fate take over. Without his protective winter gear, Alan ran across to the café. Halfway there he noticed a light on in the saloon. The full bar was not open, just a hint of lighting, but he decided he would take a look to see who he might find.

The smell of apple pie was a welcome distraction when he entered the diner. No one looked up or greeted him to escort him to a table, so he took a couple of quiet side steps toward the Squeaky Saddle. "Mitochondria." Rachels' voice filled his void, a huge bold checkmark flashed in the romance box on his list. Destiny had spoken.

Not being obvious, but not hiding either, his feet carried him to the back booth. Neither lady saw or heard him.

"What was the first US fighter plane that eluded radar?" Alan knew the answer immediately but wanted to let Rachel answer first.

"Don't tell me. I know this one. It's on the tip of my tongue."

Alan waited, but couldn't stand to watch her struggle. "F-117 Nighthawk."

"Doc, hi there. Figures you would know that. It's a guy thing." Patsy greeted him first. Rachel looked his way without saying a word. Alan did his best to guess what might be going through her mind. A cloud of unease settled. Then her warm smile, that he would do anything to see, appeared.

"I'm practicing. Want to join us?" Rachel shoved a chair at the end of the booth toward him to take a seat.

"Can I have a slice of pie while we work?"

Rachel jumped from the table and flew past him before he could tell her he'd go get it, that she didn't need to get up. He watched her leave the room and then decided he shouldn't allow himself to get caught enjoying that type of activity. He abruptly swiveled his view to Patsy. "How are you feeling?"

"I'm fine. Oh look, my husband is here to pick me up. You can help Rachel with the trivia, can't you?" Patsy struggled to remove herself from the booth.

Alan saw her coat on a nearby stand and helped her into it until Patsy's husband reached them and took over the task. She made a polite introduction, then the new parents to be made a fast exit out the side door. Alan moved the chair back against the wall and occupied the warm spot Patsy had created in the booth. He was organizing the stacks of questions when Rachel returned with warm pie and a glass of water. "On the house." She placed them in front of him. "I'm guessing Patsy went to the ladies' room?"

"Thanks. No. She and her husband just left."

"Oh… Okay, but… that means we'll be here alone. This isn't the office." Rachel kept looking at him, the door and then into the restaurant.

Alan didn't know what to think of her newly exposed anxiety. "We have a reason to be together outside the office." He held up the game cards. "Mrs. Jameson made it clear my participation was required." Rachel had not climbed back into the booth. Alan took a bite of pie to give her a bit of space. "This is so good. Did you make it?"

"My recipe, but Olga made this batch so I could give you nursing hours." Rachel looked away yet again and was still standing. Her view landed on the chair he had just put away and she stepped toward it.

"We're not going to get fired. We don't need a chaperone." Their eyes met. He swallowed hard. She seemed fixed to the floor unable to respond. He didn't look away, neither did Rachel. Alan had no idea how much time passed. He was near her and seeing her head to toe beauty. He was content to sit like a mannequin in a store window display. But he didn't want to leave her standing there. "Or do we?"

"Do we what?" She finally came back to life.

"Need a chaperone?"

"Don't be silly."

Alan continued to scarf down his dessert and was pleased when she made her way to the other side of their booth. They traded questions and talked strategy. The slab of thick wood was between them. They never touched. But, being with her made him so happy. Seeing her long lush hair and mesmerizing smile refueled his resilience. She had quirky little behaviors like the way she tucked her hair behind her ears over and over was endearing. He couldn't get enough. Alan didn't need to touch her to enjoy her company. *Could this be enough?*

They decided to divide the subjects between them so that they could try to cram on a wider number of potential questions. Alan lost track of time until he saw Parrot coming his way in a pair of Superman pajamas and his ever-present cowboy boots. "Auntie Rach, I'm ready for bed. Brushed my teeth and everything." Alan could see the genetic contributions from his Welch relatives as he climbed into the booth to give Rachel a hug goodnight. "What're you doing?"

Rachel laughed and relaxed again, comfortable in caring for the child. The affection between them was palpable. Alan looked upon the two of them with joy and a bit of envy. He had no siblings, no nieces or nephews. He and his *madre* had a special bond, but he looked forward to the day that he could start his own family. "Dr. G, wanna play my game?"

"Sure! I've been looking forward to it." Alan sat up straighter and tried to wake up his tired mind.

Parrot jumped from the bench using his cape to help him fly, if only for a split second. He took his place at the open end of the booth like he was on center stage. "Will you stay with me forever?" Parrot delivered the line with as much drama as he expected from this fledgling actor.

Alan searched his mind. "Gosh Parrot, that could be from so many places. How about a hint? Was it a local person, movie or TV?"

Rachel interrupted with her own question. "Why did you pick that line?"

Parrot looked at Alan. "It's on TV. A soap opera." Then he turned his attention to his aunt. "Dr. G gets all mushy when he looks at you Auntie Rach, just like they do on that show." His attempt to portray a lovesick hero missed the mark, but its intent was clear.

"Alright, that's enough games for one night. Off to bed with you young man. March. I'll be up to tuck you in shortly." Rachel got up, taking Parrot by the shoulders, and turned him toward the stairs for the apartment over the café.

Parrot escaped from her grasp and came back at Alan. "Aren't you even gonna guess?"

"General Hospital." That was the only name of a daytime soap that Alan knew.

Parrot did a bit of a jig and had Alan chuckling. "Good guess, but the answer was As the World Turns." Then he and his heavy boots made clunking sounds all the way to the base of the steps with his aunt keeping him from straying from his path.

Once Parrot disappeared into the apartment, Rachel came back to the study area. "If Parrot sees what he thinks relates to a romance between us, what might other people see? I think you should go."

Rachel conveyed her concern with politeness, but the message was cold. The snow falling outside seemed warmer.

"Thanks again for the pie." Alan went to gather his things but realized he had left them at his office. Before heading out, he added. "We weren't doing anything wrong. We can't let what people might think control our every move." He pushed open the side door. "I would never let anyone hurt you or your career." But, she had fled back to the café leaving her trivia games behind. *Had she heard him? Would she still want to work with him?*

CHAPTER 14

DREADING THE NEED TO MOVE, Alan stepped out of his office, heading to his Jeep. The sheriff had warned him he might be sore for days, and he wasn't kidding. *I thought I was in shape.* His leg and back muscles were yelping. But he didn't tell a soul. If he walked a bit slower, folks would have no idea he was limping. Well, maybe that wasn't the right word since both sides ached equally. Just before he opened the door of his vehicle, a flash of light caught his eye.

The sun was shining in the bright Montana big sky, but something metal caught a ray and reflected the light in his face. Looking in the direction of the glare, he was surprised to see a man swinging from the scaffolding around the church's bell tower. He made a point of walking slowly as he meandered his way to the pharmacy. Alan raised his hand to block out the sun's glare and called out to Bodie, who seemed to be directing the action. "What's all this?"

"Putting up our signature snowflakes," replied Bodie. "Look this way tonight. I think you'll be impressed." With a wink and a wave, Bodie went back to calling out orders to Monkey. Glad to not have an outdoor occupation, Alan continued on his journey to becoming better acquainted with the town's only pharmacist.

Once back in the office, Alan kept passing Rachel in the hall. She was cheery and professional, but she seemed to be holding something back.

"Are we good?" he asked.

"Absolutely!" But then she carved an enormous circular path around him to pick up a patient file.

So, we're good as professionals, but we can't be friends or heaven forbid be seen allowing any part of our clothing to graze the other's as we pass. This would not do, but Alan took one look at the number of people standing in the cold because the waiting room was packed and decided his relationship with Rachel would have to be put on a shelf for now.

He had just closed himself into an exam room when the CB radio came to life. "We've got a serious car crash with multiple wounded at the intersection of SR-2 and Vista Peak Rd." The sheriff's beyond loud voice quivered as he shouted.

Alan threw the door open and ran to the microphone. Rachel arrived first and their skin touched before grasping metal. She flung his hand back with such force his jaw dropped. Then he realized he was witnessing fear. Not concern about what people might think, but some other type of terror.

"Rachel here, the doc and I are on our way. Be there in five. Over." Rachel grabbed his coat off its hook and threw it at him. The down-feather sleeve swatted him in the head when Alan caught the bulk of it. Next, his gut took a sucker-punch from his emergency medical-bag. "Move it. Lives are at risk."

As Alan gasped for air and jammed his arm down a sleeve, he wanted to ease her concern, but Rachel ran toward the back door where she stored her rescue gear. She was out of sight, keys jangling in an instant. "Sorry everyone, we'll work as long as necessary to accommodate every appointment once we return." He ran to catch his ride before she left without him.

Not a good time for his mother to be out of the office, but she deserved to see her family for the holidays. Alan wondered if Teresa would have thought Rachel's actions were as out of character as he did.

By the time he raced into the parking lot, Rachel had turned her truck around facing the exit, opening the passenger side for his leaping entrance. "What..." Alan bit his tongue due to the whiplash effect Rachel caused thrusting the gas pedal to the floor. He swallowed hard and tried again as he clung to his free-flying seatbelt. "What other rescue equipment can we expect?"

"If we're lucky Brett and Betsy are nearby. I keep a backboard and a repelling apparatus in my truck bed." She didn't take her eyes off the road, but she kept honking her horn and the drivers who recognized her truck pulled over to let her pass.

"Did you restock the pain killers?" Alan ripped open his duffle and began to take inventory.

"Can't chat and drive." She crossed over the double yellow. "Maybe you should let me triage and you treat?" After a check in the rearview, Rachel yanked the wheel back returning to her lane.

Alan said a silent prayer as he watched Rachel's anxiety consume her and hijack her rational mind. "I'll follow your lead. You know this intersection."

"The bane of my existence."

He had more than he could handle trying to put himself into emergency medicine mode, so he didn't have spare energy to console her. *I'm ready, she'll be fine.* He just kept telling himself to stay alert, calm and positive.

The sheriff's car with lights flashing was just ahead straddling both lanes. Words began to spew as Alan assessed the situation out loud. "Motorcycle on its side, SUV into a guard rail. Sherriff Wilson wants us to drive past, why?"

"We use my truck as a barrier to protect us from oncoming traffic."

"Oh! Good thing it's such a beast."

That put a smile on her face. But she put the double cab into park and jumped out coattails flapping in the wind. "Where's the bike driver?"

The sheriff pointed to a dent in the snowbank. "He's in and out of consciousness."

Just as Rachel ran toward the snowy ditch, a man stumbled out of the passenger side of the SUV. He appeared to be the driver, but the damage to his door made him crawl out the other side. He held one hand to a head wound, and the other carried broken glasses. *Airbags and seatbelt?* As Alan sprinted to the victim, his peripheral vision caught a glimpse of Betsy chugging up the icy pavement.

Alan concentrated on his assessment of the man in front of him until he heard Rachel shout. "Brett, take Vista Peak." Alan was surprised to see how fast the big man could move. Long graceful strides that didn't look fast, but he covered large chunks of ground at a rapid-fire pace, placing caution flags as he went. "Faster Brett! You've got to stop other drivers, or we'll have more victims."

Okay, she's on the edge. Not safe for her or the injured. "You think you'll be okay for a minute? I'll be right back." Alan's patient nodded and leaned against his back bumper. In four strides, Alan reached Rachel. He laid his gloved palm on her coat sleeve and whispered, "Rachel, focus on stabilizing the motorcyclist."

"What?"

"Rachel?" Alan feared he would soon be treating her as well. Her actions resembled a skipping record. She was moving, but not gaining ground.

"Let's trade patients. I can't. Not again. Too much."

"Good idea. Probable concussion, check his neck, collarbones and ribs."

"Sure, right." Rachel stumbled a bit but managed to pull herself together by the time she reached the guy at the guard rail.

Practicing medicine on a snowy road was a first for Alan. He liked that the cold conditions helped to lessen the injuries. Better to be thrown into snow than drop-kicked onto asphalt. The driver's helmet had no scratches, and he had regained consciousness. As time passed, more deputies and volunteer firemen arrived on the scene. Brett helped Alan secure the man onto a backboard. Eventually, an ambulance showed up from Kalispell. Once Alan gave the

EMT's his evaluation, he was cleared to go back to his patients and Rachel.

Rachel didn't say a word to him the entire trip back. Alan didn't know if she had recovered or was a volcano ready to erupt. As they both hopped down from her monster ride, Alan decided he had to do something. "Why don't you take the rest of the day off."

"What? Why? No!"

"That's an order soldier." Alan wished he hadn't been so harsh, but his adrenaline was running high, too.

"Are you firing me?" Rachel raked her knit cap from her head.

"No! Gosh, no." Alan forced himself temporarily to think of Rachel as a patient and turned up his bedside manner. "You're a bit too emotional to provide medical care right now. That happens to us all." He took a step in her direction, but she was faster. Rachel lowered her face, pivoted and hauled herself back up into her truck. "You did good work today!" He called out to her but doubted that she heard him over her roaring engine.

Alan snuck into his office and did a full-body shake, head to feet, trying to release his pent-up energy. Everyone had secrets and demons. Rachel's torment about her parents' accident must run deeper than she had let on. Alan started a new list: Save her from herself.

AFTER EIGHT O'CLOCK, Alan heard the jingle of the holiday bells that hung over the clinic's front door. Rest was not in the cards for the weary healer. *Not another walk-in. My mind is mush.* "Hello, can I help you?"

"I'm here to help you." The sound of Mrs. Wilson's boots accompanied her to Alan's office. "My hubby told me you had a rough day. I hope you like lasagna?" She held out a clear glass dish covered in foil.

Alan's mood lightened at her offering. This was like the Red Cross providing doctors in the field with food, he told himself, not him accepting charity. He would never do that. "Hot anything sounds wonderful. You're a lifesaver."

Mrs. Wilson plopped the tray on his desk with a clank and yanked off the covering. "Nah, I'm the life saver's handyman." She scowled. "Handy-woman." She let out one of her bellowing laughs and snorted. "You know what I mean."

Alan rooted through his desk and found an errant plastic fork. "I'm afraid I don't have a clean plate."

"Go ahead, eat right out of the baking dish. I won't tell anyone." Mrs. Wilson repositioned the plastic chair and tried to get comfortable. But she wasn't.

Alan inhaled a couple of bites of dinner, enjoying the smell of basil and oregano as the steam warmed his face. He hoped his guest would say what she really came to tell him. "Your husband has a good head on his shoulders. Pleasure to work with him."

"True, true. But that's not why I'm here." Irene crossed her legs and a clump of mud hit the floor with a thud. She didn't notice. "That Rachel gal now she's good people and a good nurse."

Alan wasn't expecting her to champion Rachel, but he welcomed it. "I couldn't agree more."

"What happened today, that's not the real woman we know and love." She took off her cowboy hat, ran her fingers through her straighter than straight, brindle colored hair and replaced it. "The injuries to her parents were beyond her control. We've all told her that, over and over and over." She rolled her face in circles until she made herself dizzy. "Since you're the new guy in town, maybe you have a shot a breaking through?"

Alan put his fork down. "She deserves the very best from me. Tell me all you know about that night. I'll do everything I can." He caught his second wind. But he needed to tread carefully. He would reach out to her as a friend, not her boss, coworker or physician. This conversation would help him attain his most important goal. If he helped her overcome her guilt, grief or fear maybe she could get past her concern about what people might think about them. Them dating. Should he let himself have that type of hope?

CHAPTER 15

RACHEL THREW herself into completing the extra tasks associated with her businesses around the holidays. She needed to keep her mind occupied. She knew Alan was right, but it still stung. *Why do I keep letting my parent's accident cloud my judgment? They're fine. It's been years. Why can't I move on?* Rachel was restocking the takeout bags as her always full of energy nephew bounded through the back door.

"Auntie Rach, you're here," Jacob's face lit up, and then he stuffed his mittens in his pockets.

Rachel felt her body relax as she hugged him. She drew strength from his excitement to see her. "Dr. Garcia let me off early so I could be with you."

"Really? At school, they said you saved people on the highway again."

Rachel reminded herself how fast news traveled in Snowflake. "Dr. Garcia was amazing, and I helped a little." That statement was true enough, she told herself. But her nagging guilt reared up like an attacking grizzly bear. "Hey, since we're both home, why don't we decorate the Christmas tree upstairs?"

"Oh, boy! I'll race you." Jacob dropped his coat and backpack on the floor then sprung up the stairs.

Rachel went to remind him that the customers didn't appreciate the sound of his boots thunking on the wooden planks, but she needed to see him smiling. After telling Olga where she was headed, she gathered Jacob's belongings. Something about holding them close to her chest made her feel safe.

Plugging in the tree's lights helped to lift her spirits. Jacob's method of hanging ornaments had the tree looking a bit lopsided, but she didn't care. She concentrated on the branches he couldn't reach while she rehearsed in her mind the apology she would deliver to Alan. She would describe her issue resolution action-plan and guarantee her work would never suffer again. If only she could believe that herself.

Alan was a medical professional. He would understand. *He seems to be genuine and kind. He might be able to help?* Her closest family and friends understood her grief and guilt, and they tried. Maybe she shouldn't get her hopes up. But she knew more about the events of that night than anyone. *What if I tell him? Bare my soul?* She worried he would think less of her, not want her to be his nurse. She didn't think she would forgive herself if she had to move out of town to find another nursing job. She wanted Jacob to enjoy the tree decorating, so she buried her tumultuous past in the darkest place she could find in her mind.

While opening another box of ornaments, Rachel found the batch her mother made by hand. The clear-coated eggshells sparkled with red, green and gold glitter. The air whooshed from her lungs. She leaned on the wall and eased to the floor, the box still in her hand. Rachel hadn't seen her parents in months. Online calling just wasn't as personal and nurturing as being in the same room.

Before she knew it, Jacob was on his knees in front of her. "I miss mommy too, but daddy said she's where the doctors can help her." Then he crawled onto her lap and laid his head on her shoulder. "It's okay. We have each other." His eyelashes flickered across her cheek and she almost lost it. Holding back tears, Rachel reminded herself that many of her neighbors were going through tougher times than being haunted by the past. She squeezed Jacob as hard as she could.

Everything would be okay. She was a good nurse. Dr. Garcia needed her. No one was perfect, and she would find a way to conquer this demon. Rachel compartmentalized her thoughts about her parent's accident. She let the celebration of Christmas fill her with joy. The sun had set and stars twinkled in the sky by the time the tree was adorned. Rachel gravitated to the window overlooking Main Street.

She gasped. Even though she had seen them all her life, their artful brilliance always made her as giddy as a child waiting for Santa. "Jacob come see. The snowflakes have been lit."

AFTER MRS. WILSON'S VISIT, Alan decided to clear his mind by taking a walk around town. Bodie had said to look at the church after dark. He walked at a snail's pace. Then he saw the church, or more correctly, the bright lights shining around the church's bell tower. The snowflakes. Alan arrived at the rectangular white building and walked around all four sides. No matter the direction, a unique piece of artwork made of a metal frame, and large brilliant white lights created the shape of a snowflake. Alan was so awestruck by the beauty he didn't hear the pastor approaching.

"Must be your first time to see them lit."

Alan just nodded his head and smiled.

"The legend says the first time you see the lights, make a wish and your dreams will come true," added the clergyman.

Alan had so much he wanted. Most things were for his mother, other family and friends. Then he thought about the people living in Snowflake who had made his transition much easier. *Maybe the wish should benefit one of them? The legend was theirs.* He closed his eyes and, with every fiber of his heart and soul, Alan wished that Rachel could find inner peace and the love of a worthy man to care for her the rest of her days.

Alan kept walking. He shivered but trudged forward anyway. Wrestling with the details Mrs. Wilson had divulged pained him more than any icy wind. To be able to help Rachel he needed her to open up to him. He couldn't let her know one of her dearest friends had betrayed a confidence. This betrayal as Alan saw it was an act of kindness, but Rachel may not see it that way. He needed to get her alone. The dreaded no dating a coworker rule would be a problem. She wouldn't let herself within a foot of him and preferred a third party be present to deter the rumor mill. The privacy he needed might prove to be the most challenging part of his plan.

Alan had learned lessons by living them while completing a residency in emergency medicine. He was certain he could help her let go of the shame, fear or guilt she must be carrying. Alan put one foot in front of the other until he was well beyond the street lights' glow. He looked up into a clear night sky, Montana's Big Sky. The dance of the stars enveloped him. He thought of his mother and hoped her view of the Milky Way was as beautiful as his. *How would my madre fix this?*

His mother was a person who followed the rules until she didn't. Sometimes a rule needed to be broken or at the very least changed. Alan knew he might be risking his job, but he was a true friend and he was Rachel's best hope of being healed. Alan was willing to take that chance. But could he get her to take it with him?

THE NEXT MORNING, Alan paced around his office while sifted through his thoughts and feelings. He replayed telling Rachel she was too emotional to practice nursing after the rescue and absent-mindedly held his stomach with both hands. At least his mother had just returned safe and renewed after visiting her family. He managed to get Teresa up to speed without divulging too much and asked for her feedback. Alan appreciated the fresh perspective his mother provided.

"What's worse, the goings-on with the gang in Miami, or a nurse with possible PTSD?" she asked. He agreed that living in Miami was no longer an option and leave it to his mother to use a description often associated with the military to give Rachel's situation a label. What had happened to her was traumatic on several levels, and he decided to review the literature on successful PTSD treatment plans.

Alan wanted Rachel to feel very welcome and needed when she returned to the office, so he decided to send her a friendly text: **Looking forward to working with you this morning. You did great work yesterday.**

A few hours later, Rachel came out of an exam room with a happy patient trailing behind her. She managed to give Alan a thumbs up sign with the patient being none the wiser. "Got a second?" He stepped into the room she had vacated and motioned for her to follow him. Once behind closed doors, he added, "Another satisfied customer?"

"Yes, easy cure." Rachel smiled, but then looked away and started adjusting the blinds on the window.

He sat on the rolling stool and did his best to present a calm facade. "I wanted you to know…"

"I'm working on it," she interrupted.

"Understood. Would you let the new guy in town help?"

"I've tried everything I know." She turned her back to him. "But talking to you at the lake seemed different. Maybe you can…" Her head dropped and she swiped at her face just below her eye.

Alan's heart fractured into pieces the size of sand grains. Easing her pain became his primary mission. In his culture hugs were an everyday thing. He didn't think the action would be inappropriate but wasn't sure. "Can the first step in your recovery be a hug? No one will know."

She shifted her stance just enough to give him the opening he needed. Vaulting off the rickety stool, he encircled her with barely a wisp of contact. She leaned into him. His need to squeeze her grew, but he didn't. Alan wanted her to come to him, trust him. Then he felt the weight of her arms around him and enveloped her. The smell of her fruity shampoo could sustain him. He held her tight with no movement or sound. *Talk to me.* Alan made a point of holding her until she broke away. When she did, a profound sorrow filled him, like he had just lost a friend.

"You give good hugs." Her voice was shaking and hoarse. "Until our next session…" Rachel patted him on the shoulder and then reached to open the door.

Good progress. She will open up to me. I'll do whatever it takes. He went through the rest of his day with a renewed hope and debated his next move.

CHAPTER 16

As the day wore on and he bumped into Rachel in the hallway, the ease between them returned. This made Alan the happiest he'd been in days. Alan worked late, but his mother had gone to buy groceries so he was the first to arrive home. He didn't notice until after he turned off his Jeep that his house was surrounded by trucks. Bodie met him in the driveway, running as fast as a man could at his age.

"Surprise!" yelled the tribal elder, leaning through Alan's truck window. "You're home right on time, but we're not finished, just cleaning up."

Alan projected a jovial and friendly demeanor. "Finished with what?" Now he understood why his mother was a bit cagey about needing to go to the store.

"I've been supervising the project. Wait till you see. Come on, I'll show you." Bodie practically dragged Alan off his seat. He appreciated the man's enthusiasm, but he had a sneaking suspicion he wasn't going to like what he saw.

"Did my mom know about this?" asked Alan, trying to keep his concern from seeping into his voice.

Bodie just kept waving Alan toward him as he walked backward, heading to the oldest portion of the building, which Alan called his bedroom. "Not until the last minute. Like I said—it's a surprise!"

The men who owned the trucks gathered as Alan rounded to his backyard. He greeted the guys he knew and was introduced to the ones he'd never met. Construction tools and supplies were strewn around the yard.

"I think she'll hold heat a whole lot better now," said Bodie, with a grin so wide Alan thought it had to make the man's face hurt. "Another roofing layer, new triple-pane windows and we resealed between the logs to make her airtight."

"Amazing! I'll sleep better tonight, but what do I owe you?" Alan slapped the man on the back and tried to make the statement a bit of a joke. But he was dead serious.

"Not a thing. We had a hell of a good time, right boys?" All of the men's heads bobbed up and down. Some men flashed Alan toothy smiles and others gave each other fist bumps.

Alan figured maybe this was Bodie's way of winning a date with his mother. He had to choose his next move very carefully. "Gosh, you guys are all right. I appreciate that you shared your time and skills. I'm honored, really." Alan gave each man a hearty high five and personal thank you. "I'd offer you all a beer, but I don't have any."

All the men laughed, went back to cleaning up the yard, and within minutes left to go home. Bodie took Alan inside and gave him the grand tour. The house was just as he had left it, maybe even a bit cleaner. The fireplace and wood-burning stove in the guest quarters were pumping out glorious warmth. The room had never been this inviting.

Just as Bodie was ready to leave, Alan asked, "Snowflake currency? Really, I need to repay everyone. It's too much."

Bodie shook his head and sighed. Walking outside, he got into his truck in silence. Alan followed him step for step, the lump in his throat so large he could hardly swallow. Once the engine turned over, Bodie lowered the window. "Doc, you know you got my vote to pass your probation. But I gotta tell you, to really fit in, be accepted in Snowflake, you need to let people help you." Alan sucked in air to speak, but Bodie cut him off. "Folks may not have much money. But they can swing a hammer or bake a pie. Sometimes people need to help others. It makes them feel good. Let them feel good." Bodie gave him a fake punch to the chin and put the truck in drive.

Waving goodbye, Alan began to search his soul. What a day. How could one man feel so good and so bad in such a short span of time?

THE TWELVE DAYS of Christmas competition arrived before Alan felt comfortable on a horse, but that was the least of his worries. Because of the holiday season, Rachel was working days with him and nights at the bar or café. The next therapy session had not been scheduled. He wanted to keep the momentum going forward but forced himself to practice patience.

Alan rarely argued with his mother, but they had a loud quarrel about the renovations to his bedroom. "You should have warned me." He had shouted. "How could you protect Bodies feeling over mine?" But then he felt guilty and had apologized. He realized Bodie had unknowingly put her in a no-win situation.

Bodie's comment stabbed him in the gut. Alan felt like the dagger was still in him, the wound remained fresh. He kept reliving the conversation and each time the knife sliced a bit deeper. He didn't know what haunted him more, this new wound or the one that still festered since his childhood. *I can't be my own man and let people help me out of duty or worse out of pity.*

For some strange reason, the appointments at the clinic seemed to have dried up. He expected a high demand until the backlog cleared and then for a steady rhythm to be established. Large quantities of patients were canceling appointments. Maybe the mill closing was affecting the economy in Snowflake more than forecasted.

As requested, Alan gathered at the sheriff's stables to mount up and begin their parade-like march through town. All of the Snowflake team was there including Rachel, Brett and Monkey. This was his first view of Rachel in her western wear. He found himself looking in her direction a great deal until he caught the mayor pointing two fingers at his own eyes then flipping his hand so those same fingers pointed directly at him. The message was clear, but the man couldn't have known what Alan was thinking. *He has an overactive imagination and some nerve.* But, just in case Alan's line of sight wandered over the whole team.

The thought of being in a saddle pained him, but the ride to the community center was short. Small blessing. Alan had thought he'd never see the day, but at Bodie's urging, he donned a cowboy hat to look the part. He was glad to be in between Bodie and Brett, even though he couldn't see Rachel—somehow the horses those men rode seemed to keep his horse calm.

With great fanfare, the Snowflake contingent blocked the thoroughfare by riding ten horses abreast all the way down Main Street. The closer they got to the playing fields, the more people lined the sidewalks, cheering and shouting well wishes. Alan was pleased to see his mother and Olga huddled together just outside the café. The day was sunny but brisk, perfect for this type of competition.

Grinning as he saw the other town's team riding from the opposite direction to set up the showdown, Alan decided to put medicine, business and romance out of his mind to enjoy the day's events. Both towns' sheriffs dismounted and faced off. At some signal, they drew their fake cap-gun revolvers and fired. Then both teams and the crowd joined in firing their own plastic firearms to declare the games open.

Luckily, Alan's only event would be the trivia challenge, which was the last competition of the night. He found his mom, and they decided which activities to watch. Those where Rachel and Bodie competed made the top of the list. To his relief, the mayor was too busy schmoozing constituents to continue keeping tabs on who he was admiring, so Alan found himself relaxing and enjoying his surroundings. Of course, Rachel won the barrel racing and Brett won ax throwing. As darkness fell, the team's scores were almost tied, and the trivia event would decide the day's winner.

Alan had made a prior visit to the Snowflake Community Center which consisted of groupings of open bleachers next to fields, but his event would be held indoors, at the gathering hall. Tonight, the hall was set up as if for a boxing match, instead of a wedding reception or other family celebration. In the center ring an oversized picnic table stood waiting, surrounded on all sides with rows of metal folding chairs.

The trivia questions would be randomly selected by a computer. Each contestant had a buzzer button connected to the laptop to identify who rang in first. If an individual answered incorrectly, the other team could consult teammates as a trio and then offer their team's answer. The questions would be read in an alternating fashion by the sheriffs to keep things fair.

Alan was pleased the Snowflake team included Rachel, and he would find a way to endure Mayor Jameson as a teammate. Of course, the mayor sat closet to the microphone and would be the center of attention. That was fine with Alan because that allowed him to be next to Rachel. He did his best to not let any part on his clothing touch her, but in the tight quarters that wasn't easy. As the contestants took their places, Alan finally came face to face with her. "Congrats on the win, you looked good out there."

With her usual nonchalance, Rachel ducked her head, but the move didn't conceal the blush that flowed across her cheeks, "Oh, thanks. Been racing barrels for as long as I can remember."

Alan wasn't certain if the embarrassment was related to the compliment or that fact that she had ducked his offer to continue therapy. But he pressed on anyway. "You okay?"

"Yeah, I'm sorry I didn't answer your text. Been working two jobs. She tucked her hair behind her ears with more force than necessary. "No accidents to rattle me, thank God."

Alan slipped into his natural behavior and gave her a sideways hug, squeezing her shoulder. She tensed up when the mayor approached the table. Then he whispered in her ear, "Yikes, busted." He winked and saw the tension ease out of her.

Mayor Jameson grabbed the microphone, "Who's going to win?"

"Snowflake!" shouted the local townspeople. A few boos could be heard from the opposing team's contestants.

The robust competition went on for about thirty minutes. Alan had to give the mayor props for being pretty smart and fast with the buzzer trigger, and Rachel's knowledge base was much larger than he had expected. But most of all, he enjoyed when the home team needed to confer before they gave a joint answer. Alan could feel her heat next to his. Her breath on his face. Could stare into her beautiful brown eyes and no one would ever be the wiser.

As the final question came up, the score was tied. The entire challenge between the two towns would come down to this last trivia question. The other town's sheriff took his turn with the question asking duties. All contestants held a palm above their buzzer, and the crowd fell silent.

"What day of the year does our country celebrate Gold Star Spouses?"

Alan slammed down on his button and shouted, "April fifth," while all the other competitors' jaws dropped. Knowing he was correct, he stood, saluted his mother and then blew her a kiss. Of course, he knew this answer. The day was special, one that he and his *madre* cherished together. Her Special Forces husband had lost his life while serving his country. She and all the other military widows supported each other on this day.

"That is correct." The visiting sheriff couldn't believe that someone had known the answer. "Snowflake wins!"

The crowd went wild, especially the residents of Snowflake. Alan's fellow teammates rushed in to celebrate the victory with him. As he accepted the gratitude of many, he also kept an eye on Rachel. She hugged and gave a kiss on the cheek to every teammate. When she turned to find Alan, the embrace she gave him was like she was at a private school cotillion, where the dancers needed to keep at least twelve inches apart at all times. She made a *mmmmaw* sound, with her lips never coming near his cheek.

Nearby, a fellow teammate was attempting a leaping high five but lost his balance on his way down, and his back slammed into Rachel's, propelling her forward. Alan instinctively caught her, and as she looked up to see who had inflicted the body blow, her lips brushed Alan's.

You're not supposed to kiss her! Alan's mind screamed at him as his body responded.

The contact was only a split second, but all the pent-up passion he hadn't known he had for her rushed out like water over Niagara Falls. Their bodies played Twister as they each lost and regained their balance in different directions. He righted himself first and shielded her from another teammate's stray body blow as the celebrating continued around them.

"I got you. You're okay." The wispy gasp of a phrase escaped from his mouth as the tingle he was feeling made his whole body shake.

Rachel's eyes shot open wide. "Um, thanks. I mean, sorry. Um I didn't mean to..." He enjoyed the inadvertent public display of affection. Until she stepped back and shouted, "Gotta go." Turning, she dodged through people like a pinball. He tried to catch her, but several other teammates grabbed him to offer their thanks. He wanted to call out her name, but he stopped himself. Too many unanswered questions filled his thoughts.

As the place began to settle down, Alan saw Monkey, Olga and Bodie keeping his mother company, so he decided to walk back to his office alone. He stopped at the lit snowflakes and remembered his wish. He would put his needs aside until he knew she had recovered. She also deserved a man who would look past her money and love her for the beautiful woman she was on the inside.

A scary thought then entered his mind. If the mayor or any other council member had seen their lips touch would they both be fired?

CHAPTER 17

RACHEL MADE a beeline for the exit and didn't slow the speed of her walking until she was alone in her apartment. *Oh dear, what if someone saw our lips connect? How am I going to explain that?* She sat in her living room watching her Christmas tree blink. She even launched her holiday station on Pandora. Nothing seemed to help her relax. Rachel must have looked at her phone ten times per minute until she finally tossed it out of her reach.

No one texted, emailed or called her to raise the panic flag.

Maybe no one saw it? Or maybe they did, but weren't aware of the new HR rules at the clinic. Her racing heart slowed to a normal rhythm. *Had she overreacted? Should she go back?* The thought of traipsing through the snow even one block made her legs hurt. She reviewed her schedule from the past week in her mind and decided she was overly tired. She started a bubble bath, lit some aromatherapy candles, poured a glass of wine and took it along with her cheery music into her bathroom.

After a good scrub and long soak, she checked her phone one more time. A text had come in from Alan: **You OK? People are asking me where you went. I'm saying you're tired. Do we need to talk?**

Rachel allowed herself to relive the moment. It wasn't a kiss but coming so close unleashed a whole new set of thoughts where Alan was concerned. Working with him was one of the better doctor-nurse relationships she had ever experienced. He treated her with respect and admiration for the knowledge and skills she brought to the practice. She couldn't wait until they could schedule some time to work on her fear of treating car accident victims on Peak Vista Road. He was her friend on every level she could imagine.

Now her romantic desire for Alan could not be denied. Sure, he was good looking, charming, intelligent and physically strong. But he treated her differently than any other man she'd ever met. He wasn't from Montana, hadn't picked up bad habits from cowboys. Well maybe not all cowboys, just the ones who asked her to marry them after one date. She wanted more and because of the no fraternization rule, she couldn't have it and continue pursuing her passion for nursing. She sighed, pushed those thoughts into a cage and slammed the door.

She replied to his text: **I'm home safe. Tired is right. If no one calls us to a city council meeting, we're good. Thanks for asking.** She had hoped his asking was meant to be personal, but she decided to respond professionally. Once tucked into her warm soft bed, she fell asleep dreaming of how sweet his kisses would be.

THE FOLLOWING morning Alan still couldn't get Rachel and her lips off his mind. She hadn't intended her lips to brush across his, but she might too embarrassed to confirm it. He knew she had been thrown off balance and had turned her head to make certain she wouldn't cause him harm as she came crashing in his direction. An accident, no doubt. But what a wonderful collision. His mouth still tingled and longed to connect with hers again.

Rachel's texted response was all business, which was understandable but not what he wanted. He hoped she would open up to him. That was still going to be an uphill climb. Concerning the city council, the way he figured it, either no one had seen the momentary lapse in balance or they recognized it as an impromptu game of Twister because Rachel had been shoved.

Alan sat at his desk trying to read the latest articles in the *Journal of American Medical Association*, but he had read the same sentence four times. When Rachel walked in dressed in her nursing whites, he couldn't say what he wanted so he punted. "Hey, there. Sleep well? Café all good?'

"Yep, I'm impressed with the two new hires." Rachel took off her coat. "All in all not too bad. Especially after the bumpy beginning, but Mrs. Jameson's heart was in the right place."

"Maybe we should ask the mayor to put in a crosswalk for you since you're running across the street so often these days?" Alan's attempt to make a joke fell a bit flat. "So, Patsy is due just before lunch, but we've got some time to ourselves before she arrives. I thought we could have another session?"

Rachel seemed to ignore the therapy request and picked up some files and sat in the chair normally occupied by Teresa. "Where is everyone? I expected a waiting room full of patients."

Maneuvering one of the rolling stools from an exam room, Alan found a spot behind the reception desk next to Rachel. "About that... it's very strange. The volume of appointments has dropped. Folks keep making odd excuses to cancel long-standing appointments. My *madre* went to help out at the Trading Post." Alan stopped his seat's movement before his lab coat touched her. "Do you think it's because their budgets are tighter due to the holidays and the closing of the mill?"

"I don't know?" Rachel took a moment to think. "Business at the restaurant seems about the same as in years past."

Alan fidgeted with a pen and pad of paper, then took out his cell to check for texts. But before Rachel was able to open a patient file, he got up the courage to ask, "Can we please schedule your next session?"

Rachel stopped what she had been doing and gave him her full attention. Being able to look deep into her sweet brown eyes had him stumbling on the stool and backing it into the cabinet with a clatter. "I've been researching PTSD in first responders. I think, well you know. Um, I can help because I'm a fellow medical professional." So much for his rehearsal in the mirror that morning. He stared at the floor and cleared his throat. "We've lived through similar experiences. I have insight into what you might feel."

Rachel tried to tuck her hair behind her ears, but her braid worn for work thwarted her attempt. *At least she's as nervous as I am.*

"Yes, that makes sense. I'm not avoiding you or my issue. I'm swamped." She smiled.

Alan waited for her to say more. She didn't. He looked up and smiled back. Her grin widened. He wanted to sit there and stare at her lovely mouth. "Okay, sorry if I'm pushing too hard." Alan's voice wavered and he wished he had some water nearby.

Rachel hesitated, pursing her lips, but eventually laughed. "We escaped the wrath of the city council. How awful would that be if we both got fired before Christmas?"

"We did nothing wrong. They wouldn't."

"You don't know this town like I do."

"Still, they would have to accept our explanation, right?"

"Gossip rules over common sense around here."

"What? Nah, tell me I haven't entered the Twilight Zone."

Blinking, Rachel sat in silence. She shrugged. Alan didn't realize he'd dug his nails into his palm until it hurt. He had to kill the stillness in the room. But before he could think of a clever way to ease the tension, Patsy arrived for her appointment.

"Saved by the principal," chuckled Rachel. "Right this way, your private suite awaits, but first we must stop at the dreaded scale." The best friends hugged and caught up on family and friends. After the check-up was completed, Patsy asked if Alan could spare a moment, and requested that Rachel stay in the exam room as well. Alan's blood pressure was rising, but he didn't let it show.

"I don't know exactly how to bring up this subject, so I'm just going to say it." Patsy slid off the exam table and waddled her way to a spare chair, rubbing her growing belly. "I got this strange call from a friend of mine. I'm not a gossip, can't stand ladies who spread vicious lies." The animated principal used her whole body to speak. "People of this town think you're some kingpin in a Cuban gang and you moved here to expand your illegal drug sales." Cocking her head and lifting one eyebrow she added, "Now, I know that isn't true. But where on earth did that rumor come from?"

Flabbergasted, Alan looked at Rachel, who looked at Patsy, who was gawking at Alan. "I couldn't help but notice, I'm the only patient in the building."

"Thank you for bringing this to my attention," choked out Alan. He wanted to pound his head against a wall or go into a closet and let loose a primal scream. "Not true. So not true!" He stutter-stepped his way to the exam table and crawled on top of the already crinkled tissue paper. Collapsing with a sigh, he dropped his shoulders, face going slack.

Rachel told Patsy an abbreviated version of the story that Alan had confided to her at the lake. At the end of her retelling, Alan added a confirming, "Right!" He thought through whom else could have found out the truth, but the facts were a jumbled mess. The sheriff wouldn't reveal his secret. And then he remembered—Irene Wilson had been in the stables when his mother's security was being discussed. "Mrs. Wilson!"

"What?!" Patsy stopped rubbing her belly, covering her mouth with a gasp.

Through his anger, Alan watched Rachel and her friend have one of those female conversations without saying a word.

Leaping up and making a dash for the door, Alan shouted, "I'm going to have a word with the sheriff about his wife's loose lips."

"NO!" Both Patsy and Rachel screamed in unison.

Halting in a huff and making a speedy about-face, Alan waited for the ladies to give him one good reason. "Why not?"

Rachel took his hand in hers and led him to his office, Patsy chasing close behind. "Just in case we get a walk-in, the exam room walls are a bit thin." Enjoying the feel of her hand, Alan allowed her to pull his chair out from behind his desk and help him take a seat. The principal closed the door. In a whisper, Rachel continued, "The sheriff and the mayor will always defend their wives, no matter how many irrefutable facts you put in front of them."

Patsy chimed in with, "Oh no, honey. You don't want to tangle with either of them. Not when their wives are involved."

Slamming his fists on his desks in a rare burst of anger, Alan ground his teeth. "I've got to do something!" Jumping back up from his perch, he began to pace. "I can't lose my reputation, AGAIN. I just can't!"

Patsy matched Alan's motions stride for stride, patting his back. "Why don't you go tidy up the reception area or something. Let Rachel and I hatch a plan. We've lived here all our lives and seen this rumor thing before."

Exasperated, Alan threw the door open, slamming it against the wall. His lab coat flapped behind him with the speed of his exit.

CHAPTER 18

LATER THAT AFTERNOON, Alan manned the reception desk alone. Not a patient in sight. The phone sat silent as if to confirm his reputation was ruined. Of all the dumb luck. He played by the rules and got his ability to practice medicine ripped away, twice in one year. *How does that happen?*

The jingle of the front door sounded. Alan's hopes lifted. A walk-in, hallelujah. And then Mrs. Jameson popped in. This meddling woman who had proposed the new HR rules for the clinic was now chasing away his patients with some rumor. Alan wanted to unleash the full fire of his fury on her. Professionalism held him in check. Tasting the blood as he bit his tongue, he became a mannequin with a pained smile.

Heidi ambled around the waiting room, then strolled halfway down the hall, one of her decorative scarves fluttering over her shoulder. "I was on my way to the Trading Post and expected to see a crowd. Where is everyone?"

Your manipulation of the truth scared everybody off. But of course, he couldn't say that. "Folks tend not to schedule visits near the holidays." His response was truth-based for most medical practices. He said a silent prayer that Rachel and Patsy could save him from this villainous woman.

"Well, how can you justify passing your 90-day probation if you're not providing medical care. Oh, and for the record as a city employee, the council has tasked me with enforcing the new rule. You know the one I mean." Before he could contemplate an answer, she darted back out into the cold. "Wait till I tell my husband."

CLOSING time took the slowest pace possible to arrive. Alan locked up the office, especially his prescription pads, just after 5 PM. The rumors were bad enough, but he couldn't let that type of fiasco happen again. He planned to go home and sulk while heating up the frozen leftovers. His mother had lovingly filled their freezer with single-serving containers for him before she left to help Bodie at the Trading Post. But the flashing neon of Rachel's establishments beckoned for him to enjoy a serving of hospitality, Snowflake style.

As Alan entered the café, the fact that Christmas was around the corner hit him in the face. Clusters of people crammed into the restaurant and saloon for holiday gatherings. Ribbons and gift wrap cluttered the floor. At the gift shop, the line to mail packages took up every inch of aisle space in the claustrophobic shop. Alan settled into the last available table, a small two-seater crammed into a corner. The noisy exuberance of the gatherings all around him only emphasized that he'd still be dining alone.

If only he could see Rachel while he ate. Because the postmaster was expected to make surprise inspections before the end of the Christmas rush, Rachel had said she needed to staff the extended hours at the gift shop herself.

Olga looked like she had the crowd under control, as she raced to get hot meals from the order pick-up counter to the customers in the bar. Alan saw two new faces through the pass through to the kitchen and guessed they were Mrs. Jameson's recommended recruits. The thought of that woman made his stomach churn, but then it grumbled a request to be fed. At least he'd be able to order some hot, non-left-over, comfort food, and he could do a bit of people watching to distract him from the two bombshells of the day. The town thought he was a drug lord and it may be weeks before he could get Rachel alone to help her PTSD. *Merry Christmas to me.*

And then, Parrot made a grand entrance. Dressed as an elf, except for his cowboy boots, the child could not have been cuter. The place went wild. Parrot sashayed from one large group to another, doing a made-up jig. Everyone understood how to play his game. He would act out a scene, and they would guess who said it. Alan couldn't help but laugh at the shouts of who the original speaker could have been. They ranged from rock stars to movie stars to the mayor.

Alan didn't mind waiting his turn as he ate his home-cooked meal. He was just a table of one. But eventually, the not-so-good dancer in red and green came up to Alan's table.

"Hi Dr. G." He bowed as if already taking a curtain call. "You ready?" He grinned and stomped his boots.

"Hit me." Alan's mood was as the best it had been all day.

But before Jacob presented the line the sheriff's cruiser sped by with blue lights flashing. His pulse ticked up a notch. The CB radio in the back not too far from his table came to life. Alan heard a distorted voice, but couldn't tell what had been said.

Since there was a second CB in the gift shop, Alan figured Rachel heard the call for help more clearly. Then a crash of glass came from where she had been working, and he heard Rachel let out a scream.

"I'm coming!" Alan yelled as he dodged Olga carrying plates of food and skidded on a stray piece of Christmas wrapping that had recently fallen on the floor. Bolting into the postal area, he saw a shattered coffee mug on the countertop and Rachel holding one hand with the other. "How bad is it?"

She looked up at him, shaking from head to toe. "Peak Vista Road."

"Your hand. Did you cut it?" Alan made a point of using his calm emergency doctor voice even though the acid from his empty stomach had splashed up into his throat.

"Peak Vista. Car Accident! Waiting for the sheriff to get on scene."

Letting his gaze dart between the broken glass, her quivering hand and her ashen face, Alan diagnosed that her panic attack was more severe than the cut. He didn't care who saw what he decided to do next. *Let them fire me, she means more to me than any job.* He hugged her leaving a gap for her injured hand and lowered his forehead to hers. "Let's get you to the clinic. I can bandage the laceration there. I'll restart my CB. We can chat." He shook his head up and down and Rachel began to do the same.

Brett, Jacob clinging to his thigh, appeared in the doorway. "I'll clean this up. You do whatever you need to do, Doc." Brett had gone pale under his dark shaggy hair and scruffy beard. "You're our only hope. Please fix her."

Alan maneuvered Rachel out the shop's side door and adjusted his embrace to shelter her from the cold. Tears flowed down her face. "Pain?"

"Brain..."

He kissed her cheek. "We'll get through this together." When he looked both ways to cross the street, he saw Mrs. Jameson get out of her car parked at the Squeaky Saddle. *Let her tell the mayor she caught me hugging Rachel. I double dare her.*

CHAPTER 19

RACHEL FIXATED on the static from the Radio while Alan cleaned the wound and applied a butterfly band-aide to her palm. She thought she would lose it, but Alan's deep soothing voice kept pinging her with questions she could answer with one word.

"Two trucks spun out into snowdrifts, but no injuries. We need a wrecker and Betsy." The sheriff's assessment of the accident allowed Rachel to exhale. But then the flashbacks she dreaded, tried her best to bury, pushed all other thoughts from her mind.

Her waking nightmare was a view of her father stumbling in deep snow while he trudged into to town. She tried to help, but he was out of reach. Seeing her mother unconscious and trapped was unbearable. *They're alive and doing well.* Closing her eyes didn't turn off the movie playing in her head. *Get to the good part already,* she thought. Rachel willed her frightening daydream to skip ahead to when her healed parents left the hospital. No such luck. The worst of the memory kept repeating, like a misbehaving slide projector only showing two pictures. "My fault. My fault." She whispered into Alan's shoulder.

With her physical care complete, he held her close while they waited for news. "I'm telling you this as a friend, I doubt you did anything wrong. I know it'll be agonizing, but tell me, not as a doctor as your friend, what you think happened that night."

Her head popped up, jaw-dropping. "What? No. I can't..."

"Take your time, we have all night." Alan shifted them to the cot in his office. He sat, back against the wall and legs sprawled out, so she did the same. The bile in her stomach churned. She wanted him to keep talking, but he stayed motionless and silent. She took in the deepest breath she had taken all day and words spewed like a confetti explosion. At first, they came at random and without meanings, but in time she pieced together sentences. Telling him her darkest secrets from that dreadful stormy night lightened her soul. The hammer in her head took a break for the night.

She felt the vice grip around her heart begin to loosen. *But now that he knows what I did, will he let me be his nurse? Could he even want to befriend the woman who caused her parents' injuries?*

"Settle down everyone. Settle down," Bodie shouted to the business owners that had gathered at the community center. "Thank you for coming. I'll be brief." The small crowd of annoyed, busy people took a seat and prepared to listen. Rachel had learned to value what Bodie had to say, and if he'd asked the Snowflake Main Street Chamber of Commerce members to gather, he had a good reason.

It had been a day since Rachel unloaded her nightmare concerning her parents on Alan. She sent him a text and invited him as a guest but wasn't sure he'd be willing to show his face until after she and Patsy made headway to clear his reputation. She couldn't help but notice the flash of white from his lab coat when he arrived late and hovered in the back.

With Sophie out of town, Brett made a point of staying close to Rachel when she was in public. She wasn't sure if it was for her benefit or his.

With no microphone system available, Bodie used his louder-than-loud outdoor voice to project his message around the room. "For those of you who don't know me, I'm Bodaway Crow—owner of the Trading Post." This brought a round of laughs. If you didn't know Bodie, you had no business being in the room. "I've been communicating with the tribal elders and some other people who will speak after me." A restless rumble went through the horde of mostly blue-collar, salt-of-the-earth people in attendance—most of them men. When the elders forwarded a message to the townspeople, if you had any sense, you took heed.

"Call it the 100-year storm or blame it on global warming, but the elders expect this winter to be the worst of their lifetime. More snow fall than they have ever seen with multiple blizzards." The crowd erupted into gasps and cries of woe. Bodie let what he said sink in and waited for the noise level to die down. "The reason I requested your attendance is to ask you all to work together, help each other plan. Prepare for the worst and do it now."

Bodie walked off the makeshift stage and Rachel felt a chill as her brother left her side to add to the worrisome news. She had no idea he'd planned to address his cohorts and friends. "I'm Brett Welch, senior manager of roads for the Montana Department of Transportation for this region."

"I've known you since you were in diapers," said an anonymous voice from the rows of people. Another chuckle rumbled through the room, but this time you could cut the tension with a knife.

"Based on intel from the State of Montana's head meteorologist and NOAA, the National Oceanic and Atmospheric Administration, our governor will close the mountain passes two weeks sooner and leave them closed at least two weeks longer."

"What about Christmas?" A little boy who had come with his dad was the first to react.

"We need supplies," shouted someone from the back of the room.

A woman in the front row stood, yelling, "That'll ruin my business!"

"The governor can't tell us what to do," hollered the veterinarian, raising his fist. The crowd supported those brave enough to speak out by jumping to their feet or making comments in loud voices, but they all muddled together and became a growing grumble. Rachel wanted to cover her ears.

Brett signaled for the masses to quiet down, and after the usual loudmouths said their piece, he was able to continue. "I'm working with my counterparts and am waiting to present a proposal to the powers that be to keep the roads open. You know Betsy and I will do everything we can to keep the roads open and safe."

"That's our Betsy, she'll see us through."

"Betsy'll tell Old Man Winter where he can go."

Making a fast exit, Brett eased into the chair next to Rachel. She winked at him. "Good job." Then she punched his arm, wishing her exhausted body had more strength. "What, you couldn't let me in on the big secret?" He winced, but then put his arm around her for a sideways hug.

Sheriff Wilson took control of the rowdy room. The buzzing swarm knew to zip it, pronto. "If you haven't already, get your survival supplies inventoried, make sure your CB radios are in good working order, keep an eye on your neighbors, and let's all be careful out there."

RACHEL POWERED through the next morning. She had only slept a few hours, but those hours had been the most restful sleep she had experienced in years. At the clinic, the patient load was anemic. Alan pleaded with her to hasten the pace of her plan to clear his name. At least discussions about that project kept him from bringing up all that she had revealed to him while on the cot. She felt a bit lighter, but still responsible and laden with guilt. Somehow, he knew she could only handle the emotional trauma in small batches. The space he gave this morning was comforting, like a hug made of silence.

"It's your turn to trust me," she said.

"You know I do, but sitting here in my empty office is excruciating," Alan threw his hands in the air and then crossed his arms over his chest. "I've always been a man of action."

"And I've always been a woman who thinks twice." Rachel double-checked her online order for medical supplies. "The rumor mill is full of land mines. Patsy and I will get you through this." She hit the confirm order button and turned off the tablet. "I'm going back across the street. Promise me you won't do anything rash."

Alan shook his head no and managed to grind out a few words between his teeth. His reputation being destroyed concerned him but knowing people weren't seeking the medical care they needed broke his heat. "I promise. Just for today. I need to see progress."

LATER THAT EVENING, Rachel snuck out through the fire exit over the saloon so her staff couldn't see her, then dashed to her truck and was on the road before anyone could stop her. Olga, Tameka and Jackie, as a team decision, had insisted she take the night off. She was in charge, but she let them tell her what to do because she knew they cared. Not wanting to hang out in her room alone and stew over her growing lists of concerns, she gathered her medical gear and decided to pay Running Wolf, a fellow tribal elder, a visit. After the town hall gathering, Bodie had pulled her aside to let her know on top of his chronic condition, Running Wolf had added the flu to his ailments.

The nurse in Rachel understood that in his depleted condition from untreated lung cancer, the flu would make him feel extra lousy. Bodie knew it too. The elder was already in caretaker mode when she arrived. Not surprising. Just as Rachel turned off the ignition, Bodie exited the tiny cabin wearing a surgical mask and rubber gloves. Mr. Cuddles the rescue dog with long white fluffy hair trotted behind him. "How's Running Wolf doing?"

"Sounds awful. Place is a mess. Need to get the germs out. Can you help with that?" Before Rachel could answer, Mr. Cuddles jumped against her thigh and licked her mittens in between barks.

"That's why I'm here." Rachel knew Bodie well enough to understand his half sentences meant he was more concerned than he wanted to let on. She guessed word had gotten out about the ailing elder, which was why Zeb had loaned Mr. Cuddles for a patient comfort visit. Rachel enjoyed her own snuggle with the companion pet before she donned a mask and gloves, then picked up the extra quilts she'd borrowed from the gift shop and followed Bodie in to evaluate the patient.

"Hi, Running Wolf." Rachel put on a tranquil, happy face as she assessed the severity of the situation. His eyelids fluttered open and he tried to respond but got engulfed by a coughing fit instead. "Easy there, you don't need to answer. Just a rhetorical question." When the coughing got worse, Mr. Cuddles jumped onto the bed, laying his head within petting proximity of the frail man.

She took his temperature and sighed—103 degrees. "Let's get you into some clean clothes and linens. How about if we air this place out?" Bodie found a fresh set of makeshift pajamas, and she stepped out as Running Wolf changed. Rachel put her own humidifier next to his bed then wrapped him in a clean quilt. "Can you have a seat in your rocking chair, please, while I get some fresh sheets on your bed?"

As Rachel became a glorified maid, Bodie hauled in a large supply of wood for the fire. She opened up all the doors and windows for a couple of minutes because the place was stale on top of stagnate. Glad she had access to an industrial-sized washer and dryer, Rachel took everything she could carry back to her truck for a hot water wash. Once she had Running Wolf comfy again in a clean bed, she heated a large batch of her homemade chicken noodle soup.

Bodie continued to remove anything that might have germs while Rachel fed the elder a slow spoonful at a time. She held the bowl just below his nose and mouth, and as she had hoped, the steam helped him breathe easier. "Feeling any better now?"

"Much," was all he could manage in a raspy voice that had been ravaged by a strong cough all day.

After setting him up with a miniature bell, a fresh pitcher of water and a sterilized chamber pot, she told him to get some rest. "I'll be here by the main fireplace if you need anything at all." Rachel closed the bedroom door, and she and Bodie continued to make the cabin as livable as possible, considering the circumstances. Rachel heard a vehicle pulled up and went to the door—maybe a fellow tribal elder had come to pay his respects.

When Alan greeted her and stepped into the small quarters, happy surprise stole her breath. Rachel's heart soared. Mr. Cuddle's wagging hindquarters showed the emotion Rachel couldn't reveal. Alan carried a bag, she knew he had medication and other items to help Running Wolf fight the good fight. Seeing him on neutral ground was nice. This wasn't his office or her café. She could be her friend-self instead of her professional-self while still honoring the intent of the clinic rules.

"Hey, the gang's all here." Alan gave their furry friend a rub behind the ears. "How's the patient doing?" He glanced around, eyes wide. "This place looks so much better."

Rachel gave him a report like a surgical nurse and then allowed herself to go back into pal mode. She escorted Alan into the patient's room.

"Hello, Running Wolf, I'm Dr. Garcia." Alan sat on the edge of the bed and leaned in. "These meds are no charge because I invited a drug representative to come to my office earlier today, and we chatted with the pharmacist by phone. Some pills are samples and others are just past their expiration date, but they'll still help you feel better." Alan smiled in Rachel's direction and it warmed her heart to see Running Wolf grinning as well.

"Here's your wellness cocktail for the upcoming week." The drugs were already in three different premeasured pillboxes, labeled Sunday through Saturday. "Take the stash in the green container when you wake up, the yellow case with lunch and the red box before bedtime. Think you can do that?" Alan held out the medication, "This batch is for right now. Let's kick that flu bug in the pants."

"I think the A team is caring for you now." Bodie pulled the covers up under his friend's chin and gave him a wink. He pointed at Rachel and hitched his finger over his shoulder. Bodie picked up a bag of trash and Rachel did the same as she followed him outside. "If he takes a turn for the worse, please call me or use the radio." The anxious look on Bodie's face stopped Rachel in her tracks.

Bodie's expression then changed from concern about Running Wolf to a glare. One of his eyebrows rose. "I'm not going to do or say anything, but I wanted you to know." Bodie tossed the overstuffed trash-bag into his truck bed with a grunt. "I saw the high five stumble that became a kiss."

Rachel could hear her pulse pounding in her ears and her heart kicked into high gear. "Let me explain."

Bodie held his index finger to his lip to silence her. "It wasn't that it happened. It's how you both reacted that's got me worried. I'm happy for you. You deserve to have a good man in your life. I'm just saying, be careful. If this gets out, there may be no saving either of you." Bodie climbed into his seat.

Rachel opened her mouth, but Bodie lips narrowed into a thin line so she changed her reply. "Understood." With another wary look, Bodie left her with a sleeping patient and a wide awake Alan. Not like Mr. Cuddles could be considered a proper chaperone. She watched his truck leave until all she could see were dirty ruts in the snow. At a snail's pace, she trudged back to the man she couldn't date.

After taking off her medical gear and giving herself a good scrub, Rachel plopped onto the love seat. A full-sized couch would not fit in the room. That left one rickety stool or the seat beside her for Alan. He sterilized his hands and gear and then sat next to her, but didn't get comfortable. He perched on the edge, straight-backed, as if he touched the material he too would catch the flu. Maybe he was observing the no hook-ups with staff rule, she wasn't certain.

Alan opened a king-sized Snickers bar and offered half of it to Rachel. "This is my dinner. Have you eaten?"

Muffling a laugh so as not to wake up the patient, she accepted the nourishment. "Nope, is it that obvious? Thanks, Snickers is my fav—" Before the whole word left her lips, she took a huge bite.

"Um, not obvious, but I know restaurant owners don't always get to eat." Alan's reply was followed by a long span of silence while the candy bar was devoured.

"Bodie thinks we're an item but will remain mute." Rachel blurted out this news after the last swallow of chocolate. Alan had the right to know about the elder's warning.

A heap of awkwardness sucked the air out of the room. Alan made a hand gesture like he was going to say something, but didn't. The silence thickened.

Rachel wanted to say so much, but where to begin? "You and your mom ready for Christmas?" It was the best she could come up with.

Alan seized the change in conversation, "Our holiday will be more about spirituality than gift-giving this year." He started to relax onto the sofa, but instead turned the conversation into a different direction. "Do you know any doctors or nurses who save everyone every time? Their patient's never have side effects or lasting scars?"

Rachel's mind raced to keep up with his equally abrupt change in topic. "No, of course not. That's not realistic."

"I agree."

He held her hand in his and her whole body relaxed to his gentle touch.

"No one else was around to help." He didn't need to say where or when. His concern for the grip that night had on her was in every line of his face. "You were still a student, and honestly your parents' only hope."

"Where are you going with this?"

"Every other medical professional would have done exactly what you did. You did nothing wrong." He squeezed her hand.

Rachel wanted him to keep talking. She wasn't ready to process his statement, let alone reply. She pressed her lips together, but so did he. She sighed, he grinned.

After a long moment, she whispered. "I couldn't make them whole."

"No one could have." He said it in a whisper, body tense as he turned to put his face directly in front of hers. They lived and recovered because of you. Happy in Arizona, right?"

"You think?"

"I know."

His gaze met hers and there was no uncertainty in his eyes. He meant it—with all his knowledge, experience, and integrity—he knew she had provided the best medical care possible.

She harrumphed and leaned on his shoulder. "Avalanches are still a problem."

"One step at a time." He tilted his head to touch hers. "Let's talk reputation rescue."

Rachel pulled away, rubbing her temples. Then she slumped deeper into the sofa. "That's going to be a long mission soldier." The anguished look on his face caused heaviness the size of an elephant to invade her chest. She used a technique that had always worked on her brother. She tickled him.

Laughing loudly, then trying to suppress his volume, he smirked. "Hey, who gave you the order allowing roughhousing? We're on the front lines of this medical care duty."

In the relief of the moment, the truth flowed out of her before she could stop it. "Other than my family, you've treated me better than any man I've ever met." Part of her wanted to suck the words back into her mouth, but most of her felt safe and loved. *Did I just think he loved me? Not like I can read his mind.*

"Told you so."

Oh, right. He did say he wasn't a gold-digger and he would prove that to me.

"No fraternization." She leaped with a laugh, in mock terror, halfway off the loveseat, but he grabbed her sleeve and pulled her back down. She relaxed and cuddled closer to him.

"How about this?" He put his arm around her. "We focus on what matters to us. Let's step off the merry-go-round and forget about the city council circus. Do you think you can do that?"

"Sure. I prefer not getting dizzy." If she was being honest with herself, she had never felt more alive with any other guy, and she refused to let the mayor's new rule take that away from her. She needed to give a romance with Alan a fighting chance. Rachel sat up so they could shake on the newfound agreement.

He had a good firm grip, and using his free fingers, he tucked a stray hair behind her ear. Part of her wanted to run away, but most of her wanted more. He leaned in and hovered. She didn't move. The backs of his fingers caressed her cheek. She trembled. He brushed the tip of his nose against hers. She let out a small gasp. He took her mouth with a tender hunger, and she fell into his arms. Their lips danced, the sweetness of chocolate and caramel lingering between them. Just as he pulled her onto his lap, a coughing fit rang out from the other room. They vaulted toward opposite arms of the loveseat, stifling cackles. Mr. Cuddles took the opportunity to lay down between them.

RACHEL SWORE she heard someone clearing their throat. *This exhaustion, am-I-dreaming-or-awake thing needs to stop.* Then it happened again. *Oh, it can't be,* she told herself. *The cushion my head is on feels too good.* Then her pillow moved. "I'm up! I'm up." She flew into a standing position, head-spinning, looking through the blur to see what kind of bed could move. Alan was sprawled on his side of the sofa, his head straight back over the top, mouth gaping. He snorted, eyes still closed. She stared—*he's beautiful when he's sleeping.*

A familiar seizure of coughing had Rachel whirling on her heels. "Running Wolf!" Oh, now she remembered where she was and why. A blinding ray of sunlight struck her face.

Alan sprung to life, sitting straight up like someone had glued him to plywood. "What's the emergency?"

The tribal elder, who was still in Rachel's hat and encased in a quilt, had hobbled to the divide of the two rooms. The sound of the tiny bell rang out from under the rumpled pile of covers. "Soup please?"

CHAPTER 20

CHRISTMAS WAS ONLY three days away when Rachel broke the land speed barrier getting back to open the café after falling asleep on the loveseat with Alan. The predictions of heavy snow had already begun to come true. Trembling against the cold, she danced a jig until Brett rumbled up, driving Betsy. The siblings met every morning he ventured out to clear the streets of snow. Rachel climbed up and passed him several packages of food through the window. She couldn't tamp down the fears that kept her up most of the night. "Did you see the news?"

Brett looked at her and cocked his head to one side. "Of course! That's a big part of my job." He went back to positioning the food so he could grab it while driving.

Rachel did her best to contain herself, as she knew how he would react, but the words sprang from her lips as if the action was involuntary. "The more snow on the ground, the higher the risk of avalanche." She put on her best gotta-love-me grin and waited.

Brett slammed his long-haired skull against the headrest, wrinkling his nose. "That's enough!" He whacked the palms of his hands onto the steering wheel. "I've already got too many people stressing out on me. I don't need you jumping on the pile." He turned his face away, and Rachel knew he was trying to hide something. She'd expected him to tease her about her fear or grumble a bit, but this reaction was over the top.

Throwing her mind into emergency nurse composure mode, she pushed up her sleeves and took a slow, deep inhale. "Brett, tell me—what's really going on?" The expression he allowed her to see was pure anguish—eyebrows pinched together and a jaw clenched so tight she wondered if he was about to break a tooth.

"Sophie's in the hospital." He yanked his hat much lower over his eyes than necessary. "She's been watching the weather reports. Her anxiety about me plowing through these storms put the baby in distress." He hung his head and shoulders, clenching his fists.

Rachel unlatched the door, and slinging it open, she launched herself around him. She clawed at the material of his coat, pulling him as close to her as possible. "It's going to be okay. Sophie and the baby will be fine." Rachel felt the moisture of Brett's tears rub onto her cheek. Her heart shattered. She had never seen him cry, never. Holding him closer, she whispered, "The hospital in Kalispell has the equipment needed to monitor them both. Sophie's going to deliver a healthy baby, and she'll be fine too. I know it. I can feel it in my bones." She squeezed him with every ounce of energy she had.

The worried Welch duo held each other for several minutes, and eventually, Brett broke away. "I've got to stay on schedule if my plan is to work. Gotta go. Love you."

Giving him one extra hug, Rachel let Brett and Betsy prepare for their battle ahead. She stood in the back parking lot of the café until she couldn't see the monster snowplow any longer. She headed for the kitchen door, and all of the responsibilities that weighed on her came crashing down at once.

How could she contribute to reopening the mill, be a nurse, manage three businesses, support Sophie during her maternity leave, continue her PTSD sessions with Alan and keep herself from becoming romantically involved with her boss? The unsweetened icing on this cake made of uncertainty was that she missed her parents terribly. Christmas was around the corner, and they would be in Arizona. Their broken bodies could no longer withstand the cold. At least she knew they were safe.

Rachel reached out to open the door but instead crumpled against it. Tears poured down her face, and the salty, stinging emotion dug in even further as a frosty wind filled with huge snowflakes compressed every part of her against the icy metal. The cry was short, but it served its purpose. She stood up straight, swiped the liquid trepidation from her face and pulled herself up by her bootstraps. Rachel made a point of giving each faux-fur boot that kept her feet so warm a good tug. She was Rachel Welch, she was strong in every sense of the word, and she would be the rock. The source of strength that everyone around her needed.

STANDING NEAR THE RECEPTION DESK, with three days before Christmas, Alan blew a kiss to his mother. Teresa had committed to Bodie, weeks before she left, to help at his free gift-wrapping table. Being a woman of her word, even with the latest batch of bad news, she went to the Trading Post for her shift.

The difficult conversation with her concerning the drug lord rumors had gone better than he had expected. She hadn't gotten angry. He wished she had. Her stone face and balancing-a-book-on-her-head posture was more than he could take. Not even a sigh. He needed one of her encouraging speeches but didn't get that either. His *madre* gave him a nod, rose from her chair and went back to her post.

At least she'd had a wonderful visit. Seeing her family and friends seemed to have strengthened her resilience. But, the city of Snowflake could revoke his contract, or the people might reject him as a person who could not be trusted. Where would they go?

Alan went back to his empty office and waited for the phone to ring. It didn't. The stillness in the clinic was unnerving. Alan decided to review the portions of his life that were going well: those folks who knew he wasn't a drug dealer gave him high marks on his ability to provide medical care, the samples of medication seemed to be controlling Running Wolf's chronic condition and minimizing his flu symptoms. But, Alan's private time with Rachel was the greatest gift.

She had fallen asleep and slid onto his shoulder. He knew he shouldn't have, but he let himself find slumber beside her. His dreams had been more than vivid with her practically in his arms. Even with the rumor stress and forbidden romance, Alan allowed himself to wonder about the intensity of their passion if they could kiss for real. That thought made him smile just as she stumbled into his reception area.

Warning bells went off on many levels. She wasn't in her nursing whites and looked like she hadn't slept when he knew she had—in fact, she looked unwell. In an instant, he considered the possibility that she was coming down with the flu. Her body language was off. All the usual inspirational light in her eyes was gone. He wanted to hug her, but instead he jumped up from his desk and bolted to the lobby to feel her forehead for fever.

Rachel batted his arm away. "What are you doing? I'm fine!" The words came out with such venom, Alan took several steps backward.

"Sorry. What's wrong?" His heart sunk to his feet. He knew she was hurting, but he couldn't diagnose how.

"I'm here to help with the only appointment still on the books today." She acted like she was standing up to the mayor, not having a conversation with the man she'd slept beside the night before.

"Thank you for that, but please what else has you troubled?"

She pushed passed him and started setting up the exam room. "The negotiations to reopen the mill broke down, Sophie is in the hospital, Brett is risking his life plowing snow, and I miss my parents." She reached for a tablet to log into the patient's records. "People are relying on me." She crumpled onto a rickety rolling stool. "And Bodie insinuated we have feelings for each other based on the way we reacted to the...well let's call it, the near-miss, after the trivia win."

"And what? He's filed a complaint with the city council?" Alan stood so straight his back spasmed, and he hoped she couldn't tell his blood pressure was on the rise.

"Nah. He thinks if we belong together, then we should be." She let her head fall back until it thunked against the wall. "What are we doing? Is it worth our careers?"

"My reputation has hit the skids. Again! So I may not have a career to protect. Besides the mayor's knee jerk reaction needs to be amended." Alan went down on one knee and took both of her hands. "But if you're feeling what I am, then I say let's see where it takes us. I'm ready to fight city hall if you are? But this is your hometown, and I don't want to put you in an awkward position."

The jingle of the bells on the front door kept Rachel from answering. Alan snuck a lightning-fast peck on her palm before he released her to greet the patient. This office visit for the Pharmacy Tech Joanna was going to be rough. She did a great job of helping patients and now she would become one. He steeled himself to deliver bad news. Rachel had requested to be present after she saw the test results.

The patient went through every emotion he expected. Rachel was amazing. Her calm, caring demeanor helped the patient so much. He gave the news along with treatment possibilities, and Rachel chimed in saying the same thing using words the patient seemed to better understand. Eventually, the wife and mother appeared prepared for the battle ahead and saw herself to the exit.

Alan then noticed Rachel had become unsteady on her feet and leaned heavily on the exam table. "You okay?"

"Not really."

Alan closed the door and locked it. Before she could object, he was hugging her, grabbing the curls she had not contained. His mouth to her ear. "With our help, she can beat this." He strained to hear her response.

"It's not fair."

"No. But she'll have an amazing network of support." His lips glided to the side of her face.

"You mean us?"

He took a step back. "Professional us or personal us?"

She almost laughed but choked on it. "Fiercely attracted and growing connection us."

He raised an eyebrow. "Oh, them. The odds-makers have *that* us as a long shot, but I'm all in. You?"

"Just doubled down."

From the first moment he saw her lips, he wanted to devour them. But now he took his time. First a fly-by, then the slightest touch. A soft kiss smoldered until her mouth parted. His mind went offline, but his body knew just what to do. She responded with a hunger that surprised him. "I like the sensual us." Rachel cut off his whisper with her voluptuous mouth.

"Alan?" The muffled voice came from the back door of the clinic. "I came to see if you wanted to have lunch with Bodie and me?"

My madre! He jumped back, sucked in air, concealed his emotions with his camouflage cloak and responded. "Sure thing. Be right there."

Rachel stifled a giggle and shrugged. Then began the post-visit routine. "I like all our versions of us."

"Yeah, me too." He opened the door and began to stroll to the lobby but did an about-face to verify the blinds had been closed. Shut tight, good. He grinned. "Thanks again for your help with Joanna."

"Sure thing. I'm heading back to the café. I'll walk with you."

Alan cocked his head at Rachel to get her attention. After verifying his mother couldn't see him, he gave a quick side to side shake of his head.

"Oh, right. I have to place a few calls first," said Rachel. She then tried to tell him something with hand gestures, but he didn't understand. She frowned and pulled her phone from her pocket. Next, she typed a text to him but didn't send it. Instead, she flipped her phone so he could read:

Let me leave first?

Alan's eyebrows rose as he scanned her screen. He waved a hand toward the door as if to say *after you*. "I'll make those calls for you later. I know the café needs you." Her index finger drew a question mark in the air and her feet didn't move. He panicked as his mother arrived from his office carrying his coat. As Alan escorted his mom to the front exit, he looked back and mouthed *sorry*. *Did I just ruin an amazing kiss by trying to be secretive?*

CHAPTER 21

On December twenty-third while in his office, Alan needed to keep his mind from plotting when next he could further his fledgling romance with Rachel, so he was thrilled to have a few emergency patients. Seeing the stack of messages his mother had placed on his desk brought him back to reality. He picked up a pen to organize his thoughts before he called the local pharmacy to refill patient's prescriptions.

Teresa had been asking him questions about Rachel at breakfast that he wasn't ready to answer. She had given him a knowing look. Heat had flowed onto his cheeks, but he had chomped down on his tongue before he said too much too soon. At Alan's urging, Teresa volunteered again to help Bodie with the gift-wrapping table. He appreciated the alone time until every thought relating to Rachel came up against a hurdle or brick wall. He sat in his rickety chair shoulders slumped and stared out the window.

The snow had been falling off and on for hours and was expected to do so for days. Living less than two miles from the clinic had been a good choice, but based on today's weather, Teresa's vehicle would not be able to maneuver in the drifting snow, so she'd be riding with him until the snow melted. Even Alan's four-wheel-drive Jeep almost got stuck more than once during the short journey. Just in case, they'd brought extra food and clothing to his office. He wanted to be prepared for anything.

After the morning rush, if he could call it that, Alan couldn't keep himself from looking across the way at Rachel's businesses. He imagined her working harder than ever to try to forget all her troubles, which now included him. *I've got to give her space. Be supportive of her dilemmas.* The thought of being close to her without touching her was painful. He also somehow needed to keep whatever she and Patsy were working on to save his career on the top of her priority list. *Am I being selfish? It is my life's work after all.* Alan made a list of chores and dove in, devoting all his energy.

Just as he was running out of self-assigned, unnecessary tasks designed to keep his brain busy, the CB radio crackled to life. "Residents of Snowflake." The unidentified speaker sounded like he couldn't contain his enthusiasm. "Three long blasts at the mountain pass. Repeat, three long blasts. All available snow blowers and manpower to meet on Main Street. Convoy ETA is 30 minutes. Residents of Snowflake, three long blasts."

More lingo came his way that he didn't understand, another reminder that he was new to Montana—and Alan had thought he was getting the hang of living under the big sky. He wanted to go ask Rachel but knew that was a bad idea. Confirming to his new neighbors that he had much to learn about local customs was as painful an idea as accepting their help. Alan dropped his head into his hands. He must make this transition on his own.

The next best thing would be going to the Trading Post and hope to decipher how people responded to this announcement, but that meant showing his face in public. The face that some folks thought belonged to a drug dealer. Determined to not let the rumors ruin him, Alan took off his lab coat and put on his winter gear, which made him look as much like a local as he could manage.

He wrapped his scarf around the outside of his knit ski cap, so only his eyes were visible to anyone trying to identify him, then used the back exit. Alan was satisfied with this covert course of action but wasn't prepared for the gust of frigid wind that caught him as he stepped out from between his office and the nearest business. The howling blast almost knocked him on his derriere. He'd heard of sea legs, but this snowstorm stuff was new territory for him. Alan literally leaned all his weight into the squally gale, and Mother Nature held him up with her frosty arms.

As he shivered, Alan was beginning to better understand what the weather people were making such a fuss about. "Snow Emergency. Expect power outages," they said. With the heavy wet snow, falling tree limbs would knock down power lines. This brought a new appreciation for the types of medical emergencies he would be asked to treat. The thought was daunting.

Alan snuck back a couple of steps, and the building provided enough shelter for him to survey the goings-on around him. The Big Sky had no sun today. He knew it was up there, but the thick dark cloud banks blocked the rays from breaking through. He was a Sunshine State guy. Winter was just beginning. *Why did I move here again?*

"Is that you, Alan?" So much for his disguise. He turned to respond before he realized that move confirmed his identity. "It's Monkey." The high wire rigging master had on one-piece coveralls that had to be lined with a quilted inner layer, based on his girth. "Three long blasts. That Brett is quite a guy, right?"

Glad Monkey couldn't see his expression, Alan asked, "What does that mean, exactly? Three long blasts."

"Oh! Right, you're new here." Monkey adjusted his ski goggles and continued. "They closed the mountain pass due to the amount of snow. But somehow Brett and Betsy made it to the highest elevation. He's on his way down. The delivery trucks are right behind him."

The thought that Brett was on his way into the center of town made Alan nervous. The things he wanted to do with Rachel when next they were alone may not go over well with her older brother. Her really big older brother. He wasn't sure if Brett would ask him to stay away and conform to the new clinic rules or caution him to treat his sister right. *That would be an awkward conversation.*

"Did you see it? Was that a flash of yellow light? I've got to go." With a couple of steps, Monkey rounded the corner and was out of sight.

Be the man Rachel would want to date. This was Alan's latest mantra. With that in mind, he struggled to make his way in the direction of the Trading Post. Then he saw what Monkey must have seen. Through a large number of huge snowflakes, off in the distance, a flash of yellow brightened up the grey sky. What resembled an 18-wheeler horn sounded. Each blast continued at length and Alan began to count. Three. Vehicles all through town honked their horns in reply. Anyone already outside hooted and hollered. Alan likened this to the cavalry arriving.

All kinds of activity launched into overdrive. Anything that had been on the road was removed. People arrived on horses, sleighs and snowmobiles to the side streets and nearby parking lots. But Main Street was empty. Then he saw her. Rachel, along with the café staff, was hovering just outside the saloon's side entrance. She had her hood up and gloves on, but he knew her walk and mannerism. It didn't matter what coat she chose, even if it was one he had never seen her wear. When she was near him, his spirit soared.

The rumble arrived before the caravan. A flying haze of white stretched from the pavement to the flashing caution lights, but eventually, Alan could see Betsy. Flanking her, but hanging back off each side of her rear bumper, were two similar trucks with plows. All three machines were going the same direction, even if that meant they were going the wrong way down the road. This set-up cleared the street and left massive banks of dirty snow almost as tall as Alan in their wake.

The triad of plows thundered past the medical clinic and slowed to a halt. Five delivery trucks lumbered up behind them with a multitude of squeaks and grumbles from having made the treacherous journey over the curvy, narrow mountain route filled with ice and fallen rocks. Alan heard the sheriff and the mayor bark orders, and the good people of Snowflake obeyed without question. These folks had run this drill before. That was obvious. Snowblowers roared to life to clear the piles of snow as other neighbors greeted the trucks to accept the highly-anticipated packages.

"Christmas is saved," cried out one of the youngsters. "Is that a real elf in the monster plow?"

The children ran to investigate while the adults hugged one another and counted their blessings. Alan watched the bystanders go from worried and frustrated to spreading joy and holiday cheer.

"Hail to Betsy and Brett," added a local business owner.

It was true, Alan thought. Many small businesses would have suffered if their merchandise or supplies had not arrived. So much more than not having a present under the tree was at risk. How did these folks manage the logistics of the weather each year? He was beginning to better appreciate the glistening of the Christmas decorations, the smell of the food coming from the café, and even the tingle of the snow melting on his skin. He added to his checklist of personal goals: live up to being a contributing resident of Snowflake. Recognize the effort and sacrifice each person makes to keep this town running.

Alan decided to help the crew closest to the Trading Post. People made a line and passed parcels one to the next, like the bucket brigade of volunteer firefighters of old. It felt good to be useful. No one seemed to care who he was, just that the boxes needed to be unloaded with haste. Out of the corner of his eye, Alan waited for Brett to leap down from his seat in Betsy's cab. Mr. Hero was dressed like one of Santa's helpers, complete with a red coat and the elf hat that Parrot had worn as part of his costume at the café. The hat's bottom was outlined in white furry piping. A ball of fleece flopped on the end of the folded-over green and red triangle.

"Ho ho ho, Merry Christmas!" shouted Brett as he stretched his legs and adjusted his costume. Alan grinned at the display of holiday rejoicing, even though Brett might choose to protect his sister's career over her having a date. Seeing the excited pack of kids gawking up at the red-suited man warmed his heart. The tossing and grasping of boxes kept Alan occupied as he watched the tallest elf he had ever seen. With a gaggle of youth following him, Brett turned away, heading toward the restaurant and his sister. Alan narrowed his focus to the task in front of him and continued to move in stealth mode.

"Mama!"

Alan knew the voice in an instant. Rachel's cry of surprise, joy and concern touched Alan's heart. He continued listening as another package made its way past him along the human conveyor belt.

"Daddy!" This Rachel said with a gasp and a sob.

Hearing the emotion in her words made Alan's throat constrict. She was happy to see her parents, but pain and sorrow were in her wail. Saving his career and outmaneuvering the no dating coworkers rule became insignificant. *She needs to make her family her priority.* Dropping his gaze to the snow, he pulled the belt on his coat tighter with a quick flick of his wrists.

Alan stepped out of the line and winced as a frosty blast blew right through his coat, chilling him to his core. He deserved this discomfort and more. He so wanted to hug her and be the man to provide comfort. Would the Welch family allow him near her? He longed to march over to profess his honorable and gentlemanly intentions toward their daughter. But, the thought of meeting her parents under these circumstances was not ideal. He still longed to get a glimpse of the people who had raised the woman who excited every cell in his body, especially those in his heart.

Peeking around one of the delivery rigs, Alan spotted the empty wheelchair sitting alone in the new dusting of snow. Brett was in the process of lifting a small, frail woman down from the elevated seat. She reminded him of his *madre*. He bit his lip to keep from calling out to Rachel, who was extending her arms to help support the transfer of her mother.

Once Mrs. Welch was settled, several men assisted the patriarch of the family. They all but carried him down as well. Once he was safely on the pavement, Rachel pushed his modified walker in his direction. And then Alan remembered—this loving couple had been in a bad car accident, leaving the wife paralyzed and the husband with severe frostbite. Alan counted his blessings that his mother had made it through the ordeal in Miami unharmed. He tried to empathize with

Rachel. Alan better understood now why Peak Vista Road and the possibility of an avalanche set off her panic attacks.

"What are you doing here? In this storm? You should have stayed in Kalispell with Sophie." Rachel hugged her father and then bent down to wrap her arms around her mother in the chair. "I'm so happy to see you! You have no idea." She swiped at her eyes and Alan welled up himself. The siblings supported the parents as they, with great effort, managed to enter the café. Alan lifted his foot to follow but didn't get very far. Parrot ran up to greet his grandparents, and Alan knew it wasn't the right moment. Time stood still as Alan watched from afar, hoping beyond all hope that he might someday earn a spot in that family.

"Hey, we've got to get these liquid meds inside before they freeze," called out the pharmacist to anyone within earshot. Giving his scarf a yank to pull it tighter around his face, Alan went to fill the request for help.

Eventually, the roar of the snow blowers faded and the Christmas gifts heading to Snowflake were unloaded. Alan couldn't believe how quickly a couple of inches of snow blanketed the street once more. He lifted his face to look at the overcast weather, wondering just how much longer this storm would last. The Christmas lights in the heart of downtown still twinkled though, and folks went back to the day-to-day tasks of the holiday season.

Snow formed high walls in what Alan guessed were designated areas. People had cleared the driveways, and the sidewalks were usable for the time being. The spaces in between buildings were stuffed with snow. The drivers of the convoy, having been given food and beverages from Rachel's restaurant, were starting the engines again and meeting with Elf Brett before heading onward.

Alan was tempted to head into the saloon instead of returning to his empty office. Maybe he could order takeout and keep his ears open for the goings-on within the Welch family, but his feet wouldn't take him in that direction. *I'm not making my own way in the world by myself.* Maybe he didn't deserve to become one of them after all.

Having lumbered to his side of the street, Alan ran into Monkey again. He had a serious scowl on his face. "What's wrong? Can I help?"

Monkey just shook his head. "I get it, but I don't like it."

Alan remembered the climbing expert had a hard time disclosing his feelings. "Don't like what?" A draft of the ever-colder wind filled Alan's throat as he spoke, and it actually hurt.

"Oh, the three plows help to get the job done, but they have to stay together and clear two more mountain passes." Monkey pulled his hat lower over his ears. "They've got a long haul ahead of them. They're saving everyone else's Christmas, but at what cost to themselves?" He tugged his hood to block the wind from his eyes. "They're gonna spend the night two counties over. But if he wants to be home for Christmas, Brett has to clear a return path by himself. I just don't like the sound of that."

"Not to change the subject, and don't look now, but Olga is keeping tabs on you from across the street." Alan needed to lighten the mood and couldn't help but notice Olga while he was watching Rachel and the Welch family.

Shuffling back a couple of steps and whipping his face toward the buildings on his side of the road, Monkey asked, "Is she still looking?" Monkey waved at Bodie, who was a block away, and who had no idea the greeting was meant for him.

"Yep. She's still sneaking glances over here."

With swift strides, Monkey arrived at a snowbank and picked up the biggest shovel he could find. As he tossed heaping piles of white to the top of the snowdrift, even Alan was impressed.

"Is she seeing this?'

"Ah, sorry. She must have been called back into the café. She's inside."

After stabbing his shovel into the ice to be ready for its next usage, Monkey slapped Alan on the back and continued leaning into the wind as he made his way down the road. "Women."

"I know the feeling. At least you're worthy of Olga." Alan's military-inspired posture sagged and his voice trailed off as he called out to his retreating friend.

He took stock of his thoughts from the past 24 hours. *I want to live here, earn everyone's trust.* Then he remembered Monkey's concern about Brett who clearly was willing to give so much of himself to help his neighbors. Between the possibilities of avalanches and frostbite, Alan knew Rachel would be worried sick. He could do nothing to help her. Rachel let him see hints of her attraction toward him but, she had a strong family commitment as a descendant of the town's founding fathers. Following the city council's edict meant more to her. If Alan tried to go against their new rules, he would put Rachel's career and reputation at stake. He couldn't do that to her. What did the Hippocratic Oath say? *First do no harm.* Ugh, he'd have to find a way to live with that!

CHAPTER 22

"AUNTIE RACH, GET UP!"

On Christmas Eve, Rachel forced her eyelids to remain still, but Rachel already knew who had run into the guest room at the ranch house. It became apparent she had not responded fast enough when Parrot launched himself onto the bed. She took an unintentional, errant knee to the ribs, and exhaled with a whoosh as most of Parrot's weight found its way to her midsection.

"Easy Parrot," gasped Rachel, trying to remove her unwanted visitor from the bed. "Santa Claus is watching. You'd better be nice." Rolling over and tapping her cell screen, she realized she still had about 15 minutes before her alarm would be doing its duty. Who needed a wake-up call when a five-year-old slept in the house on Christmas Eve?

"I gotta send Santa another letter. You work for the post office, so you can get it to him, right?" Instead of pouncing on her, now Parrot was poking Rachel's arm and nudging her shoulder.

Flopping back onto her pillow, Rachel tried to appease her nephew and find a way to ease into her morning like she usually did. "Why? Santa's busy loading the sleigh."

"But sometimes I sleep here and sometimes I sleep above the café.

How's Santa gonna know how to find me?" The look of obvious concern on Parrot's face was adorable but didn't make up for the rude awakening.

Rachel pulled the covers up to her chin, trying to talk while simultaneously yawning and stretching. "He sees you when you're sleeping. That means he also knows where you're sleeping. Get it?"

Parrot's bottom lip protruded and his nose crinkled as he contemplated this explanation. Rachel had to bite the inside of her cheek to keep from laughing. She could almost see the inner workings of Parrot's well-above-average intellect kick into high gear.

"Oh, like a superpower." Still in deep thought, Parrot made his way to the door. "I need to set out the milk and cookies here, then." His eyebrows shot up as a new idea formed. "I better do it NOW! Santa needs to save his energy to deliver all the presents."

Scrunching as deep into the covers as possible, Rachel called after him, "That's very thoughtful of you." Grateful to be alone again, she ran through her to-do list in her mind. She was thrilled to see her parents, but their surprise arrival had her a bit discombobulated. She had intended to sleep in her bed. Now she was needed at the ranch to fix everyone's breakfast and then had to drive to the restaurant. The additional snow that had fallen overnight would lengthen her travel time. Joy.

Guilt made her sit up like the flag on an expired parking meter. *I'm grumbling because I'm in my brother's house, but Brett is sleeping who knows where.* She sighed. She'd give him an extra-long hug when next she saw him. But when would that be? Bile began to rise in her empty stomach. *I can't think about that. Christmas, that's a better topic.* Her body melted back into the sheets and she ran through her day's tasks: food she needed to prepare, items people would pick up for their loved ones from the gift shop. Oh, she needed to give Mrs. Garcia the quilt Teresa planned to give to Alan. Since all the silk flower arrangements had sold out, that delivery would include extra cash. Being a Santa's helper did have its redeeming moments.

Alan. The thought of him brought up more emotions than she could process before her coffee. Rachel closed her eyes. Maybe she'd fall back to sleep. Slumber was less complicated than attraction. No, she felt more than that for him. What word best described her feelings? Rachel's phone played the wind chimes she had used of late to start each day on a lighter note. Well, that peaceful sound helped for about a nanosecond.

She replayed her last interaction with him. She had gotten angry that he left her at the clinic to have lunch with his mother when she needed to get back to the cafe. She had tried to use impromptu hand signals to tell him to flip-flop the order so she left first. Where had that come from? It hadn't worked. Why was she being so selfish? Alan was only trying to conceal their alone time and the kiss.

Oh, the man could kiss. He had also kept his word to treat her like any other gal, not someone with high-end finances and influence to spare. The way he helped her with the PTSD issue earned him major good-boyfriend-material points. *He could have fired me, but he saved me instead.* She gathered all of his appealing qualities so she could list them for her parents. He's a loving son and good doctor, boss, neighbor, friend and kisser. *Well, I'll keep that last attribute to myself.*

Her whole body began to wake-up as she thought about his luscious lips. *My parents will like him for sure.* She pondered how best to make his introduction. And then the mayor's rant ping-ponged around in her brain. The new rule! She had finally found a man she wanted to marry, but she'd have to sacrifice her career. Thoughts of marrying had never crowded into her daydreams. *What have I done to deserve this?*

Yesterday, when she'd seen Alan helping to unload the trucks, she had wanted to run over, throw her arms around him and kiss him again so all of Snowflake could see the passion she felt for him. Rule be dammed. But then she'd seen her mother's wheelchair and everything had turned upside down. If only her need for him to be part of her life could be as high a priority as everything else she was juggling. So many people needed her, now was not a time to be selfish. He wouldn't stay unless he was the town's doctor. Maybe giving up nursing wouldn't be so bad since she had the café, saloon and gift shop to fall back on? She was a seesaw of contradictions.

She heard her parents banging around in the kitchen and her shoulders slumped. Rachel couldn't let herself think past their immediate needs. Dragging on a robe and her slippers, she made her way down the hall. "Merry Christmas Eve!"

On the morning of Christmas Eve, Alan looked out his living room window and noticed someone had removed the snow from Main Street to his driveway, again. He asked his mother if she had heard the snowplow overnight, but it seemed that both of them had slept right through the noise that activity must surely make.

Brett and Betsy's monster-plow couldn't have made these tracks—a smaller, bucket-and-blade setup, maybe? The sheriff wanted him available for emergencies. Alan needed to know who to thank, but until his suspected drug dealer status was reversed, he didn't dare ask around. He had promised himself he would let Rachel and Patsy work their magic and stay out of it. He'd think of the drivable road as a gift from Santa himself. That put a smile on his face.

Alan had expected the day at the office to be slow, so as he reviewed his day planner he was pleasantly surprised that his mother had made a few future appointments. She was granting payment extensions for folks who wanted to pay with real dollars. Teresa knew best how to survive in Snowflake with a good reputation intact.

Five o'clock took its sweet time in arriving. Alan relished helping his mother with end-of-day tasks so they could go home to relax and enjoy the holiday. But just as he was about to put on his coat, Bodie popped in the front door, asking, "Teresa, may I walk you down to the community center?"

His mother looked Alan's way and shrugged. "What's going on down there?"

Bodie was no actor, so Alan believed the look of complete surprise. The shock turned into embarrassment. "I'm so sorry. We don't get many new folks." Stepping further into the office, he took off his hat.

"Snowflake doesn't advertise the dinner. It just happens. We all know about it. I should've told you. I'm an idiot."

Alan's mother got up from behind the reception desk to comfort her new friend. "Don't say such things. You're one of the smartest people I know."

Alan chimed in, "No worries, really. You do so much for so many. What's up with the dinner?"

Bodie hesitated. "Well, people bring a dish. It's a big feast. Folks come and go whenever they'd like. No charge, no rules."

Alan stifled a smirk. The man always managed to convey his message well enough.

"I won't go unless I bring a dish," said Teresa.

It must be a womanly thing, always having to bring a homemade item. Seeing the look of disappointment on Bodie's face, Alan tried to find a solution. "How about the flan you made for tomorrow?"

"No, people here won't know what that is." Teresa's voice ticked up an octave and she fiddled with the buttons of her Christmas sweater.

Bodie looked confused but encouraged. "What's a fl… who?"

Alan chuckled. "Flan. It's a Cuban dessert. It's kind of like a custard with a caramel sauce over it."

"Oh, dessert of any kind is always welcome. My taste buds are watering. If you made it, I'm sure it's delicious." Bodie put his hat back on. "I'll use my sleigh to get you home and back in no time."

Alan watched his mother review her options. A silent conversation also went on between her and Bodie. "Well, I guess I can make another one tomorrow for Alan and me." Bodie gave Teresa the biggest smile Alan had ever seen grace the man's face.

"Back in a jiffy." Halfway out the door, Bodie turned back. "Oh, and I'm a part of the plan Ms. Patsy and Ms. Rachel have been working on."

Alan tried to conjure up a polite way to ask for more details about the plan, but Bodie rushed out of the office like a child needing to be in bed before Santa arrived. Well finally, action would occur. That didn't mean his reputation would be restored any time soon. But he enjoyed seeing the new glow on his mother's face.

A wonderful thought came to his mind. "*Madre*, before you jump into Bodie's sleigh, come into my office. I have something for you." Alan had to turn his back to her so she couldn't see his mischievous grin.

"What!?" Teresa followed him halfway down the hall, then took a detour into the supply room. When she arrived at his desk, she carried a huge paper bag at her side. "We decided to not exchange gifts. I hope you didn't get me anything."

Alan gave his mother a long hug then bent to retrieve the box he had hidden under the cot. "I can't begin to thank you for moving here with me. I'm sorry your life has been disrupted. I'll find a way to make it up to you." His voice wavered as he made the promise. But he didn't care if his *madre* saw him getting emotional. She was his rock. Teresa had raised him on her own, sometimes taking on two or three jobs to make ends meet when he was in college. He knew the bond he had with his *madre* was more special than most.

Teresa squeezed him like she had done all her life. Her unconditional love was all the gift he needed this year. The finger wag she gave him had him feeling guilty, but he could reconcile that against her years of devotion. "I came by this item because of Snowflake currency. I hope you like it." Alan presented her with the unwrapped box. *This can't begin to say thank you for all you've sacrificed for my happiness.*

"Well, that barter money thing is a two-way street." Before she accepted the gift, she lifted the oversized bag. "When I saw this, it reminded me of home and how happy you've made me over the years. I'm so proud of you."

With a quick air-blown kiss, Alan took the gift but waited to watch her open her package before looking at his. Once the lid was off and she grasped the scarf, the other half of the box fell to the floor. "Oh my goodness! How did you know? It's the one I've wanted." With dramatic flair, Teresa flung one side of the colorful cashmere over her shoulder and then the other. "It's so soft. I love it. Thank you!" Tears began to roll down her face.

"I'm glad you're happy, but no tears, please. They'll freeze in

Bodie's sleigh." Alan dropped his gift and gave her another hug. "A wise man told me this is what you wanted."

Drying her face with her new scarf, Teresa asked, "Could that man be Bodie?"

"I'll never tell." Alan winked and tugged at the scarf. "It looks really good on you." Pawing around in the bag, Alan pulled out a thick quilt in orange and green. "Go Canes! I can definitely use this." Alan smothered himself from head to toe in the warm comfort of the gift. "Thank you!" He pulled his *madre* into the cocoon of the over-sized quilt. And for that instant, all of his cares faded away. No worries, just love and fond memories.

He didn't want the moment to end but knew his mother needed to bundle up for the ride to his house. At least she'd be warmer with the new scarf. Alan was certain Bodie would notice she was wearing the gift he had recommended. He escorted his mother to the back entrance, still holding her tight.

Before he could pull the door open for her, Teresa pushed him away. "I want to make something clear." Her solemn expression gave him cause for concern. "I've made it clear to Bodie that I miss your father every day, and no one can ever replace him. He gets that I'm not focused on myself, and he's fine with us being just friends for now."

As Alan gathered himself a long hush lingered. "I wish I could have met my *padre*."

"He's watching over us. He'd be proud of the man you have become." Teresa kissed him on the cheek and made her way to the horse-drawn sleigh, which was decked out with holly sprigs wrapped in red ribbons and lanterns to guide the way.

As Bodie gave the horse the command to move forward, he yelled out, "We'll meet you at the community center in a few."

Alan watched the back of the red carriage until he could no longer see the oil lamps. Going back into his office, he realized the plan was still in motion. He'd have to show his face at a party where some people wouldn't have a very high opinion of him. Tugging the quilt around him, he prayed for courage. Hopefully, the good people of Snowflake would be on their best behavior for the holiday.

Another thought that made the whole trip worthwhile came to mind. Rachel would undoubtedly attend. He wanted to talk to her, but should he? What could he say? How could he show her the adjustments or sacrifices he was willing to make to earn a first date? If all he got to do tonight was watch her from afar, that would be enough.

CHAPTER 23

Walking alone to the Christmas Eve celebration, Alan realized his feet were taking their sweet time moving forward, despite the temperatures dipping close to zero. For the first time in his life, he dreaded the thought of having to face his patients. In Miami, he could talk about cooperating with the FDA. In Snowflake, a rumor—unsubstantiated gossip was the problem. Why did people believe he might be a drug dealer?

Pushing that anxiety out of his mind, he decided to enjoy the Christmas decorations.

Each business he passed had its own theme or creative flare. Some were classic, elegant and simple, while others were flashing extravaganzas that helped to promote the business as much as celebrate the holiday. One business had even sponsored a snowman-building contest, with pictures of the winners proudly displayed in the shop's front window.

As he got closer to the community center, the church with its giant snowflakes on all four sides commandeered his focus. He rounded each side, and as he had the first time, he saw them lit up and remembered what the pastor had said about the legend. Could his wish come true? Would Rachel make more progress to overcome her PTSD? Was he meant to be the man of her dreams? Alan envisioned her on his arm instead of some local cowboy. Maybe if he wished harder or worked harder toward the goal he could improve his chances.

Making a point of entering through the rear entrance, Alan took off his coat and hoped the more casual clothes he wore would help him stay in the background. The lights were dimmed to let the ten-foot Christmas tree be a centerpiece of the decorations. The glow from the stunning white angel tree topper glimmered near the rafters. Seeing this symbol of the season made Alan feel comforted and watched over. The smell of bayberries filled the air from the branches that adorned the fireplaces. Without hesitation, Alan found a lone rocking chair by the wall along with some stray mismatched seating and settled in for some people watching.

His mood lightened when he spotted Monkey in a corner, so Alan started to walk over to join to him, until he saw Olga just behind Monkey, giggling and tossing her hair. The thought of those two finding a way to have quality time at the soiree gave him hope. The rest of the men gathered around the largest fireplace. Alan overheard what he guessed was claims of who had shot the buck with the most antler points.

Some extended families used the gathering to exchange gifts, while others made the trip into town to see everyone and anyone. A long row of tables covered in red and green tablecloths stood in the center of the room. Every type of food made up this feast. Bodie had been correct, there were no rules. Folks made their way to the tables and took whatever they desired. The holiday spirit was alive and well in Snowflake, even with the series of bad winter storms predicted over the next couple of days.

Alan considered it a miracle of the season when he saw that Running Wolf felt well enough to join the festivities. He was holding court by the tree with Mr. Cuddles on this lap. Most of the younger children had gathered around him, sitting on the floor, enthralled by every word he uttered. Their mouths gaped open and their eyes twinkled along with the tiny lights wrapped around the tree. The kids' oohs and ahs made the K-9 companion bark, which brought a smile to Alan's lips and reminded him why he'd become a doctor. It soothed his soul.

No doubt, he wanted children and knew Rachel would be a terrific mom. *Geez, can't get her to say yes to a date and in my mind, she's already the mother of my children. Sigh.* Conscious thoughts of Rachel returned with the faint sound of her laughter coming from the kitchen. If he leaned forward just enough, Alan could see the top half of the goings-on over the counter of the pass-through window. This was the women's watering hole. It seemed that Rachel, even though this should have been her night off, was still cooking. Other ladies were making last-minute enhancements to the dishes they'd brought before adding them to the feast.

Alan spied the top of a head gliding past the opening. Rachel's mother in her wheelchair, he realized. Maria Welch was obviously still an important part of Snowflake, even though she had moved away. Several hugs were given and questions asked. He so wanted to meet the woman who had helped to mold Rachel into the woman she had become. The thought of being introduced to her father was a bit scary though. Alan now knew where Brett had gotten his height gene. He didn't know if the Welches had been told about the no fraternization rule. *I can't think about that tonight.*

With a silent prayer, Alan thanked his lucky stars when he was saved by his mother's arrival, with Bodie close on her heels. A sudden bout of bashfulness had him glued to his rocker. He took the time to see for himself how well his *madre* had adapted to her new home. While Bodie made a beeline for some male bonding, Teresa found the kitchen. Alan suppressed his urge to giggle when he kept hearing the word flan. For his mother's sake, he hoped her dessert would be well accepted.

His heart skipped a beat as he heard Rachel introduce his *madre* and her mother, Maria. The trio chatted for what felt like hours. *Oh, this could be very bad or very good.* His memory went back to the stunt pulled by Mrs. Jameson and Mrs. Wilson. The pseudo blind date. He felt bad for Rachel but had enjoyed the opportunity to get to know her better. The connection between them had ignited that night and been dowsed at the city council meeting. *Why did the poor behavior of the prior doctor get to derail his love life?*

Laughter came from the kitchen and the whole powerhouse grouping of women was now there. *Oh, no. Speak of the devils.* Alan sunk lower into the chair and stopped rocking. He wanted to become a Christmas decoration and blend into the scenery. His doctor's senses kicked in. Something was wrong. The tension among the ladies doubled. Alan rubbed one palm down the front of his pant leg while giving himself a protective hug with the other. No matter what he thought of this gaggle, they all deserved to enjoy the festivities. He contemplated what might be troubling them, and it dawned on him that the mayor, the sheriff and Brett had not yet arrived.

But then the word flan was mentioned, and they all started cackling. Leave it to his *madre* to be able to break the ice. Maybe that was his cue to enter the estrogen zone. Nope, the testosterone in him liked his chances with Bodie and friends better. Alan made a stealthy approach and stood just far enough behind the master trader as not to interrupt, but close enough that he looked like part of the group. This trick had worked for him at many hospital events. He certainly didn't miss that part of living in Miami.

Several topics bounced among the gentlemen, and Alan was content to be an active listener. His nerves began to stop complaining and just let him be.

"It's gone!" The tug on his shirt and familiar voice had Alan making an about-face. Bodie turned too. Teresa was beaming. "I didn't even get to put the plate on the table. The ladies in the kitchen gobbled it up."

Alan gave his mom a big holiday hug and a kiss on the top of her head. "Of course they loved it. You make the best flan ever!" Everyone within earshot joined in the revelry of her success.

"But I didn't get a piece." Bodie protested and rubbed his belly. "You'll have to make it again for me. Speaking of food, let's eat." He led a large contingent of merrymakers to fill their plates. Just as the group settled for their holiday meal, the mayor made a grand entrance. Mrs. Jameson acted out a faux-faint, then blew him a kiss.

Per his request, someone handed him a microphone. The mayor climbed up on a chair as a makeshift platform next to the tree, his antics upstaging Running Wolf. The children moved away to find their parents. "I'm sorry to interrupt, but this is too important." The room quieted down. "The details still need to be worked out, but the money needed to open the mill has been found!"

A roar of celebrating and congratulations filled the room. Hugs were aplenty and even some tears slid down the faces of the families most affected. "Merry Christmas," shouted the mayor as he motioned for the crowd to pay attention again. "The city council has been working with financiers, and an angel investor heard about our plight. She chose to give us the money because she liked what she heard about the fine people of Snowflake and Lodgepole Valley. Give yourselves a round of applause." The celebrating kicked in again.

"What's an angel investor?" Somebody asked.

Another person shouted, "When do we get to meet her? I want to thank her myself."

Mayor Jameson took control of the room again. "An angel investor is someone who has spare cash, but usually doesn't want to be involved in the day-to-day running of a business. Our angel is a recent widow who lives in New York City, but she wishes to remain anonymous."

Several conversations erupted simultaneously. This time the mayor gave up the mic and stepped down from the chair. But before the din got too loud, the pastor hopped up. The celebrating died down to a low roar. "Can we please have a moment of silence for the loss that our angel endured and send our heartfelt thanks in a group prayer to this generous woman." As the whispers came to a halt, the sound of silence was deafening. Most folks bowed their heads, right hands to their hearts. "Amen."

The cheer of the season launched into full swing. More food was eaten and drinks flowed. Dancing even broke out in one corner. Alan did his best to fit in.

HEARING the mayor was about to make an announcement, Rachel helped her mother maneuver out of the kitchen to join the crowd. She wished she hadn't been trapped in food prep mode most of the evening. She'd noticed Alan sitting alone, and she wanted to keep him company. If only she could explain that she'd had no idea about her parents' surprise visit. But one guest after another chained her to the stove or some other food-related emergency.

The mill will open again at last. This was wonderful news of course, but it didn't resolve her long list of concerns. Maybe more people could soon afford to eat at the café, but would the profit be enough to keep her two new hires after the holiday rush ended? Poor Sophie. Could she carry this baby to term? And if she did, how long would she take to stay home with the newborn? When Sophie returned, would she lay off the other two?

If Rachel had written a letter to Santa, she would have asked him to throw the mayor's new rule out in the snow so she could work for and date Dr. Garcia. Alan. She needed to talk to him, but with her parents in town and Brett out on the roads, how could she step away? Be so selfish? Too many people needed her right now. Where the heck was the sheriff? Irene was putting on a brave face, but Rachel could tell she was worried.

Someone held out an empty platter at her like she should be bussing tables. Kicking herself for being such a people pleaser, she dutifully went back to the kitchen to wash the dish and place it on the table to be retrieved by its owner. As she was scrubbing, the hot water must have triggered her internal boiling point. This was the community center, not her restaurant. She deserved a night off.

Taking off her the apron, Rachel grabbed her barrette, let down her hair and gave it a fluff—it was now or never. Making a beeline to the table where Alan sat, she stood directly in front of him. "There's a service at the church across the way tonight around 11:30. If you'd like, I'll save you a seat." Rachel rattled off her statement with such haste, she wasn't certain if all the words came out in the correct order. Alan stood up, bumping the table on the way and sending folks reaching for their drinks to keep them from spilling.

Alan's face matched the scarlet shade of the tablecloth, and he apologized to his dinner mates. "Yes, please. Sounds like a plan."

"Speaking of a plan, Patsy will join us at the church later," added Bodie.

"Oh, right. I nearly forgot. Good timing. Looks like the pews will be full." Rachel looked for the pastor. That was another person she needed to pin down for a conversation. She snuck a glance at Alan. He was staring at her, an expression of concern on his beautiful face. Maybe she could whisper what the plan was to give him a heads up. She was rounding the table to do just that when someone called out her name from the kitchen. She stopped and wanted to curse but didn't. It was Christmas Eve after all. "Excuse me. Duty calls."

As she headed to assist once again, she looked back over her shoulder. Alan's visage had softened. If she wasn't mistaken, he was making a circle with his arms. A hug without touching, maybe? She'd take that.

Mrs. Jameson called Rachel to the food prep area. "How dare you. The council just implemented the new rule and you broke it already. The mayor has asked me personally to make certain it is strictly enforced. Do you want to be fired?"

Think fast! Stay calm. "But Heidi, I didn't. If you had a new coworker who had just moved to town and you invited that person to church, wouldn't you save them a seat?" She touched Mrs. Jameson on the arm with a there-there-now pat.

Mrs. Jameson became flabbergasted. "Well, maybe. But mark my words. If something is going on between the two of you, I will catch you. I have spies everywhere." With a huff, she stormed out of the room, but with an over the top smile like she hadn't just run Rachel through with words.

Rachel suspected something else was bothering Heidi to make her lash out, but today was Christmas Eve. She would broach that problem after solving the others on her growing list. Straightening her posture against her exhaustion, she put a holiday spring in her step. Many people needed to be made merry. *Everything and everyone will be all right. They just have to be.* Eleven-thirty couldn't arrive fast enough for her.

CHAPTER 24

WAITING for the clock's minute hands to move was almost more than Alan could bear. Rachel hadn't come back from dish duty at the Christmas Eve party to talk to him. You'd think she was the guest of honor based on the number of people calling out for her assistance. Her parents always seemed to be hovering nearby making him hesitate to speak. How was a guy supposed to get in a word with that kind of competition for her attention?

It did, however, give him great joy to see how well his mother seemed to be enjoying herself. He could tell Bodie was keeping tabs on her with a sideways glance every now and then. But he didn't crowd or cling to her. Hopefully, the "just friends" agreement his mother had mentioned would meet both their needs.

Keeping himself busy, Alan helped clean up the aftermath of the holiday meal without crossing the threshold into the kitchen. He dutifully stacked chairs and offered well wishes or safe travels as folks came and went. No one mentioned his reputation issue. Maybe the residents of Snowflake were giving him a reprieve while they celebrated Christmas. Alan would accept that blessing and smile.

When he stepped outside to make the short journey across the street, he was surprised at how much new snow had fallen. Because he was trying not to stare, Alan had lost track of Rachel and hoped she was already in the church. He and Bodie helped his mother stand up against the howling winds and icy pavement. The bright lights of the Snowflake bell tower lit the road enough for the faithful to complete the crossing.

Due to his hectic schedule, Alan had not yet been inside this church and was taken aback by its simplicity. The building was historic, he knew, and the spare furnishings consisted of a few plain wooden pews and a small platform that served as the altar. Bodie told him that this service would be lit and heated using only natural elements—not because of a fear of a power outage, but to pay homage to the original settlers of Snowflake. In each corner, a fire roared within a deep brick hearth, and chest-high shelves supported oil lanterns, spaced every foot or so along the walls. Each parishioner was given their own small red or green candle, complete with a round holder to catch the dripping wax.

Fighting the need to find Rachel, Alan moved along with the crowd. Mrs. Jameson and Mrs. Wilson made themselves useful by giving out programs at the front door. Alan wanted to roll his eyes at the thought of the two controlling women wielding their influence over the Christmas service too. But being in the holiday spirit, he refrained. Bodie led him to the front row pew, as it held the only seats not yet filled. Just before he sat down, he saw Rachel locking the wheels of her mother's chair adjacent to the pew where her father already sat, and his tension eased. They were across the aisle and a couple of rows back. He watched as she requested that people shift over so she could squeeze into a slot narrower than most people would need.

With an almost unnoticeable twitch, he got her attention. She mouthed back at him, *I tried, sorry.* The mournful grimace Rachel wore told him that she wished to be sitting next to him.

Alan smiled at her with his entire body and soul. *It's okay,* he said, moving his lips without saying a word. She placed both palms over her heart and a gentle mist filled her eyes. It gave him hope.

The pastor started the service and gave a holiday-related greeting.

Looking around the room he stated, "I see a few new faces tonight. Please stand in introduce yourselves to everyone."

"I'm the new business developer at city hall. My name is Horace, Horace O'Grady." The well-dressed middle-aged man bounced from one foot to the other and waved a greeting as he turned to all four sides of the room, then retook his seat.

Mayor Jameson popped up and added, "He's being modest. Mr. O'Grady found the angel investor for the mill." A round of applause, welcomes and well wishes filled the tiny chapel.

The pastor gestured at Alan and he froze, choked on air and dug his fingernails into his palms. How could he stand up and endure speaking to this congregation when some of them thought so little of him? Head spinning, mind racing, Alan searched for the appropriate words. But his *madre* beat him to the punch. "Feliz Navidad, everyone. I'm Teresa Garcia. Recently moved here from Miami. This area has such natural beauty and friendly neighbors. I'm pleased to be here with my son. You know him, the doctor." Giving Alan a nudge and a wink, she glided back into the pew, grinning from ear to ear.

Alan's legs shook, and he wished a pew for him to grasp was in front of him. Locking his knees, he searched the faces that were waiting for him to speak. He saw Principal Patsy giving him a sign to speak up. Rachel offered him a silent head bob of encouragement. "Um. I'm Dr. Alan Garcia." His voice wavered, and he cleared his throat. "I'll do my best to keep everyone healthy and well. Merry Christmas." Alan crawled back into his seat before he collapsed. An unsettling silence hung in the air. *What else could I have said?*

"Welcome! Welcome to one and all," offered the clergyman, ignoring the awkwardness that marred the celebration. "You know, when the holidays roll around, we chat more with our friends and neighbors. We need to be vigilant that what we say is fact-based and charitable. Our hearts may be in the right place, but at times our tongues can wag into an un-Christian direction." The pastor wandered over and stood in front of Alan. "Good people of Snowflake, I think we've wronged this fine man. Some of you may have heard Dr. Garcia deals in illegal drugs, or that he is a gang member."

The blood drained from Alan's face. No one had told him the plan would be so humiliating. What if it didn't work? Alan's knees locked tight together, and his lifeless arms fell to his sides as he looked only into the eyes of the head parishioner. He couldn't risk seeing the reaction around him. *On Christmas Eve no less. This "plan" may be the worst gift ever.*

"I'm not sure how this game of telephone got out of control, but we need to reverse it. We need to invite Dr. Garcia into this congregation with open hearts and trusting minds."

Bodie stood, interrupting. "I can confirm that the city council completed a thorough background check for every medical clinic applicant. Dr. Garcia is all kinds of squeaky clean. Don't believe anyone who tells you otherwise." Leaning past his mother, Bodie gave Alan's shoulder a hearty squeeze.

Another voice called from the back, "As the town's pharmacist, I can endorse Dr. Garcia's practice of prescribing medications. The clinic is so busy he doesn't have time to mess with illegal activities." The last comment had a multitude of chuckles cascading from the pews.

Making his way back to the altar, the pastor closed out the subject, "Okay. I think the point has been made. It's un-Christian to spread rumors. I think we can all rise above it." Opening his Bible, he continued with the service that included a sermon more appropriate for Christmas Eve.

Although he tried to participate and enjoy the worship, Alan couldn't keep his mind focused. He couldn't convey how much he appreciated the efforts of those involved in saving him. But was it enough? Rachel's parents heard that the townsfolk had thought of him as possibly being a drug dealer. Would they want their only daughter to date him? Or even work for him? Well, at least no one was trying to hurt his mother. He appreciated that silver lining in his set of problems.

The pastor asked everyone to open their hymnals and sing "Silent

Night." This helped Alan to get out of his head and be more in the moment. It wasn't a glorious choir, but the many voices made for enjoyable listening. In the middle of the second verse, a rush of cold air blew out many of the lanterns and candles closest to the entrance. Some of the worshippers stopped singing.

"Daddy!" Parrot ran down the aisle, clopping away in his ever-present cowboy boots.

Alan turned to see the shadow of the giant of a man. Allowing his eyes to adjust, he realized he saw more ice and snow than clothing. The shadow didn't move. Stumbling past the walker and wheelchair, Rachel raced in Brett's direction. Alan remembered Rachel's motto. The words she'd spoken in the cabin during the rescue of Monkey ran though his head on a loop. *No frostbite on my watch.* Alan went into emergency medical mode—shut down the emotions and save the patient.

I must save Brett for Rachel. But what if the town sees how I feel about her as we work together? Let the city fire me. Leaping from the pew, Alan rushed to assist. As he closed the distance, he saw the Sasquatch shiver, eyes closed. Bracing himself for the cold, Alan ducked under one arm and Rachel followed him under the other. Together they dragged Brett to the nearest fireplace. An old wooden folding chair that had seen better days appeared from behind Alan.

"Get the icy clothes off. Check the hands and feet first." Alan knew Rachel understood this protocol better than he did, but he pulled down his camouflage cloak and acted like he'd never seen anyone around him before. That way, the treatment he provided would be his very best. He, with Rachel's help, managed to get Brett seated in the chair, towing him as close to the fire as they dared. She worked on the feet, so Alan snatched off the hat and the scarf. Pain racked his fingers as he pushed the layers of ice away to find a zipper on Brett's coat.

The singing had stopped. People gathered around the spectacle. "What happened?" asked Rachel, her voice the only sound in the church.

Without opening his eyes, Brett tried to speak, "N...n...no. G... ga...gas!"

To Alan's utter surprise, people started tossing him things. Somehow someone else's warm hat was put back on Brett's head. A wool scarf sailed through the air, falling over his face. Grasping it, Alan wrapped it around Brett's neck. Gloves made their way into Brett's lap. After examining the half-frozen man's extremities, Alan took great care putting his patient's hands into the warm offering. A pair of socks that had clearly never been worn toppled toward the icy boots. Without hesitation, Rachel yanked them over the pale, almost-blue feet. Even a Saint Christopher medal was pressed into Alan's palm. The patron saint of travelers couldn't hurt. Alan stuffed the medallion into Brett's chest pocket. A couple of quilts and blankets were then wrapped around and tucked under the Christmas saving giant.

Alan saw Brett's parents on the edge of the onlookers, their faces full of concern for the well-being of their son. "He'll make a full recovery," Alan said. The tension drained from their bodies. Alan did his best to relax, but the camouflage cloak remained firmly affixed in place.

"Agreed. He was lucky," replied Rachel. "How far did you walk?"

Brett didn't answer. A small version of a shrug was all he could manage.

"How could you see in this storm? Know which direction to walk?" asked Mr. O'Grady.

A still shuddering, newly woolen mitt pushed through the top of the quilts, pointing toward the ceiling.

"Does he mean God?" Mr. O'Grady scratched his head.

The pastor stepped closer. "No, I think he means he followed the guiding light of our giant snowflakes decorating the bell tower."

Brett did his best to show his agreement, but his attempt became more of a shiver than a nod.

The clergyman clutched his Bible to his chest. "It's not the first time our snowflakes have saved a soul." The lead parishioner made his way back to the front of the church. "Mr. Welch is getting the best medical care in town. Let us get back to our singing and prayers. Why don't we start 'Silent Night' from the second verse?"

Before the singing began, Alan heard a familiar crinkle. Parrot appeared next to his father, holding up a piece of candy. Brett opened his mouth and Parrot popped it in.

"Mmmm...pep...peppermint. My fav...favorite." Brett's voice still stuttered, but that seemed to be lessening.

Suddenly, a young boy about Parrot's age darted out from behind Brett and ran to one of the pews. This child had given Parrot the candy for him to give to his father. Alan watched as this generous youngster jumped into his father's loving embrace. He didn't have to hear it to know that the dad said: "I'm proud of you, son."

With the service nearing its end, another blast of frigid air blew through the chapel. The sheriff made quite the entrance, wiping the snow off his uniform coat and hat.

"There you are! I've been looking all over for you," the sheriff said as he moved toward Brett, but was cut off by his wife, whose face showed all the worry she had been carrying about him. Giving her a quick peck on the cheek, the sheriff stepped around her. "No cell or radio signal I take it?"

The ice hanging from Brett's long hair scratched across the blanket as his head went back and forth.

"I get it." The sheriff shifted his weight. "This is good news, but brace yourself. They decided to do an emergency C-section, but mother and daughter are doing fine."

Brett's face snapped in Sheriff Wilson's direction, and Rachel vaulted up from the massage she had been giving Brett's feet. "What?! When?" Rachel's voice was two octaves higher than usual.

"About four hours ago. The sheriffs relayed the message from one town to the next because no one has a signal strong enough to transmit over the mountain in this storm." Sheriff Wilson was clearly enjoying delivering the message. "Your daughter is in an incubator in the neonatal unit, but she's strong and is expected to be fine."

"I have a baby sister?" asked Parrot. Brett opened the layers of quilts and his son climbed onto his lap.

"You do!" Brett cocooned his boy as the covers tightened around him. Rachel flung herself around them, and Alan saw the Welches making their way over to savor this joyous news. Feeling a bit out of place, Alan stepped back and watched from afar.

As the people began to make their way to their homes, Alan took stock of all the Christmas gifts he had already received. The orange and green quilt of course, but he'd seen Running Wolf telling stories, his mother's flan was a hit at the feast, the angel investor for the mill, a hope that his reputation would be restored, Brett made it safely back to Snowflake, and now Sophie and her daughter would be fine too.

Merry Christmas to me! Continuing to people watch, Alan noticed the man about to walk out into the below-freezing weather without a hat. He had given it to Brett. Then he realized that man worked at the mill and had been one of the guys who had winterized his home. The man carried the boy who had given the only thing he had to give: a piece of candy. These people who had fallen on hard times had no trouble giving. Then he remembered what Bodie had said the night that now-hatless man had donated his skills. "Allow a man to enjoy the act of giving. Even if it is just to swing a hammer." Now that wonderful father was teaching his son the joy of giving.

People could accept help without it being a sign of weakness. The action showed respect and compassion. *I get it now!* The dark hunk of imaginary coal that he'd been carrying around in his chest disintegrated and vanished with a poof. *I get it now!* Tears welled in his eyes, and he didn't care who saw them. Searching the crowd, he found Bodie. Alan raced to his side.

The words rushed from his mouth before Alan could put them through his internal filter, startling poor Bodie. They were straight from his heart. "I get it now! What you said about being accepted in Snowflake. It's not about the rumors. It's about how I behave." He waved his hands over his head in celebration. "I'll gladly accept any type of help from anyone. I don't have to do everything on my own. That makes me a better man." Before Bodie could react, Alan gave him a mammoth bear hug.

"Ah, I see Santa Claus came early for you this year." Bodie grinned as he slapped Alan on the back and hauled him close again. "Merry Christmas!"

CHAPTER 25

ON CHRISTMAS DAY, Rachel was not surprised that she found herself in a kitchen again, but this time she was exactly where she wanted to be. The guest room bed at Brett's ranch had never felt so good. She had fallen asleep when her head hit the pillow and woken up in the same position when the sunlight filtered around the edges of the curtains. Even Parrot had managed to let her sleep in. Her parents had quietly made breakfast and kept Parrot entertained because Brett had slept longer than she had.

Still in her pajamas, Rachel was in the process of converting the kitchen from the breakfast bar into the cookie-making area when Brett stumbled into the room. "What time is it? Does the radio work? Have you heard from Sophie?" Brett yawned and scratched his beard.

Laughing, Rachel did her best to provide rapid-fire answers to ease her brother's mind. "Who cares what time it is? The radio is spotty, but a text with video should be on your phone. If not you can watch it on mine."

Kissing the top of the head of each parent and then Parrot, Brett made a beeline to his phone. He plopped down into his well-worn, overstuffed rocker, then signaled for everyone to gather around as he played the footage. Sophie was in a hospital gown and had also donned a Mrs. Claus hat. She sat in a wheelchair and held her phone's camera so they could see her and the incubator. The baby squirmed and let out a soft cry. Most of the necessary tubes had been disguised by the swaddling. "She's 4.8 pounds with a strong heart. What do you want to name her? How about Christina in honor of the being born on Christmas Eve?" Sophie waved feverishly as tears of joy fell down her cheeks. "Miss you all so much! Love you."

A timer on a batch of cookies rang, so Rachel and her parents went back into the kitchen while Brett and Parrot watched the video over and over again, and then sat by the radio for hours, trying to get either it or a cell phone to work. Back in the kitchen, Maria was the master decorator while Luke was in charge of monitoring the oven. "So dear, tell us what's going on in your life? We haven't had a chance to catch up since we got here." Maria's question was broad, but Rachel knew she wanted to know about the café, saloon and gift shop.

"It's Christmas. Do you really want to talk business?" Rachel did her best to evade the inquisition.

"Would you rather talk about your love life?" Maria knew how to maneuver a conversation to get to the heart of the info she wanted to hear.

Turning off the mixer, Rachel slid into a dining room chair. "I hired two ladies for the café, but now that the mill has reopened they may get their old jobs back." Two could play the control-the-conversation game.

The trio took a break from the confections and sipped hot chocolate while they chatted. "How about city politics?" grumbled Luke as his eyebrows pinched together.

Parrot ran through the room, playing with his radio-controlled car and everybody laughed. Rachel took that as a sign and let her guard down. Her parents were good people and might have some sage advice. "The mayor has been his pompous controlling self. He created a new rule at the clinic. No dating coworkers."

"But why? Is this about Dr. Remington?" Maria took a sip from her cup.

Rachel let her hair fall across her face in an attempt to hide. "Yes."

She drew out her pronunciation of the word. "Like I had any control over that." She started decorating cookies. "And Heidi has it out for me. She wanted me fired because I offered to save Alan a seat at church last night." She sighed. *Things are so complicated. How do I explain?*

Just as her parents opened their mouths to launch a slew of questions, Brett sauntered into the room, biting the head off of a gingerbread man. "What? Fire who?"

"Walk into the middle of a conversation much?" Rachel reached up and broke the feet off the cookie Brett was holding and stuffed them into her mouth.

He grinned at her diversion. "Doesn't Heidi have better things to do?"

Maria touched her hand. "Shouldn't you be calling him Dr. Garcia? Isn't he your boss?"

"What she said." Rachel winced as her dad jumped in to support her mother's inquisition.

"Dr. G has helped her more than I could with her post-trauma issue. She can call him whatever she wants." Brett picked up a replacement cookie and went back to the radio.

"Tell us about this new doctor." Her dad used his protective tone.

Rachel hung her head and gave a half-hearted shrug. Her father put down his cocoa and leaned in, so she knew she wasn't going to get out of talking about this topic. "He's a highly competent physician, generous and kind. Work is great and it's like we were meant to be together." *Oops, did I just say that out loud?*

"Be together how?" Luke began to move the cooled cookies from the baking sheet into a storage tin, but his questioning look made her feel like she was in high school again.

"Daddy! We haven't. It's not like that." Rachel choked up. *How do I say this?* "Finally, someone I want to date wants to ask me out but can't. It's like we have to pick our jobs or romance." She turned to stare at her father. "We can't have both like you and mom did."

Luke struggled to his feet without his walker, and with great effort tugged Rachel toward him. She went willingly into his embrace. The emotional floodwaters she'd been holding back for so long flowed over the walls of her self-made dam. "I want to be loved for who I am, not because I'm a Welch. No potential boyfriend has ever treated me like he does." Maria's chair bumped her thigh and her mother yanked on her arm. Rachel lost it, collapsing into the support of both of her parents. She clawed at their robes to pull them as close to her as she could.

"Honey. We want you to be happy." Luke stroked her hair away from her face and lifted her chin. "If you really care for this man, can't you get a nursing job somewhere else?" He gave her one more big squeeze and let Maria in closer.

When Rachel looked down to see that her mother's face was streaked with tears, she sobbed again. "I want to live in Snowflake. Keep an eye on the café and all." Rachel handed her mother a napkin for her tears. "The clinic is the only nursing job in town." She swiped at her face. "You know how much I want to be a nurse, right?"

"Oh, my darling, the night you saved our lives, I knew what you were meant to be. You're an amazing nurse." Maria sniffled.

Her dad grabbed his walker and slammed it on the floor, then stood up as straight as he was able. "Then you'll just have to take on city hall. You are a Welch after all."

"THANKS FOR MAKING ANOTHER FLAN." Alan leaned back in his seat to give his stomach more room to do its work. Then he got up to help his mother with the dishes. As he reached for a glass to dry, the sweet smell he associated with Rachel wafted past his nose. "Mom, can I ask you an odd question? Have you changed your soap or shampoo lately?"

"I did." Teresa put the pan she was washing down. "How did you know?"

"Well, it smells different. I like it, but it's not like anything from Miami." Alan opened a cabinet and leaned into it to help hide the awkwardness he felt.

"It's an indigenous plant called huckleberry. Mrs. Wilson makes products with it and Rachel carries them in her gift shop."

Mystery finally solved. Feeling like himself again, Alan stepped back into the light, but since he had promised himself he would spend quality time with his mother today, he changed the subject. "Where did the flank steak come from for the delicious ropa vieja?"

Teresa's face filled with a rosy glow and she grinned. "Bodie introduced me to the Welch family's favorite butcher. He's so thoughtful that way."

Making his way to the sofa, Alan added, "Yeah, Bodie's a great guy. I don't know if I would have made it this long in Montana without him. And how about how popular your flan was?"

"Well, Maria is half-Cuban. You know, Rachel's mom." Teresa let the water out of the sink. "She said my flan was the best she'd ever had, and now Rachel wants me to make several at a time so she can sell it in the café."

Alan choked on his sip of red wine. "What?" Hauling himself up, he turned to face his mother. "Come again...Cuban?"

"Oh yes, Maria Hernandez Welch. Her father was from Cuba. I didn't expect to find fellow Cubans in Montana either." She picked up her drink and lifted it to make a toast. "To my mother's recipe. I think I've found my new calling."

"So that's why her hair is dark and wavy."

"What dear? Who's hair?"

"Oh, um...Rachel, I mean Ms. Welch."

The sound of a vehicle pulling up the drive kept his thoughts from revealing his true feelings about her. "Is somebody lost? Who would be on this road on Christmas day?" Teresa came alongside Alan as they both peered out the window.

"That's Bodie's monster double-cab truck. It looks full of people. I don't have enough food for all those people." Teresa ran through the house, picking up things to make her home presentable.

Alan continued to spy on the unexpected visitors. "I don't believe it! *Madre*, it's the mayor, the sheriff and their wives! What are they doing here?" He put down the wine, adjusted his sweater and ran his fingers through his hair.

Flinging the front door open wide, he shouted, "Merry Christmas! How nice to see all of you. Welcome. Welcome, please come in."

The crowd made their way inside and shuffled about the living room, giving holiday greetings in return.

"Please have a seat," offered Alan as his mother joined them coming back from the kitchen.

"Sorry for coming unannounced. We won't stay long." Something in the mayor's voice sounded a bit off. Almost agitated. He thrust an envelope in Alan's direction. "Special delivery. Go on, read it aloud."

Alan did his best to control his grip, but the paper almost slipped out of his grasp. He looked at Bodie for guidance, but the man wasn't paying attention. Fumbling past the glue, Alan unfolded a letter complete with the embossed seal of the city of Snowflake. He cleared his throat.

"Dr. Alan Garcia has hereby passed the requirements of the 90-day probationary period and thus is now officially the permanent physician of Snowflake's medical clinic." Alan stopped speaking. He needed to reread the statement to himself. Looking up, all he saw were smiling faces. "Thank you. This means so much."

The men of the city council each shook Alan's hand, and then his *madre* smothered him with a hug.

"We decided we've seen enough of your good work to forego the rest of the timeframe. Glad to have you on board. Merry Christmas." The mayor was all business, and Alan couldn't figure out what had the man so put out. The words were positive, but the body language was stiff all over.

"How thoughtful. It's a wonderful gift. Thank you, again." Alan wished his glass of wine could be turned into champagne. *Oh, I am so going to celebrate.*

A small female voice came from the back of the pack. "I wanted to apologize." Mrs. Wilson stepped forward. "I shared confidential information. What I forwarded was accurate, but if I in any way played a part in harming your reputation, I'm deeply sorry." She stepped back behind her husband and stared at the floor.

"I need to add my apology." This came from Mrs. Jameson. "I thought what I said to several people was also fact-based, but if my actions kept patients from seeking your care, I am humbly sorry." She adjusted her scarf on her shoulder and looked away.

It took Alan a good stretch of time to absorb, comprehend and react to what had just happened. "I appreciate your honesty and accept the apology."

The tension in the room sucked out all the oxygen. Alan deliberated what to do next. *Now I understand why the mayor looked so steamed and the sheriff never looked me in the eye.* Alan wanted to hug the ladies, but that didn't seem like the right thing to do. Then his amazing *madre* saved him again.

"Look at this fine custom-crafted quilt I gave Alan for Christmas. It has the school colors of his alma mater." Teresa picked up the neatly folded blanket so that the guests could see it.

"Did you get that from the gift shop? I think my wife made that." The mayor began to relax.

"Did she?" Carrying the gift, Teresa made her way toward Mrs. Jameson. "Your work is impeccable. The design is so unique. What a talent you have."

Alan watched as the faces of his guests loosen a bit. How did she know what to say and do to make everyone so comfortable? She should be teaching a class on bedside manner.

Heidi regained her courage and became her usual chatty self. "You know, it's the funniest thing. My beloved gave me the same present as Irene's hubby happened to give her. Can you believe it? These silk flowers were like nothing I'd ever seen. So colorful. I know they'll brighten up my winter blues."

When Teresa gave Alan a sideways glance, he couldn't help himself. He burst out laughing and in between chuckles he managed to say, "My mother made those flower arrangements."

Everyone laughed at the Snowflake currency coincidence. The three women gave hugs all around and made plans for a ladies' night out. The men began to make their way back toward the truck. But Alan's mind strayed to Rachel. He didn't dare push his luck and ask for the new rule to be reversed. He wanted to date her without getting fired. They just had to find a way.

The short Christmas visit ended up being a very merry one, and the days ahead held great promise. As Mayor Jameson climbed into the passenger seat he called out to Alan. "You got my email, right? We need you on the team tomorrow."

"Yes, sir. I'll be there bright and early. It's my pleasure to serve."

CHAPTER 26

When Alan arrived at the pavilion by the lake where he'd first met Rachel, he feared he had misread the email and was late. Even on the day after Christmas, the site was already teeming with activity. The mayor, sheriff, several deputies, two snowplows and many other vehicles filled the snow-covered pasture that served as a parking lot. Clusters of people gathered, having animated conversations. Since the request had come from the mayor, Alan sought him out as soon as he jumped from his Jeep, with his medical bag at the ready.

"Mayor Jameson." Alan spied him as he rounded the corner of the wooden pavilion wall. "Wasn't I supposed to arrive at nine o'clock?"

Tucking a clipboard under his arm, Mayor Jameson surveyed the staging area while he replied, "Is it nine already? You're on time. These other folks had more prep work." Climbing atop a picnic table, the mayor shouted to all within earshot. "Gather round everyone. Let's go through the checklist together."

A gust of wind pushed at his back, and Alan was pleased he'd asked Monkey where to get some all-in-one winter coveralls. Having tightened the Velcro around the wrists and ankles, he could endure the cold without any unwanted gaps to chill him to the bone. With his hood cinched over a knit hat and insulated mittens drawn over gloves, he could stand outside alongside the native Montana men with some measure of comfort. He still needed to work on breathing the frosty air, but that would come in time. The extraordinary vastness of the Big Sky helped to distract him from the cold. The fluffy billowing clouds seemed to like to gather within the surrounding expansive space.

A man dressed in all orange joined Mayor Jameson on his makeshift stage, as did Monkey and Brett. The mayor continued his speech. "For those of you who haven't met him, this orange-man is Major Jamal Washington, retired special forces. He will be managing all of the dynamite." The Major saluted and bowed as a round of applause went through the crowd. "The map shows the three areas where the governor has granted permission to proactively cause snow slides. We need to reduce the weight of the ice and powder in a well-supervised and meticulous manner. This prevents avalanches that block the mountain roadways."

Stepping to the side, Alan allowed Sheriff Wilson and his deputies a closer look at the map. He knew his presence at this maneuver was deemed to be a safety precaution, but he was pleased to use this opportunity to become more ingrained in the day-to-day happenings of Snowflake. Hearing the mayor's comment about the roadways reminded Alan of how Mr. and Mrs. Welch had been injured. He wondered if Rachel would be able to feel the ground shake at the café. She'd be a nervous wreck, he figured. If he hadn't been needed here, he'd rather have been with her, to protect and comfort her.

Regaining his focus, Alan picked up the next sentence of the always long-winded mayor. "Monkey will be our backcountry guide, Brett will supervise debris removal, and Dr. Garcia and his nurse Rachel are on-site to administer first aid." *What?! Where?* Alan searched the bystanders. *Maybe she hadn't arrived yet?* The blasts would cause avalanches. The thought of being near them had to have her on edge. *Maybe she's hiding from the sounds?*

Finally, he could have some long-awaited alone time with her. The list of thorny items they needed to discuss grew longer as each day passed. She'd wanted to sit next to him at the Christmas Eve service, but they'd treated Brett and then gotten interrupted by the baby announcement.

Once Mayor Jameson had completed his instructions, he released various groups to begin their portions of work. Alan overheard Monkey congratulating Brett on the birth of his daughter and jumped on the opportunity. "Hey Brett, how are Sophie and your little girl today? Have you been able to see pictures of them?"

Climbing down from the project management pedestal, Brett searched his pocket and brought out his phone. Alan and Monkey got a private viewing of a video. "Christina is a fighter and Sophie is holding up well, considering. Her aunt's there, so they're not alone. I'm not sure Betsy could make it over the mountain pass on her own or I'd be with them already." Brett looked rested and relaxed. Being the savior of Christmas and knowing his daughter was healthy had him in a great mood. *If I could get him alone, maybe I could ask him how to get the new rule overturned.* Alan wanted Brett to know his feelings for Rachel were more than just a passing attraction.

With a trembling hand, Alan gave his hood a shove away from his face, and his heart leaped into his chest, but he continued. "Um, if you have a second, I'd like to speak with you alone." Stuffing his mittens into his oversized pockets, Alan looked up, trying to look the giant in the eye. Brett stepped away from the crowd and headed for a cluster of rocks by the lake. Alan broke into a trot to keep up with his massive strides. "I saw your parents are in town. How are they?"

"Alright, I guess. They hide their discomfort from being back in freezing temperatures well." Brett looked at his watch.

"Do you think I should invite them to a session with Rachel?"

Brett's beard flicked as his chin lifted. "I hadn't thought of that. They're here, might as well see if they're willing."

"I'll do that. And another thing, I don't think of Rachel as a patient, it's more like I'm helping a friend. I enjoy time with her away from work and our sessions."

Brett held up his oversized leather glove like a stop sign. The shouts of the people around them fell silent at that moment. Alan assumed Brett had signaled for all onlookers to cease activity. "Wait. Are you asking for permission to date my sister?"

Alan gulped the icy air, and then wished he hadn't. Brett had cut to the meat of the matter. *I like this guy.* "Yes. I want you to know I respect the city council, but the rule could use an overhaul."

Brett howled with laughter. Alan wondered if any wolves nearby might respond to his yowling. He wasn't sure if this reaction meant good news for him, so he remained motionless and waited. "Look when it comes to my sister's love life, I have zero influence." A few more chuckles caused steam to rise from his mouth. "I'll say this, Rach lights up when she talks about you."

"Thanks, but do you really think the mayor will try to fire me if I ask her out?" Alan's entire body tensed as he asked and for some reason that made the cold stab through his layered gear and he shivered.

"Absolutely, and that sucks." Brett made a motion to let Monkey know he'd join him soon. "Just because he'll try doesn't mean he'll succeed. You have to know you have more votes than he does." Brett grabbed Alan's shoulder and gave him a hearty shake. "Get it? I gotta go."

Alan dug his heels into the snow to keep himself upright. "I think so. Should I go for it?"

Brett was already halfway back to Betsy when he called back. "The mayor has a long memory, but if you think you can make her happy then, yeah."

Alan paced among the rocks allowing Brett's suggested strategy to sink in. He mulled over the pros and cons of every scenario. He needed to learn more about each council member before he decided. His immediate priority was to find Rachel, so Alan began to wander among the clusters of people. He couldn't help but be distracted by the sheriff, who was barking orders at his staff. The man could be compassionate and a tyrant at the same time, but the deputies were holding their own.

Alan couldn't see Rachel's truck, so he decided to search near Betsy. Maybe the massive machine was obscuring his view. He was striding with more confidence after his chat with Brett, but he didn't get very far.

"Sheriff, are you okay?" asked one of the officers.

Alan heard the question and turned in that direction. He caught a glimpse of the man clutching his left arm to his chest, like he had a cramp, and picked up his pace. Before Alan could get to him, Sheriff Wilson doubled over and fell to the ground.

"Chuck, it's Dr. Garcia. What hurts? Can you talk?" Alan kneeled next to his patient.

Sheriff Wilson gasped for air, but instead of responding, became unconscious. Flopping his medical bag to the ground, Alan unzipped it. Out of the corner of his eye, he saw a pair of fuzzy boots he knew well. Alan looked up to see Rachel appear with her nursing backpack and a rectangular case.

She dropped to her knees across from him. "He has an arrhythmia."

Putting his fingers to the side of the sheriff's neck, Alan called out, "No pulse." Yanking Chuck's coat open, Alan started CPR.

"Get the backboard out of Betsy!" Rachel ordered. "Alan, I brought the AED."

Alan was shocked and thrilled all at the same time. The medical clinic didn't have an AED. But he didn't care where it came from. He gave the patient's shirt an energetic tear, and buttons went flying. Rachel had the AED open and handed him the pads in a blur of activity.

Heart monitors in place, Alan waited for the machine to analyze the situation. "No heartbeat. Preparing to shock," announced the machine.

"Everybody, step back. Give us some room. Don't touch him," shouted Alan with authority.

"Clear!" replied Rachel.

"Administering shock." The electric whirl grew louder and then Sheriff Wilson's body jerked as the energy was pulsed through him.

The AED went back into monitoring mode which caused an agonizing pause for Alan.

"No pulse. Prepare to shock," announced the machine.

"Come on Chuck, come back to us. Fight!" Alan said as he gave Rachel a worried look. She had her arms raised, palms facing him in the "I'm clear" stance.

Sheriff Wilson jerked again. A couple of seconds later, the AED said, "Normal rhythm restored." A cheer went up among the people who had gathered to offer assistance.

"Where's Brett? We need to load the sheriff into Betsy and get him to the hospital in Kalispell." Rachel began to slide the backboard under the patient.

Keeping the pads from the AED in place, Alan covered the sheriff's chest with a blanket and connected the straps from the board to hold him into place. He was still incoherent, but at least his heart was beating as it should. Hearing Betsy clamor to life, Alan instructed the deputies to stand at the ends of the wooden board to lift the patient.

"Is there enough room for all four of us?" asked Alan as the rescuers worked in unison to get the beloved sheriff into the plow's custom cab.

Rachel had picked up the AED and kept pace alongside the team. She snuck a quick peek in Alan's direction. "It'll be uncomfortable, but we can make it work."

"Where? What happened? Oh, my chest hurts." A mumbling sputter of thoughts escaped from the sheriff.

"That's a good sign." Alan watched the tension ease from Rachel's body. He let his sense of emergency mode reduce to cautious optimism. "You're okay, Sheriff. Your heart acted up. We're gonna take you to the hospital as a precaution. Just relax and try to take a nap if you can."

Hoisting the patient up into the cab of the monster snowplow was no easy feat. Brett had modified the rig to his liking with storage space behind the two bucket seats and had installed a low shelf that went the width of the cab. The backboard was strapped to the sturdy wooden bench-seat. Rachel scrunched between Brett's seat and the patient, her back supported by the metal frame. Alan did the same on the passenger side, with the AED on the floor between them.

Once Brett put the plow in drive, Alan had a chance to regroup with Rachel. "If we need to do CPR, it could get dicey. Where'd the AED come from?"

Alan watched as Rachel tried to respond. She shook a bit. A branch scraped the metal roof of the cab sounding like fingernails on a chalkboard. She stiffened and the color drained from her face. He didn't think she was cold and had seen her be all kinds of calm under the pressure of providing emergency medical care. She wasn't telling him something, Alan could see the tension in her facial muscles.

"Irene brought it to me. She said that Chuck hadn't been his normal self this morning. "

"Good to know. So, the sheriff's office has an AED, but the medical clinic doesn't. We'll have to fix that."

Rachel could only smile because the chatter on the CB radio drowned out her effort to reply.

"The avalanche operation still has a green light. Please keep us informed of your whereabouts," someone said on the radio.

"Roger that," responded Brett.

Alan's new winter coveralls also doubled as a cushion against the cold, hard metal of the plow's interior. *Uncomfortable was right.* He pulled out his stethoscope. Placing the listening end onto the patient, he sighed. "Weak, but steady."

Sheriff Wilson sometimes seemed lucid, but not always. Alan asked Rachel to take turns with him monitoring the AED and pulse manually. He was pleased to be with her, but not under these circumstances. At least he had unburdened himself with Brett. Alan wanted to tell Rachel that the city of Snowflake had made his employment permanent, but the timing just didn't seem right. The responsibility of his patient's wellbeing came first.

Betsy began to climb the mountain, but their pace slowed. The knobby treads of the mammoth tires could not maintain traction. Alan watched as Brett shifted gears trying to find a speed that gave his custom machine her best chance. But then she stopped and slid back down the icy road about a foot. Alan's eyebrows shot up before he could contain his reaction. *Are we going to make it over the peak?*

"I don't like the looks of that." Brett opened the door and was gone before Alan had a chance to ask. He joined Rachel in bending forward over the back of the bucket seats so they could peer out the windshield. A haze developed around the edges of the glass as the defroster couldn't keep up with the demand caused by the below zero temperature of the higher elevation.

Rachel reached forward from her unfolding crouch to roll down the side window and stuck her head out for a better look. A rush of fresh air entered, but the next breath he took threatened to freeze his lungs so he cut it short and pulled his scarf over his mouth.

"Rockslide under the snow." She frowned, checked the sheriff's pulse and then crawled into the driver's seat for a better grip to put the barrier back in place. "Keeping Chuck warm is more important than the view."

Brett trounced through knee-deep snow to get back to the plow and opened an exterior equipment bin nestled into the side of the rig, but all Alan could do was watch. Brett took an old street sign pole back to the windswept snow and repeatedly stabbed it into the dirty ice. When he found a large rock, he'd shovel around it and then roll it like a snowball out of the main throughway. Ice crystals began to form on Brett's mustache and beard with every labored exhale. At least the heater was on full blast for the guests Betsy carried.

As he continued his work, Alan better understood why this job was best completed by a Sasquatch-sized man with hair that could keep him warm while out in the elements. The process was painstaking lengthy, but at least Sheriff Wilson's condition remained stable. The static of the radio lessened as the mayor's voice took the airwaves. "Is everyone in position for the first blast?"

Rachel launched herself at the CB's handheld microphone. "Standby. Brett's clearing boulders. Let me get him inside. Repeat, standby." She eased down the window and yelled to her brother. "They want to blow the dynamite. Please get inside Betsy until the coast is clear."

Bringing his tools back to safety with him, Brett made his way up into the plow, which seemed to be another layer of clothing to him. This man was in sync with his machine—a good thing, Alan decided.

Rachel maneuvered her stance behind the seat, straining the cord on the microphone of the radio. "All clear. You are green to blast. All clear."

Rachel had transformed into her emergency room persona, but the way she grabbed onto Alan's sleeve after replacing the mic gave her away. She hunched back into her seated position on the floor, eyes squeezed tight, quivering. Alan found himself clenching his teeth while he waited together in an unsettling stillness. He knew what was about to happen, but that wasn't a good thing.

CHAPTER 27

Rachel swallowed hard and watched Brett settle into his seat, then met her brother's eyes in the review mirror, her anxiety rising.

"You saw the map, right? This first blast isn't anywhere near us." She knew what Brett said was correct, but her stomach cramped and her heart raced. She forced the corners of her mouth to tick up, knowing he would see it as her painted-on attempt at bravery. Alan may have caught on to her interpretation of the veil. He had mastered his, but she still needed to practice her feminine version.

"Three, two, one..." counted the Major's voice over the radio.

Knowing the blast was coming only made it worse. Rachel stared at the snow-covered branches of an evergreen tree, trying to stabilize her nerves. The sound was a muffled boom.

"See, no big deal," laughed Brett as he opened the door to return to his life-saving work. Then the ground shook. Just a tiny bit. The rumble in the distance grew louder and louder. Rachel envisioned trees snapping in half as thundering blankets of packed snow were forced to take flight by the blast, gravity doing the rest.

Closing her eyes again, Rachel told herself the dusting of flakes that fell from the branches as they swayed was beautiful, and not scary at all. Before she could stop him, Brett was outside the cab. He ran to a clearing to keep the falling snow off the hood of his coat. *You're fine. Everything is good.* But then the flashbacks she dreaded, tried her best to bury, pushed all other thoughts from her mind.

She had made progress, but that was in a warm place with Alan there as her anchor. *I need Alan to hold me, but you can't. The sheriff will see us.* She heard Alan say something, but she couldn't decipher the meaning. *Go to your happy place.* She used a meditation version of biofeedback to slow her breathing and pulse. That seemed to be working, a minuscule bit.

Disobeying lungs were also a part of this dreadful mirage. Rachel had no idea she hadn't inhaled until she swayed and the tunnel of her vision grew smaller.

"Rachel. Look at me." She heard Alan's patient-calming voice. Mr. Wonderful Bedside Manner was still talking to her, but her fuzzy brain refused to comprehend.

"Rachel, focus on my voice! No fainting on my watch."

Ah, he's trying to make me laugh. Attempting to do as she was told, she opened her mouth and sucked in. No air. Why couldn't she get the oxygen in? She tried again. Not working. Warm skin cradled her cheeks. Alan to the rescue, she hoped. Moisture. *Oh no, not tears! Why now?* Rachel didn't want Alan to see her cry again. No man wanted to be saddled with a crybaby. *Get a hold of yourself.*

"You're safe. I'm here. I'll never let anything hurt you." Rachel could feel the heat of Alan's exhale on her ear. "Breathe. I'll give you mouth to mouth if I have to, but maybe a kiss will do." The softest brush of his lip caressed hers. *Not here. The sheriff will see.* Her body did not respond. Good thing Alan didn't give up easily. His fingers slipped into her hair as his mouth took her lips, distracting her from her panic. Alan's diversionary tactics worked like magic.

The kiss was seductive and heartfelt. Oh, this was more than a clinical technique, this was unbridled yearning. He deepened the kiss, tugging her closer. Rachel had wanted his caresses, craved more of his kisses, since the night at Running Wolf's cabin. She parted her lips to allow the allure of his heat to sweep her away into a dreamy haze of passion. Her pulse still raced but in a good way. The vice grip on her stomach vanished. Air found its way into her lungs. She inhaled and the scent of his musky man soap filled her nose. The taste of hot chocolate slipped across her tongue. Her feeling of 'I'm about to faint' became a blissful melting into his strong arms. *Much better.*

"Whatever you need. I just want to be a part of your life. Get to know you more, be the man you long to see," Alan whispered, then his mouth came back to explore her lips some more.

Rachel wanted to speak but didn't dare make any move that might diminish the heat rising within her. She had kept her desire to be attracted to a man blocked for so long, she wasn't sure she still had it in her.

"I'm drawn to you. Care about you. I respect and trust you, but mostly I care." The words flowed out of him like the sweetest honey.

"I care. Care about you too." Rachel uttered the words through a gasp.

Alan with a massaging touch weaved his fingers through the hair at the nape of her neck. This was a pleasure she didn't know a woman could feel.

"Where am I?" The sheriff stirred on the makeshift gurney.

She sprung backward, startled beyond explanation. Rachel turned to engage her old friend's blinking eyes. She didn't care how pink her cheeks had become. The sheriff's re-awakening was a relief, a good sign he would pull through. "Chuck, your heart skipped a beat again. You're in Betsy, going to the hospital."

"Hi there." Alan grabbed his patient's hand and leaned in so he could be easily seen as the sheriff lay on the makeshift gurney. "It's Alan. Glad you were able to catch a power nap. How're you feeling?"

"Got an elephant on my chest. Left-arm aches real bad."

"I think we have something to help with that." Alan grappled with his bag. "I'll start an IV and—"

"What?" Sheriff Wilson interrupted. "Forget I said anything."

"I've got this." Rachel gave Alan a look she hoped he'd understand. She knew the sheriff was afraid of needles.

"So Chuck, tell me what Irene got you for Christmas?" Alan presented Rachel the vial of medicine and gave her a hand signal to tell her the dose. "That's too funny that you and Will gave your wives the same gift."

"What do you get a woman who has everything? Those silk flowers were a godsend. Hey! What did you do?"

"Oh, nothing much, but you should feel better soon." Stuffing the outer wrapping of the IV kit into her backpack, Rachel winked at Alan. He grinned and pointed at the AED. Sheriff Wilson's pulse was growing stronger.

The pounding on the door made Rachel jump, again. The after-effects of her panic attack were hanging around longer than she'd like.

"I need help. Both of you." She could barely hear Brett, but his demand seemed urgent.

"Do you think you can behave yourself?" Rachel asked the sheriff, hanging the IV bag on a hook she'd requested that Brett install during the customization of Betsy.

The sheriff tried to laugh but grimaced and changed his mind. "I'm not going anywhere."

Stepping into the snow, Rachel called out, "Chuck is conscious and looking much better." Brett gave her two thumbs up. She looked around and was a bit puzzled by what she saw. Rachel found her bearings and realized they were almost to the mountain pass, between the top and the curve in the road before the summit. Brett had dug a bunch of holes in the deep powdery layer of snow that covered the pavement. Large rocks were sitting on top of the frozen drifts closest to the cliff wall, away from the road.

"The plow can only push aside rocks of a certain size. I need your help moving these boulders or we can't go forward." She knew her brother had a plan, so she awaited further instructions.

Brett led her with Alan following close behind, to a massive hunk of rock. He distributed sturdy metal rods. "Each of us is going to stick a pole under the base of the boulder and use the leverage to flip it. This one is heavy, so it could get messy." Brett gave everyone an assigned angle. "The goal is to get it over the guard rail."

On her brother's signal, Rachel lifted her entire body off the ground trying to push down on the lever. The ice cracked as the stone lifted. Alan and Brett were both grunting and digging in their boots trying to get traction. A gust of glacial wind almost knocked them all off their balance and some of the largest snowflakes she had ever seen began to collect on top of their nemesis.

To Rachel's surprise, Brett ducked down like Atlas lifting the globe and gave the boulder a final shove over the edge. The massive slab tumbled with abandon, taking out everything in its path. Big sheets of snow and ice broke free. Frozen in place, Rachel could do nothing but watch the avalanche begin and widen as the original rock tumbled down the face of the mountain.

"You're fine. I got you." Alan had grabbed her around the middle, hauling her away from the edge. He carried her several yards back and suddenly kissed her, distracting her before he put her feet back down on the ground. Her knees buckled. Squeezing her tighter, holding her weight, he held her until she could stand on her own. "I kinda like being at the top. Mother Nature's strength can be exhilarating." Rachel looked around his shoulder but regretted it when her insides did backflips.

"You good?" Alan asked. "I want to go check on the patient."

Tightening her shoulders and trying to stop the rapid blinking of her disobedient eyes, Rachel gave Alan permission to leave, even though she was nowhere near good. *Close your eyes and think about something else.* Losing one's breakfast into the snow would leave marks, and Brett would never let her live that down. Rachel doubled her meditation efforts. But, remembering Alan's amazing kisses did the trick better than anything else she tried. When she got the courage to peek at the aftermath, Brett was standing toe-to-toe with her.

Straining her neck to look up at her giant of a brother annoyed her, but he blocked the view of her biggest fear, so she'd give him a pass.

"I saw that," barked the Sasquatch.

"What?"

"It's bad enough that Betsy becomes a hospital—don't make her a county-fair kissing-booth too."

Oh, no! Brett had helped her scare off her unwanted suitors. Would he ruin her chances with Alan? "Um, but I..." She tossed her hood back so she could see more of Brett's face. "It's not what you think."

"Do I need to ask him his intentions?" Brett leaned in further, towering over her.

She pushed at his chest. "No! He's been a gentleman at all times." Rachel gave Brett a finger wag, not that she thought it would deter him. "I don't recall asking you to get rid of him."

Brett burst out laughing. "I'm just messing with you." He bent over to slap his thigh and the snow on his hat fell and dusted her face. "You two have been making goo-goo eyes at each other for weeks. It's about damn time you played kissy face." The big man snickered some more.

Rachel was stunned, confused and happy all at once. "So you approve?"

"If you're happy, I'm happy," added Brett between chuckles. "Let's get this show back on the road. I wanna see my wife and daughter."

Climbing back into the rig, Rachel saw that Alan had regained his place behind the passenger seat. Sheriff Wilson seemed to be stable and resting. When Brett put Betsy into high gear the debris she pushed over the guardrails caused miniature avalanches, but Rachel was getting a bit more comfortable with each new tremor and rumble. Once they passed the continental divide, Brett radioed Mayor Jameson the second blast zone was cleared for detonation.

Brett managed to maneuver down the curvy roads on the backside of the mountain, and another plow and ambulance waited at the bottom. Taking every precaution necessary, Alan supervised the transfer of the patient to a proper emergency vehicle. Rachel joined him and the EMT as the ambulance followed behind the tandem plows, with lights flashing to get the precious cargo to the Kalispell hospital as quickly as possible.

Rachel allowed herself to have hope that she could remain Alan's nurse and maybe manage to have a real date with the first man she'd cared about since her parents' accident. Now she needed to figure out if Sophie wanted to come back after maternity leave to manage the restaurant. Something always seemed to take priority over her love life. What would life throw at her next?

CHAPTER 28

About an hour later when they arrived at the hospital, Rachel was impressed with how Alan gave his triage report to the emergency medicine doctor on call. She and Alan decided to stay with the sheriff to provide moral support and give Brett some privacy to see Sophie and Christina. While Sheriff Wilson was wheeled in and out of his treatment bay for tests, Rachel stepped out to call Irene with updates on her husband's condition.

A few minutes later, when she was talking to her parents on her cell, the updated weather forecast stopped her in her tracks. She heard Alan tell his mother he needed to call her back. She stood next to him as they both stared up at the map showing anticipated snow over the next several hours and days. Saving Chuck's life was all she'd thought about when they'd jumped into Betsy and taken on the icy mountainous climb. Now it looked like she and her fellow travelers would be in Kalispell for the night.

Sometimes the timing of tragedies and miracles collide, thought Rachel, when Sophie's discharge was confirmed for later that afternoon. Brett and his wife could sleep at Sophie's aunt's house, but the limited floor space prohibited additional guests. Rachel had spent some time in this hospital while in nursing school and remembered many of the doctors and nurses on duty. The staff said she and Dr. Garcia could bunk with the physicians working 24-hour shifts as part of their residency, but Rachel opted for a hotel. She knew the local area, so she made reservations online for two rooms. One of her nursing school buddies offered to drive them after her shift ended.

Sheriff Wilson was scheduled for several stents and a pacemaker to be implanted the following morning. With the approaching storms, Irene would not be at her husband's side, so Rachel and Alan agreed to become his surrogate family.

The proactive blasting of excess snow had worked well, but with the latest predictions, Brett would need help from his pals again to return home. The plow-triad proposal that had saved Christmas would be the blueprint for future storms, but the main pass to Snowflake would shut down again just before sunset. Rachel couldn't decide which scenario was worse: being in Snowflake without the ability to receive supplies or being snowed-in at Kalispell.

Having confirmed the logistics and notified everyone of the plan, Rachel decided to put herself on vacation for the rest of the day. She couldn't help Olga in the kitchen at the café, the Snowflake medical clinic was closed, her parents would take care of Jacob, Sheriff Wilson was resting comfortably, and she had a new niece to meet.

Later that afternoon while sitting in the hospital waiting room with Alan, Rachel dug into her reserve of courage. "There's a place walking distance from the hotel that I adore. Let me take you to dinner tonight?" asked Rachel. She had no nerves or apprehension—the offer fell out of her mouth before she had a chance to analyze it. Maybe she should try using a vacation mentality more often.

Alan's eyebrows shot up, but then a huge grin crossed his face. "That sounds wonderful. I'm looking forward to it." His demeanor changed, like a knot in yarn had been clipped and the scarf began to unravel. His air of being on his best behavior vanished and he relaxed.

Being medical personnel had its advantages in the hospital. The NICU nurse let Rachel and Dr. Garcia closer to the incubator than most visitors. Using the attached gloves, she was able to caress the tiny baby. "Oh, look she's squeezing my finger. That's right Christina, you tell them you want to go home as soon as possible." Rachel smiled until her face hurt. "She's stronger than she looks."

To her surprise, Alan used the glove on the other side of the machine and massaged the baby's head. He cooed and used a high-pitched voice while talking to the infant. He had compassion, she knew, but Alan also had a paternal side that Rachel had never seen.

Not that she was keeping score, but over the past several weeks, Alan had earned checkmarks on her imaginary Mr. Right list. Now she could add "not afraid of infants" to the growing number of good marks. He must have noticed that she was staring. With a grin and an almost unnoticeable shrug, he went back to soothing Christina. She responded with a good long yawn.

"What, Miss Chrissie? Too many visitors today? You got to meet your daddy, didn't you? Yeah, he's the big guy that saved Christmas. Yes, he did." Alan's falsetto voice tickled her funny bone, and she was delighted he kept using it.

Before leaving the hospital, Rachel made a point of visiting Sophie. She had changed into street clothes and sat in the reclining chair while Brett was gathering her cards and gifts. "I missed you so much!" Rachel held back tears as she bent down to give her best friend a giant hug. "I'm so glad you and Christina are okay. She's beautiful! Looks just like you."

"Hey, I'm in there too," hollered Brett from across the room. "She's got my feet, poor thing." He whispered a few more traits under his breath as he went back to his task.

"I hear they're springing you before the storm arrives. Congrats on having a healthy little girl. I knew the two of you'd be fine." Alan patted Sophie on the shoulder and then stepped out of the way of the family reunion.

With a childlike fidget, Sophie adjusted in the chair, trying to find a comfortable position. "I love my aunt. She took wonderful care of me, but I can't wait to get back to work. This bed rest thing makes me stir crazy. I'm not a sit-around kind of gal."

Rachel hugged her again. "You want to be promoted to manager? Working at the café and as a nurse has me tuckered out."

Sophie beamed. "Yes, ma'am and thank you.

Knowing a Welch would be onsite at the businesses her parents had created made Rachel's decision to continue being a nurse a whole lot easier.

"Oh, right. Brett mentioned you'd been working for Dr. Garcia." Sophie smiled and blew her husband a kiss. Rachel laughed out loud when he caught it and popped it onto his mouth. "And the mayor," Sophie continued. "New rules and all, he's got some nerve."

"I'm so pleased to have her as a coworker. She's an exceptional clinical talent," interjected Alan from the peanut gallery. But then he rubbed the back of his neck and examined the diagnostic equipment in the room.

Before Rachel had a chance to bounce her take-on city hall thoughts off of the important people in her life, an orderly appeared with a wheelchair to discharge Sophie into Brett's loving care.

WITH A RENEWED HOPE, Alan met Rachel at the designated time, taking her hand in his as they strolled a couple of blocks to her favorite steakhouse. Kalispell was not metropolitan Miami, but the three blocks of downtown Snowflake seemed minuscule by comparison. The snow fell thick and heavy, but he had gotten used to it. The decorated lamp posts and shop fronts provided a perfect atmosphere for a real first date. Alan decided that was what he would consider this dinner. He had passed the 90-days hurdle early and no one in Kalispell would know about the new measure implemented by the Snowflake City Council. He could finally relax and enjoy being himself around Rachel.

"I've been meaning to tell you. On Christmas Day, I received a present from the city, confirming I passed the probationary period." Alan guffawed to himself as he remembered the look on the mayor's face when he'd given him the letter.

Rachel threw her arms around his shoulders, knocking him off balance, and they both skittered across the icy sidewalk, grabbing onto anything solid within reach. "Sorry, I forgot you're a warm-weather guy." She hugged him again with less enthusiasm. "That's wonderful news!"

Without hesitation, Alan kissed her on the cheek, then defended himself. "I'm adapting to the white stuff." Picking up a handful of fresh powder, he tossed it in the air and walked under it. "See..." He brushed the flakes off his hood and made a point of dumping them onto Rachel, chuckling. Hearing his laughter excited the pleasure synapses in his brain. He hadn't felt this carefree since before the trouble in Miami. His newfound happiness had to do with living in Snowflake, the barter currency, the community's generosity, and people like Bodie. Of course, Rachel had a lot to do with it too.

"Wow, that smells good!" Alan filled his lungs again with air that smelled of beef.

Rachel increased her pace, towing him around a corner. "Wait till you taste it. And the side dishes are to die for."

As they walked through the broad glass doors, Alan surveyed the linens on the tables and shimmering chandeliers made with elk antlers, wondering if his attire would pass. But seeing most of the people in blue jeans, sweaters and flannel shirts made him feel at home in an instant.

"Ms. Welch, so nice to see you again. I'm glad the weather is keeping you in town. Your table is right this way." Alan guessed the guy was the manager or someone important. The rest of the staff seemed to quicken their steps when they saw him.

Their secluded booth faced a row of windows that opened to the west. The sun had just gone down over the mountains in the distance, but the orange glow still lingered. Mesmerized by the extraordinary view, Alan stilled and enjoyed. He hadn't seen the mountains' majesty in this light before. *And I live there. How lucky am I?*

Noticing Rachel was removing her winter gear, he did the same. The well-varnished wooden seating had plush padding, and easing onto it, Alan exhaled, allowing himself to decompress. Between the windows was a stone hearth fireplace that crackled and popped as the flames danced. The music was low but added to the ambiance. Tongue in cheek, Alan asked, "You come here often?"

Rachel smiled, "As often as I can when I'm in town." Her genuine elation built until it lit up her face. She cackled and didn't seem to care who heard her.

Oh, good. The attempt at a joke landed, thought Alan as he put his napkin on his lap. "Was that the manager? He seemed to know you."

"The owner. This place has been serving Welch beef for generations."

Alan had to let her last statement digest in his mind. *Welch beef and the word generations were plurals.* She must have seen his puzzled look because she continued. "Brett owns the ranch now, but the foreman my dad hired before the accident still runs it. Brett's always been fascinated by plows. He and Betsy deserve each other."

She had mentioned the Welch family dynasty and people treating her differently if they knew her last name. Should I Google Rachel and Brett, Alan wondered? Some of his earlier conversations with Rachel made more sense now, especially about guys jumping the gun on popping the question. Her family must have had a bigger part in founding Snowflake than she'd let on. One of the things he liked about her was that she was unassuming. Some women in her position would be uppity, but Rachel was as modest and down-to-earth as they came. *And she'd asked him out.*

Easing further into his seat, Alan let the weight of his shoulder lean onto hers. She leaned in too until they found a comfortable balance. They sat in companionable silence, watching the skylight dim and the fire roar. When the waiter came to take their order, Rachel knew exactly what she wanted without looking at a menu. She rattled off extra details to make certain her order came out as she preferred. Alan chimed in with, "I'll have what she's having." She made it sound so mouthwatering. He'd had her cooking—the woman knew food.

They opened a bottle of merlot and honey buttered rolls arrived, followed quickly by a salad. They took their time with the medium-rare steaks and garlic mashed potatoes. Alan smiled as they both asked questions they'd been wanting to ask. The more they talked, the more in sync they became. Alan thought he'd cared for her before, but now his heart hurt with the love he carried for her. His spirit soared being around her and his heart banged in his chest with a quickening beat. *I've never felt like this before.*

At the end of the meal, she ordered red velvet cake. "We'll share it." By way of making a joke, she bounced a bit in her seat and bumped his shoulder. Rachel's willingness to share her dessert with him spoke volumes. It shouted intimacy and romance at the same time. Their forks comingled as they fed each other big, messy bits, laughing and enjoying themselves, not thinking about anything else. Or who might see them.

As Alan helped Rachel put on her coat, a middle-aged woman approached them. The scowl on her face reminded him of Mrs. Jameson. Bile rose into his throat.

"Rachel you should know better." The woman's graying hair was pulled back into a tight bun and the crooked finger she wagged reminded him of a broomstick.

Rachel who was only half in her coat dropped it to the floor. "Mrs. Baxter so nice to see you. Know better about what?" As she bent down Alan wasn't certain if she was stalling or hadn't grasped the implication that had him shaking in his shoes.

"Heidi asked me to come see how the two of you acted when you thought you were alone. You're blatantly breaking the new rule. I've already called to tell her so." The matriarch stomped to the exit with a huff but turned back to spew more hurtful words. "What is it that has doctors throwing themselves at you? You've shamed your name again."

"What?" Rachel went pale and gasped. She started to run after her accuser, but Alan captured her hand just in time.

"Anything you say will only make her thoughts about us worse." Alan let go and dropped his head, staring at the well-polished wooden floor.

"I never dreamed, but I should have known. Mrs. Jameson said she had spies." She turned toward him. "So much stress these last few weeks, I haven't had this much fun since I was a little girl." She sighed. "What are we going to do?"

"Tiempo para un nuevo trabajo."

"What?"

The confused look on Rachel's face helped him realize he had reverted to Spanglish. "Time for a new job." He began helping her with her coat again. "I won't let you lose your place in Snowflake. I'll take the fall and try to save your job."

"No! Oh, hell no. Mrs. Jameson isn't going to win this battle. The town needs you. Our relationship has only improved patient care." Rachel yanked her hair out of the back of her coat as he brought the collar up to her neck. "No."

Rachel rounded on him and poked at his chest. "No. I mean it."

"How much sway do you have over the council? If it comes to a vote, can you outmaneuver the mayor?" Alan tried to grin at her, but his upper lip quivered.

"Oh, I like it."

She jumped at him throwing her arms around him and he caught her mid-air. He liked this feisty side of Rachel. "Well? Can you?"

"Not sure. But I'm gonna try." Rachel yanked her phone from her purse and starting texting like mad. "With the storm, these messages may not get through, but not like anything else will either.

One of the decorations on their way out reminded Alan of the wish he had made on the brilliant white lights of the four giant snowflakes that encircled the church's bell tower. Rachel's flashback caused by her trauma had lessened. If he was meant to be the man of her dreams, then the council wouldn't fire him. He closed his eyes and repeated the wish in his mind. Would the legend come true for him? What would tomorrow bring, and the tomorrow after that? He said a silent prayer.

As they walked to the hotel the wind howled and the snow blew sideways, but Alan didn't care. He had a newfound hope, and he was with Rachel. Wherever that happened to be was quickly becoming his home. So sunny beaches would be replaced by snowdrifts. As long as he had her, he'd be happy.

When they arrived at her hotel room, he kissed her on the forehead. "Put the professional us aside for a minute." She looked up and when their eyes met it gave him the courage to toss his camouflage cloak aside. *I'm still in control without it.* "I want the personal us to find a way to be together no matter what."

She looked at him for a long time, a mist gathered in her eyes and a tear escaped down her cheek. "Me too. I can be the real me around you. It means so much..."

He smothered her mouth with a deep kiss. He'd heard all he needed and no longer cared who might see them together. She was his now and he would do everything possible to fill her life with joy. "May there be many merry Christmases to come."

CHAPTER 29

As a courtesy, the local sheriff's department transported Rachel and Alan to the hospital in one of their all-terrain vehicles. Christmas had been two very long days ago, and a foot of new snow had fallen overnight and was still falling in heavy, wet flakes. Rachel had to put thoughts about her growing passion for Alan and the possibility of being fired out of her mind. No one had responded to the multitude of texts she had sent last night. She knew her ability to get a signal for any type of communication would be spotty at best. Sheriff Wilson needed her and everything else would have to wait.

Once they were in the sheriff's room though, Rachel put the weather out of her mind too. She did her best to ease his nerves and found a radio to keep Irene informed when her cell signal failed. Alan, as she expected, did a wonderful job of explaining to Chuck how the procedures worked and what to anticipate when he came out of the anesthesia in the recovery room.

Sheriff Wilson put on a brave face, doing his best to crack jokes with the nurses and only show the jovial portion of his personality. "Gotta think positive," he kept saying to everyone, but Rachel figured he needed to for his benefit. At about eight in the morning, the orderly and surgical resident came to wheel Chuck away for his operation.

Rachel knew it would be several hours before she would be allowed to see him, so she and Alan went to visit Christina in the NICU. Since the time of her birth, the tiny girl had gained several ounces and her lungs had strengthened, which became obvious when she decided she needed a diaper change.

Sophie had planned on sleeping in and continuing her recovery from surgery, so Rachel was glad to be Christina's family at her side. *How awful, Sophie must have felt leaving the hospital without her child.* But the fact that Christina was reasonably healthy and could come home in a matter of weeks must have given Sophie the will to go back to her aunt's house. Rachel knew when Sophie's goofball of a husband was around, he eased anxieties as well.

Eventually, the NICU nurse hinted that Rachel and Alan needed to let Christina get some rest. Rachel showed Alan to the cafeteria, where he bought her breakfast and coffee. She picked a table in the corner, away from the bustle of the early morning food rush. This area of the hospital offered a view of the park across the street. She knew the big pine tree in the center was decorated for Christmas, but so much snow had fallen that most of what she could see was blanketed in white.

We're not in vacation mode anymore. She could tell Alan was worried about the sheriff, his mother and any medical needs that might arise since the Snowflake clinic was closed for the second day in a row. Of course, having to deal with the city council had to keep invading his thoughts. Their conversation was pleasant, but a bit more businesslike compared to their date. She had to think twice about that, but she decided it had been a real date. It made her grin. She had never asked a guy out before, but something about Alan put her at ease. She could be herself around him.

"I'd heard you were in the hospital. I hoped I'd find you here."

Rachel wasn't pleased to see her mentor but always wanted to act in a professional manner. She was here for family and friends today, not for work. She raised her head with dignity but halted when an envelope was stuck in her face. Rachel did everything she could to keep a frown from forming. She had a sneaking suspicion what it contained. Her feet took control of themselves and shuffled under the table.

"I've been able to get higher wages for the nurses. That's a revised job offer. The door is always open for you here. Because you're such a great asset in the emergency room, I can authorize a signing bonus, but you have to accept by January fifth."

Rachel fingered the envelope but didn't open it. "Alan, this is Veronica Rawling. She's the director of nursing at the hospital." Rachel began to stand and continue the introductions, but Alan spoke over her and jumped to his feet faster.

"Hello, I'm Alan Garcia. Nice to meet you. I've heard good things about this hospital and staff." Alan shook Veronica's hand and found his seat again.

"Sorry, gotta run. You know me, busy-busy. I can't wait for you to work, here again, so please say yes soon. Happy New Year!" With swinging arms and wide steps, the ball of energy Rachel looked up to and admired was gone as quickly as she had arrived.

Not wanting to think about it, Rachel set the letter down and went back to eating her breakfast. It struck her as odd that Alan had not introduced himself as a doctor. He had privileges as an attending physician, she'd helped him get them. She remembered Alan lost a bit of refinement on his social skills when he was nervous, but that was part of what she liked about him. His demeanor fit the patient base of Snowflake. She took another forkful of scrambled eggs, not having the courage to view Alan's reaction. Her morning meal grew heavy in her stomach.

"Are you going to open it? At least you can still find work as a nurse since that is your true calling," Alan leaned across the table and stroked her fingers with his own.

It felt self-centered of her to do so, but she guessed that was the only way to get rid of the elephant that had entered the room. In no hurry, she took another bite, but then with extra effort to keep the fork from shaking, she put it down. With a sigh, she retrieved the envelope. The base pay was noticeably higher, and the signing bonus leaped off the page at her. "I could put a down payment on a house with that." *Oops, why did you let Alan hear you say that?*

"Good nurses are hard to find, and you've got mad skills." Alan was smiling, but nothing else about his body language agreed with that sentiment.

"I didn't apply for a job here." Rachel felt the need to profess her loyalty to Dr. Garcia and the Snowflake medical clinic.

Alan came around to her side of the table and sat next to her putting his arm around her shoulders. "You don't have to explain. I get it. Veronica's just doing her job." He paused to choose his words. "We both might get fired. I'm going to fight like hell, but each of us needs to think about plan B for our medical careers. With Sophie coming back to the café, you can consider this opportunity." Alan's palm dropped to her back, gliding across it with a soothing side-to-side motion.

Of course, Mr. Logical is correct. But she couldn't let herself entertain the possibility, could she? Sophie might be out twelve more weeks after Christina came home. She couldn't let the mayor and his wife push her out of town. Whatever was beginning to grow between her and Alan needed to be explored. Would Alan and his mother move to Kalispell? Would he be willing to look for a local physician position or move back to Florida?

Thinking about it another way, she agreed she did well in emergency medicine. *No avalanches and seeing car accident victims at the sight of a crash.* Kalispell had more variety to offer for entertainment. She had friends and relatives in the area. No one in the bigger city cared what her last name was. She could eat at her favorite restaurant whenever she wanted. And she would never have to endure the mayor's abuse of power ever again.

But Snowflake had more natural beauty. She'd be closer to Brett, Sophie, Jacob and Christina. What did she have with Alan? Should she let him fall on his sword for her? This fiasco was her fault. She should have remembered Mrs. Baxter had moved to Kalispell. She shouldn't have asked Alan out on a date. *Maybe I can save Alan's job if the mayor knows I'm willing to move to Kalispell?*

She looked up to meet his gaze. She couldn't help but notice he had grown paler and tense. "I need time to think about this." There, she'd said it. That's what she needed—time, and advice from her parents, with input from Sophie, Bodie and even the mayor.

"Of course. That makes sense." Alan kissed the top of her head and returned to his food.

Putting the envelope in her medical backpack didn't make the offer or her apprehension go away. But she made herself stop thinking about it, at least until the sheriff came through his surgery.

"It's going to be several hours, let's go for a walk." Finishing her breakfast, she donned her coat and made her way to the park. Alan trailed behind her without comment.

Trudging through knee-deep powder wasn't necessarily the type of walk she'd wanted, but the physical activity helped to exhaust her over-excited nerves. She played tour guide and told Alan about the history of the area and how her ancestors had played a part in making the mountain settlement of Snowflake. The cloud bank that had gathered overhead must have triggered a light sensor because when they reached the massive Christmas tree, the lights turned on. It touched her inner child—the dazzling display was just what she'd needed.

Alan stumbled, then jerked back when the lights came on. "Did you do that?" His eyes sparkled with glee as he took in the beauty.

"No." As she looked up to admire the twinkling lights, a huge snowflake landed on her nose. She chuckled and started humming "Oh Christmas Tree." She didn't care that the holiday had passed—she needed to play, to go back into vacation mode. Rachel landed a snowball to the side of Alan's hood, catching him off guard. "Take that!"

"What was that for?"

Without answering, she lobbed a frozen fastball at his chest.

"This means war." Alan made his own snowball, using the tree as cover. "Did you know I was a pitcher in little league?" His first attempt disintegrated as it flew toward her. Rachel howled at the puzzled look and full-body droop that came over him.

"Have you ever made a snowball?" She pummeled him with another strike. "You gotta pack the powder."

"Huh?"

She let him watch her make her next glistening ball, and then she nailed him with it. Knowing he learned fast, she retreated behind a life-size Santa. Rachel made an arsenal and prepared to attack. As she peeked out to zero in on her target, a masterfully made snowball ricocheted off her shoulder.

"Score!" Alan's victory fist pump was a welcome distraction from her obligations.

This was the side of Alan she needed right now. She had to admit she liked that he could be her playmate and business consultant. Rachel needed to be silly, blow off steam. Finding a place where the snow had blown away and wasn't as deep, she flopped down and flapped her limbs. "Have you ever made a snow angel?" As she got up to admire her artwork, Alan raced to her side.

"Oh, I've heard about those, but I've never seen one in person." He hauled her into his arms before she knew it. "It's beautiful. Like you."

Her jaw went slack and cold air rushed in, suddenly being replaced by warmth as Alan took her mouth. He kissed her feverishly, long and strong. She loved it, wanted more, didn't care who might be watching. *That cowboy's already been bucked from his bronco.* Rachel pulled back just enough to whisper, "Do you really think I'm pretty?" His response was to squeeze her tighter and kiss her again.

WAITING HAD NEVER BEEN Alan's strongest skill, but he chalked this situation up as a reminder of what his patients went through with their loved ones. His emotions were on edge, his body was sore from sitting in uncomfortable chairs, and all he wanted was for the surgeon to come out and confirm the sheriff would enjoy a full recovery.

The job offer Rachel had received at breakfast put everything about his world off-balance. But he was determined to double his effort to show her he should be her choice. He would become the man of her dreams. Why couldn't their life be more like their steak dinner or snowball fight?

I might have to step away from a second medical practice in less than six months. With my career hitting rock bottom, I need to keep the women in my life happy. Rachel and my madre deserve better. His situation resembled an avalanche. Alan now better understood why they caused Rachel such fear.

To be honest, he knew his future wasn't the only one at stake. Alan wanted Rachel to be happy. What was the saying, if you love someone, set them free? Her passion for nursing already competed with her café job, but how could the clinic's salary live up to the offer made by the hospital? *Maybe I should encourage her to accept the big city job?* No one said life was fair. But could his love win out over her ambitions? He didn't want Rachel to regret staying in Snowflake, so he made a point to not let the director of nursing know he was the competition, the doctor she currently worked beside. *Well as long as they didn't get fired.* What if she woke up one day and blamed him for holding back her career? He wanted to be supportive, but that action caused him pure agony. The thought made his throat constrict, and he shifted in his chair with more force than intended.

Noticing Rachel flinch, Alan realized a doctor was walking in her direction. "He should be wheeled back to his room within the hour," said the cardiologist, taking off his mask. "The surgery was a marvelous success on every level."

Alan patted the man on the back after Rachel hugged him. "Great news. Thanks for your expertise. Job well done." They'd cleared one hurdle, but how many more would be thrown at him over the rest of the day?

Alan realized when he and Rachel were away from Snowflake, the locals had no access to medical care. So, Brett had begrudgingly arranged to get an additional plow to make the trip back over the mountain. Alan felt for the man who'd risked a lot to embrace his wife and meet his daughter, just to turn around and leave them again. But his skill set with Betsy was rare, and very few men could hoist a sizeable boulder over the guardrail.

As he and Rachel escorted Sheriff Wilson from recovery back to his room, the patient managed to spread a bit of fleeting joy. *He looks good, better than expected.* The sheriff made everyone around him laugh. "I'm fine. Stop being a fussing hen. You guys need to get on the road before the sun sets," said Sheriff Wilson as Rachel adjusted everything around him to ensure his comfort before she left.

Saying goodbye to loved ones in Kalispell was not easy for the Welch siblings, but by mid-afternoon, Alan found himself sitting on the floor behind the passenger seat of Betsy. The sturdy snow pusher had been loaded with supplies for the snow-bound town. His muscles were more discontented on the return trip than they'd been during the rescue transport. "What's up with you two?" asked Brett. "The boxes in the front seat are better travel companions."

Stifling a grimace, Alan knew Brett had a point. Both he and Rachel, who sat across from him, hadn't said a word since they left the hospital.

"Mrs. Baxter caught Alan and me on a date at Dusty Trail Steakhouse. She's already ratted us out to Mrs. Jameson," replied Rachel, her voice flat and lifeless.

"Oh." Brett perked up to participate in the conversation. "Oh." His voice lowered a bit as he began to think through the ramifications of the statement. "Oh." The sound was barely audible as the magnitude of the situation made its final landing.

Brett fell silent once more. Alan wanted to tug Rachel onto his lap and make everything okay. But he knew she needed space to think. Instead, he revved his gray matter into hyperdrive and created a plan of his own.

CHAPTER 30

Mrs. Wilson entered the room making a point of letting the door slam against the wall. "I take the minutes of all city council meetings, even the ones behind closed doors. If the snow is going to keep me in town, I might as well make myself useful."

Last night when Irene logged onto her husband's work calendar to postpone his meetings, she saw that the mayor had called an emergency gathering of the council. It didn't surprise her to see her best friend was already sitting in her designated seat for city staff. She covered her mouth with her hand to keep unkind words from escaping. It had been a minor miracle that Rachel's text had reached her last night. *Rachel and Dr. Garcia saved my husband, now I'm going to save their jobs and romance. If anyone deserves happiness, it's Rachel.*

"Fine," grunted the mayor. "Let's get started." He shuffled some papers in front of him. "For the record, the full city council is present."

Irene took a moment to make eye contact with each council member, their faces showed various levels of disdain to full-on disgruntlement. A flutter in her gut sought to distract her, but she doubled her efforts to focus.

"Heidi Jameson, please proceed with your prepared statement." The mayor leaned back in his chair with a glib expression.

Irene wanted to give her friend a dirty look but decided to stare at the floor. She knew Heidi had fallen into a dark place of late, but taking out her frustration on innocent professionals who had just barely started their careers was not the way to make herself feel better. She would find the right time to give Heidi a piece of her mind but now was not it.

Mrs. Jameson stood and read a paragraph typed in large font. "Mrs. Margaret Baxter, a former resident of Snowflake who now lives in Kalispell, forwarded the following information to me yesterday evening. She witnessed Ms. Rachel Welch and Dr. Alan Garcia sharing dessert at a steakhouse in a fashion that could only be described as flirtatious. The two people in question were most likely on a date." She sat, crossing one leg over the other and giving Irene her back. Irene wanted to yank her friend's scarf since it had been thrust in her face but sat on her hand instead.

The mayor cleared his throat. "May I remind everyone of the new no fraternization rule this council implemented at our last public meeting. The repercussion for such action is immediate dismissal."

Irene jumped up. "You can't fire someone based on a former resident's assumption."

"They broke the rule and must pay the price." Heidi stood toe-to-toe with Irene.

"We'll talk about this privately."

"No. We all know each other here. Say what you have to say."

"You really don't want me to do that."

"Ladies!" Ms. Brenda Ito, the attorney stood, hands on her hips. "I didn't get dragged away from my Christmas vacation to listen to a coworker spat. Kindly take a seat. We've offered enough time for explanatory discussion. Let's vote."

The mayor patted the lawyer on her forearm, and she plopped into her chair. "Does anyone else have any compelling evidence to corroborate Mrs. Baxter's accusations?"

The room fell silent and Irene hid her grin from Heidi.

"I second the motion to vote," bellowed Bodie.

"Fine. All in favor of the immediate termination of employment for Dr. Alan Garcia and Nurse Rachel Welch raise your hand." The mayor's arm shot up with exacting urgency.

As Irene had hoped, the other four council members' hands rested in their laps.

Mrs. Ito stood again. "I make a motion to grant an exception for the two previously mentioned employees if they agree to a 60-day notice of intent to leave their positions and their personal relationship doesn't interfere with their ability to provide medical care."

"You can't do that." The mayor banged his gavel.

Brenda laughed.

"I second the motion proposed by Attorney Baxter," Bodie's deep voice rang out over all other sounds in the room. "All in favor raise your hand."

Every council member, but the mayor, held their hands up high. "The motion carries. I'm going back to enjoy my family." As Brenda packed her belongings she added. "I'll send an official notice to the employees in question on behalf of the city and copy the people in this room."

Mr. Jameson slammed the gavel some more and shot out of his chair with such speed, it toppled over, the wooden back cracking as it shammed against the tile floor. "I'm the mayor. I control these meetings. You can't just make a motion."

"Read the bylaws, Mr. Jameson. I most certainly can." Brenda sauntered passed the red-faced mayor and the other council members began to follow.

"Hold on. Everyone stop." The mayor yanked on the lapels of his suit-coat.

Irene couldn't withstand his boorish behavior one minute more. "Hey Will!" She pointed to the flashing red light that confirmed the camera was rolling. A warm sense of relaxation soothed every nerve that had been on rapid-fire mode.

"What!? I didn't ask for that." Mr. Jameson's fists pounded on the table.

"Just doing my job, sir." Irene decided to make a copy of the tape for her records. Then she joined her co-conspirators for a drink at the

Squeaky Saddle Saloon and wondered how Alan and Rachel would react to this news.

ALAN SLEPT on the cot in his office. He had spoken to his mother around midnight to let her know Betsy and passengers had arrived safely. He couldn't bring himself to tell her about the encounter with Mrs. Baxter. *She's already been through so much.*

Sleep did not find him. *I've got to save Rachel's career. I hope Bodie received my voicemail.* Alan took a cold shower to help himself wake up and then started pacing.

He had the office ready for patients by 4 o'clock in the morning and had nothing left to do but worry. That task just gave him a headache. He was saved by the jingle at the front door. Rachel entered carrying a thermos of coffee and a bag of the café's famous muffins.

"I see you got as much rest as I did." Rachel grabbed one of the patio chairs and made herself comfortable while she set out breakfast. "Heard anything from anyone?"

"No. You?"

"Nah, but didn't expect to this early. It's the holidays, remember."

"Right. I hate waiting."

Rachel reached out and took his hand as he sat in the paired plastic furnishings. "I told Irene if she had the chance to save one of us, I wanted it to be you."

Alan squeezed her hand and swallowed twice to get his voice to work. "Wait, no. My instruction to Bodie was that he save your career at any price." He let out one of his whole-body laughs. Not because the situation was humorous. He didn't know what else to do.

"We're officially booked solid for the first week of the new year," said Teresa, having made a stealthy entrance via the back door.

Alan acknowledged her statement with a wave but hadn't comprehended a word. "I ordered more medical supplies to get us back to the preferred levels like you asked."

Alan continued to stroke Rachel's palm. His *madre* could see them as a couple. She would understand. The feel of Rachel's soft skin served as a dose of anesthesia to his frayed nerves.

"Looks like we'll get a break in the weather for the New Year's Eve celebration. Are you going, Rachel?"

"Huh?" Alan's head popped up. "Were you talking to me?"

"Yeah, I figured you weren't listening, so I said her name." Teresa took a seat at the folding chair in front of Alan's laptop. "You two are acting weird. What's up?"

Alan looked at Rachel and then back at his mother. "It's complicated."

"Okay. Should I be worried?" Teresa tapped his keyboard to refresh the screen. "Are you expecting an email from the City's attorney?"

"What? No. Let me see." Alan raced around his compressed particle desk as his mother vacated his chair.

Alan's palms got sweaty and a lump formed in his throat. Alan recalled his anguish when he received his med school acceptance letter all over again. He glanced at a couple of sentences and rubbed his eyes. Starting over, he read aloud. "An exception!"

Rachel ran to stand behind him, but he caught her and pulled her onto his lap instead.

"Oh? Hey!" She didn't resist, instead, she laughed. A truly relaxed chuckle.

"Read! We got a get out of jail free card. Both of us!" Alan hugged her around the middle and put his face next to hers.

She gasped. "Well, what do you know. Maybe being a Welch isn't so bad after all."

"Will one of you please tell me what's going on?" Teresa stood beside the desk but leaned in to catch a glimpse of the screen.

"We can date and keep our jobs." Alan stood with Rachel in his arms. Giving her a quick peck on the lips, then he dropped her feet to the floor and began to lead her in a dance around the room.

"Oops, your toes. Sorry, I don't know this one." Rachel pulled away from him, but her embarrassment just brought out her beauty.

"That's a cha-cha. Here let me show you how it's done." Teresa stepped up to Alan, and he twirled her around like he had so many times as he was growing up. The dancing continued until Teresa saw Bodie in the lobby.

Alan raced to hug him. "Gracias!"

Bodie stood like a pillar of rock at Stonehenge but patted Alan on the back. "Welcome. I guess you saw the email?"

"Yes! Cha-cha with us." Alan went back to Rachel.

Teresa stepped up to Bodie. "Do you dance?"

Bodie made a beeline for the door. "Oh, no. Not me. Not like that. Sorry, gotta go." At least a brilliant smile graced his face as he was leaving.

"Hey, can you two-step?" Rachel asked.

Alan stopped and searched his brain. "Dosey-doe and allemande right..." He took her hands and did the best he could to remember elementary gym class.

Rachel burst out laughing and followed the steps he led her to take. "No, no, no. That's a square dance." She stumbled into the wall in a fit of giggles.

Another jingle along with a cold blast of air made Alan stop celebrating. *What if it were the mayor himself?* He adjusted his lab coat and prepared to greet the next visitor.

"Irene. What brings you out this early? Here please let me help you." Teresa darted to accept the outstretched dish of food wrapped in a towel to keep it warm.

"The mood at city hall ain't too festive so I decided to join you folks for breakfast. I brought a coffee cake with plates, forks and everything."

"You did it! I can't, I mean we can't thank you enough." Rachel gave Irene a long hug.

Alan saw Mrs. Wilson tear up and wasn't sure if she missed her husband or if it had to do with city hall. He wrapped his arms around both women. And leave it to his *madre* to join in for a full group hug.

Irene stroked Rachel's hair. "Well, we Welches have to stick together."

Alan's head swiveled like an owl. "What?!"

"You didn't know I was a Welch before I became a Wilson?" Irene gave Alan a playful punch in the arm. "Luke is my cousin."

Ouch, man Irene is strong. I'm glad she's on my side. Alan allowed himself to think past the immediate moment for the first time in many days. His *madre* had mentioned a New Years' Eve party. Now he had something worth celebrating.

CHAPTER 31

"YOUR NEXT PATIENT isn't due for another hour. Do you want to talk about it?" Teresa asked her only child.

"Not really." Alan crossed his arms over his chest. "But I'm useless at the moment, so I guess I need to get a few things out in the open."

Teresa waited for her son to say something. Her only movement was an occasional blink.

"Um, I don't know where to start." Alan leaned back in his chair and let his head fall back against the wall.

Leaning forward, Teresa asked, "Did you argue?"

Alan continued staring at the ceiling. "No."

"But she's not here. Is she not going to be your nurse?" Teresa started putting stray paperclips into a holder.

Alan's arms fell to his sides and his body went limp in the chair. "It's complicated."

"Because you love her?"

He lost his balance and almost fell out of the chair. As he struggled to regain his equilibrium, Alan looked at his mother—his lips twitched, but no sound came to his voice.

"I figured out you love her." She stopped tinkering. "I'm your mother." A small grin lifted the corners of her lips. "Please tell me you recognize the feelings you're having for what they are."

"I've never felt like this before." His arms crisscrossed his chest again. "If this is love, I'm not sure I like it."

"Why?"

"These feelings have me all out of whack. I can't stop thinking about her. I can't sleep. I can't focus. I'm a mess." His body stiffened as each word got louder. "I can't be a mess."

"Uh-huh. Because you're a doctor. No mistakes."

"Right!" Now Alan's whole body became animated. "You get it." He could tell she was biting her lip and doing her best to keep a serious face. "What are you laughing at?" Standing, Alan wandered the floor behind his desk.

"I'm sorry. My son's in love. You're adorable."

He rolled his eyes, then made his way to the window to look toward the café. "I don't feel adorable. She may not think I'm adorable."

"Ah, now we're getting somewhere."

He saw her eyebrows squeezing together, and his chest tightened. "What do you mean?"

With her usual grace, Teresa got up and cradled her son in her arms. Alan couldn't move. She cupped his face. "You're afraid you love her more than she loves you."

"Right. I mean, maybe. Well, how am I supposed to know?" He stepped away from her grasp, going back to the window.

"I'm no expert, but I think I can spot a woman in love." She stood next to him and pointed at Rachel's apartment above the restaurant. "The way she acts around you, I'm thinking she's in love with you."

"Really?"

"Really!" His *madre* took hold of his shoulders and squeezed them. "Alan, my beloved, think about it."

Inhaling deeply, he shook his head, "I'm not seeing straight. Remember, I'm a mess."

"Did I ever tell you how your father won my heart?"

This got Alan's attention. He turned to look at her and saw tears welling in her eyes. The lump in his throat did not allow words to escape. So, he leaned in and kissed her forehead.

"Your father, may he rest in peace," Teresa crossed herself, "was always there when I needed him. Sure, he was gorgeous, and he made me laugh. But I knew I could count on him through the tough times." She brushed away a tear and stood up straighter. "Think about what you and Rachel have dealt with in a short span of time. You've always had her back and she's done the same for you."

Alan thought back over the difficult situations they'd faced together, and he began to unwind. "But the job offer." De-stressing halted, and a vise grip surrounded his chest instead. He began to rub his chest as if to massage the pain away.

"What offer? The one you gave her?"

He explained about Veronica, the higher salary, the signing bonus and working as an emergency room nurse.

"Hmmm..." Teresa stepped away from the window, tapping her finger to her lips. "She's a modern woman and all, but I think family's more important to her."

"How do you figure?"

"She's lived here all her life, right?" His mother took her turn to traipse in a circle. Alan allowed a bit of levity to comfort him as he realized from whom that trait had come. He loved his mother so much, and if they were both pacers, that was okay. "Except for when she went to nursing school, then she came back to live here." Teresa turned toward her son, her demeanor asking for confirmation.

Alan's head gave a slight flinch backward, and he narrowed his eyes. Then doubt crept in again. "But what about the bump-up in pay? She has been helping her parents with their medical bills."

"Money's not her thing. She'll find a way to help her family."

"Agreed, she's not a material girl. She doesn't need to be rich. That's one of the things I love about her." The last phrase flowed out of Alan before he knew he said it. His *madre* wagged a finger at him with affection and a knowing smile. Alan squirmed in his boots as he let a bout of lightheadedness subside. "Okay, I said it." Throwing his arms wide, he shouted it again. "I love her!"

"Great!" The volume of his mother's voice matched his. But then she got quiet again. "So, what're you going to do about it?'

"Oh." Alan collapsed onto the cot that sat just under the window. "I know what I want to do, but how?"

Teresa sat next to her son and leaned on him, shoulder to shoulder, teasing him. "I have something I think'll do the trick."

Thank goodness for Olga, Tameka and Jackie. Rachel sat in the dining room of Brett's house, playing Chutes and Ladders with Parrot and her parents. The gals had things under control and were even thankful for the extra income. Poor Brett was still out plowing the roads, which had her worried, but for the most part things were going well in her life.

Because of the back-to-back storms, Rachel's parents had decided to stay until after the New Year. Their new employers were being very understanding. Rachel was so proud of them. Her father worked in the test kitchen of a frozen food company. They wanted him for his ingredient combination ideas and his palate and were willing to accommodate his physical challenges. He always taught the steady stream of chef school interns valuable lessons. They did the chopping and carrying while he imparted wisdom. Rachel was dumbfounded to find out her mother narrated audiobooks. Maria was an accomplished actress. Rachel had had no idea.

This all came out once Rachel returned from Kalispell. She had mentioned the new job offer and how accepting it would make it easier to support her parents, even if the other Welch businesses were struggling. The mill closure made Rachel think of the long-term financial viability of all of the stores in Snowflake. But her parents surprised her by saying they no longer needed their children to send them money. In fact, they were prepared to help pay for the accident-related medical bills.

Of course, Parrot won the board game and then ran outside to build a snowman with his friends. Rachel began making dinner and her parents did what they could to help. Having this quality time with them was a cherished gift. Rachel relished every moment, no matter how they spent the time.

"Are you going to take the job to challenge your nursing skills? Live in a town where there are plenty of young men to date?" These questions came from her dad. Stirring the chili, Rachel gave him a stupefied look. "What? I used to be young once too. Just because I'm your father doesn't mean I've forgotten how difficult it is to find a date. There are slim pickings in Snowflake."

"Oh Luke, don't be silly. There's already one really good catch, and that's all she needs." Maria, who talked with her hands, shook a cookie at her husband, so he mimicked her, oscillating one of his own. Rachel treasured watching her parents enjoy each other's company. She wanted a love like that.

"I know about the doctor, dear. I'm just giving her options."

"Guys! I'm right here." Rachel opened the refrigerator door, pretending to look for something, but really just wanting to change the subject.

Her mother started in with the embarrassing questions. "Well, you just spent most of two whole days with him. What did you think?"

Sighing, Rachel closed the fridge and leaned her back against the door. She couldn't avoid these exploratory questions forever, so she might as spill the juicy details. "He's a magnificent doctor, great to work with, and Bodie likes him." She went back to stirring.

"That's not what I meant, and you know it."

"Okay, I took him to dinner at the Dusty Trail Steakhouse. We had a great time, he can be funny and playful, and he makes me feel safe." Out of the corner of her eye, Rachel saw her parents reach out and hold hands across the table.

"So, you really like this guy?" asked her father.

"I do, but I've kept my distance and been a bit of a jerk." She averted her gaze and turned away. Rachel was annoyed with herself for being commanded by her guilt. Trying not to fidget, she smoothed down the front of her apron. Where was a witty comeback from either of her parents? She put the spoon down.

"That doesn't sound like you." Her mother wheeled toward her. "What happened?"

When Veronica pounced on me at the hospital, I panicked." Rachel cleared her throat, but it went dry. She twisted her wrists. "The comment I blurted out when I saw the amount of the signing bonus." Rachel squeezed her eyes shut. "You should've seen his face. I don't know what he would see in me." Sheesh, it felt good to unburden herself of those misdeeds.

Inching his walker forward, her father joined her at the stove. Having her parents on either side of her made her feel stronger, but that didn't mean Alan could forgive her behavior. She gave each of her parents a pat on the arm.

"And how did he react to hearing about the job offer at the hospital?" asked her dad.

Rachel took a moment to review the pictures of him in her mind. "He was happy for me, then hurt and concerned. But in the end, he was supportive of whatever would make me happy."

Stirring the chili and taking a smell, her father said, "Sounds like a man with a level head on his shoulders."

"Who cares a great deal for you," added her mother, wheeling her way back to the table. "Do you want the hospital job?"

"When I thought we needed the money, I thought I could be happy doing that job. I'm good at it. But I belong in Snowflake." That statement hit Rachel like a snowball between her shoulder blades. *I belong in Snowflake.*

"So, let Sophie and Olga run the café and go work for the good doctor."

Rachel's father made everything sound so easy. *One more hurdle cleared.*

Her confidence was short-lived. "But what if he doesn't want me anymore?"

Maria did a rapid turn in the chair. "Of course he wants you! From what Parrot and Brett say, he's always wanted you."

Cocking her head, Rachel raised one eyebrow at her parents. "Wait, you talk to my brother about my career or my love life?"

In unison, her parents replied, "both."

Rachel stirred the chili more than it needed. This was a bit too much. But she was also grinning inside to know how much her family cared about her happiness. "The two of you think I should date Alan? Is that what you're saying?"

"Do what makes you happy," replied Maria. "But I like the thought of my beautiful daughter dating a caring doctor who's a real looker."

Rachel encircled her mother within her wheelchair and her father hobbled behind her to join in. "You think he's good-looking, really?"

"Of course—he's Cuban, you know."

Rachel joined her parents in a snicker that turned into full belly laughs, but she also thought about when next she might see Alan.

CHAPTER 32

ON THE MORNING of December thirtieth, Alan set his alarm for an hour earlier than he normally did, determined to catch his snow-clearing benefactor in the act. He had internalized his new philosophy of accepting help from others. But he still wanted to thank the selfless person who gave of himself almost every morning. With both sets of fingers encircling a cup of coffee, still in his pajamas and wrapped in the quilt his *madre* had given him for Christmas, Alan waited, peering out from behind a drawn curtain.

Sure enough, a pair of headlights pierced the blackness of pre-dawn. The truck was considered regular-sized for these parts, retro-fitted with a heavy-duty plow that scraped along his rural road. As expected, the truck passed his driveway, made a u-turn, and headed back toward town. The generosity of this man did not surprise Alan. But he hoped he didn't feel beholden to him for having stitched him up.

Alan considered this bill paid several times over. No other debt existed on Monkey's account. The Saint Nick of snowplows was busted. Alan would ask around town to see if Monkey gave this gift to others. He wanted to find a way to ensure this goodwill would be reciprocated. It didn't have to be a one-to-one exchange, but Alan wanted to do his part to keep the kindness merry-go-round of Snowflake operating under its own power.

With a newfound goal in his personal life, Alan made his way through the workday with renewed energy. Sure, it involved nerves, but his happiness meter was off the charts. And his smile was contagious. Even though the patients coming to see him too often weren't feeling well, they left his office with a lighter step and heads held high. His mother could only be described as giddy. Between the two of them, the holiday cheer they sent out into the world was overflowing. They could have bottled and given away joy for free and had enough left to fuel their own reserves for some time.

Alan made a mental to-do list to keep himself focused. But as each task was checked off, his nerves frayed a bit more. He wanted to find a way to speak to Rachel's parents without her being aware. He wasn't sure he believed in fate, but he had to credit this coincidence to something. Alan was given the opportunity he wished for when he found out Rachel and Patsy were going to meet Bodie and his mom to decorate the community center for the New Year's Eve dance.

Alan, running on pure adrenaline, checked off the tasks relating to the next chapter in his life. First, he sent a text to Brett asking for assistance. Next, he made an appointment to meet Bodie about an hour before the Trading Post closed for the night. Alan knew he needed a new outfit for the party.

Later that same evening, Teresa put a plate of food for him on the table before she darted out to meet Bodie. But, Alan's stomach made it clear no additional content would be welcomed at this time. He sat motionless except for his eyes darting every few seconds to check his watch.

Alan had been asked by several women in town to help with the party planning but had a legitimate excuse it each time. He knew that Bodie was the designated carrier of boxes and climber of ladders all afternoon. The tribal elder could handle all of those tasks. The ladies didn't need him too. Alan also realized that being on the decorating committee allowed Bodie to be closer to his mother, and this made the man happy, so he decided not to mention his mother's current stance on dating.

Double checking that the address Brett had texted him was properly loaded into his GPS, Alan started the drive to the Welch residence. Between Brett's, Monkey's and who knew how many other folks' efforts, his route was drivable in his Jeep. He had driven this direction before but seeing it at night with the holiday lights all aglow gave the area a warm feeling. The houses weren't close together, so each batch of decorations shone with a higher level of brightness.

Following the GPS, Alan pulled his white-knuckled hands from ten and two as he turned down a narrow but well-paved street. It ended up being a private road with no other houses. The final turn listed on his phone's directions came up, and the navigation app's voice told him he had arrived. *Okay, so this is supposed to be a driveway?* Alan kept driving. He had Googled the Welch family and found that their land for cattle grazing was not in Snowflake. *What is all this land for?* Was it the front yard? The acreage was big enough to be a hunting ground or an Audubon sanctuary.

Twinkling lights shone through as the trees became more sparse—not that these decorations could be seen from the road. Maybe they were hung for Jacob's benefit because Brett was working so much this time of the year. Then the house came into view. Well, house didn't do this structure justice. Maybe grand lodge or ranch-style hotel suited it better. Big. This place was bigger than big. Alan's stomach grumbled. *Now it wanted food—figured.*

With great caution, Alan took his sweet time, backing his foot off the gas. The two-story log and stone home had a porch that stretched the entire length of the front of the house and beyond. Alan couldn't see it in its entirety. Three dormer windows jutted out on the second floor, and each of them had a set of dancing Christmas lights. All of the gutters and porch support poles were decorated. The natural pine branch wreath on the front door covered the entire top half of the entrance and shimmered as the nearby lights twinkled.

Looking to the side, Alan saw a separate building that had to be the garage. It had three mechanical doors, each wide enough to hold two vehicles. Alan knew Betsy was stored at the M-DOT facility. The cattle ranch equipment wouldn't be stored here either. Alan's mouth went dry. Dress slacks and the business tie under his sweater had been the right way to go. He had chosen them to give himself confidence, but this place looked formal. When Brett had texted him the address, he'd also said three generations of the Welch family had lived here. The full meaning of that fact began to resonate. Parking in a spot that didn't block anyone's access, Alan's Jeep seemed small. Or maybe he was the inconsequential person, with his single-parent upbringing.

Get a hold of yourself. You love her and you are worthy of her love.

Ringing the doorbell, a bottle of Champagne ready to be offered, Alan lengthened his posture and puffed his chest out just a bit, adding his prefab smile. Brett answered the door, Parrot hot on his heels. "Hey, happy New Year! Come on in. My parents are in the living room." Brett's workout pants, house shoes and well-worn Packers sweatshirt allowed Alan to remove the proverbial rod from his spine and enter with ease.

"Dr. G! Daddy and I are gonna build a robot, wanna help?" Alan drew courage from Jacob's enthusiasm and hospitality. The tension in his shoulders relaxed.

Well, until he followed the father and son duo into the living room. This space had to be about the same size as the entire apartment where he'd grown up. "Are Sophie and Christina still doing well? When will they get to come home?" *That a boy Alan, talk about what you know. Medicine.*

"Sophie's gonna stay in town until they release Christina. Maybe another couple of weeks." Brett motioned toward a six-foot-wide brick fireplace complete with a mammoth big-screen TV hung above it. Maria's wheelchair sat next to a recliner that was being put back into its upright position. "Have a seat." He turned to his son. "Hey buddy, let's let the grown-ups talk and go work on that robot."

Parrot jumped on his father's back, piggyback style, and they exited before Alan could think of another clever thing to say. He took a few steps forward, the arm supporting the Champagne levering out as if on autopilot. "Happy New Year! Thanks for seeing me on such short notice." Alan saw Mr. Welch struggle to corral his walker, while Mrs. Welch turned off the television.

"Please," said Alan. "Stay comfortable in this lovely home, I'll come to you."

Luke leaned back in the chair but smiled at him.

Placing the bottle on a coffee table, Alan seated himself in a nearby plush chair and faced Rachel's parents. He could see each of their visual contributions to their beautiful daughter. What an attractive family. *Okay Alan, stop stalling and get to the point.* "Since I moved here things have been challenging. I'm not sure how I would have gotten through it all without Rachel's help. She's an amazing woman."

Alan adjusted his seat on the plush cushion. "As I'm guessing you know, I've offered Rachel a job to work as a nurse with me, but Veronica has sweetened the offer from the hospital." He stopped to allow the Welches to say something, but they didn't, so he kept going.

"Let me tell you a quick story, but feel free to interrupt anytime." The expressions of the parents were warm, but also a bit unreadable. *Just keep going.* "Before I met Rachel, I saw her working in the kitchen at the café and thought she was a short-order cook. No offense—I'm new in town and know very little about the history of the founding families." One side of Alan's mouth tweaked up as a trickle of sweat rolled down his back. He absent-mindedly tugged at his dress shirt's collar.

Poker faces stared back at him.

"I was mesmerized, couldn't wait to get to know her." He laughed at the memory and also as a release valve to his nerves. "I didn't find out she was a nurse until a couple of days later. Anyway, I've grown to care a great deal for Rachel." He swallowed hard. "I love her." *Gosh, it felt good to say that out loud again.*

"I'm here to ask for your blessing to ask Rachel to marry me."

With a whoosh of a forceful exhale, Alan waited for a reaction. The

Welches looked at each other and then back at him, their faces unchanged. *Geez, tough room.*

"I understand this may seem sudden. I'm willing to have a long engagement. I just want Rachel to know how I feel before she makes her decision. You know, continuing to work with me or take the job offer at the hospital." He moved his tongue around in what had become a desert in his mouth to try to get his voice to keep working.

"If she chooses the hospital, I will find a way to make that work. If she chooses the clinic, I know we can keep our personal feelings separate from our work. I mean, look at the two of you, happily married and you worked together." *Okay, you're babbling on. You can shut up now.*

Mr. Welch stumbled toward his walker again. Alan jumped into action to help.

"I've got it. Sit down," Mr. Welch said. "Maria and I may be slower now, but we're very self-sufficient." His bark was stern like he was giving the ranch foreman a dressing down. *Ugh, you blew it.*

"Yes, sir. I can see that you are both very capable." Alan wanted to check his pulse but didn't dare.

Mr. Welch moved his walker up to Alan, and Mrs. Welch swiveled right up beside him. He stuck his hand out. Alan hesitated. The stress of the moment jumbled his ability to see reason. Maria leaned forward, placing her palm against the back of her husband's offer of goodwill. "You have our blessing." She smiled and tears welled up in her eyes. When Alan dared to look at Mr. Welch, tracks of salt stain glistened on his face.

Standing, grasping both hands, Alan shook them with great vigor. "Oh, thank you! That means so much." The muscles in his face softened except for the grin he couldn't hold back. He quelled the urge to jump up and down, but couldn't still the slight tremor running from his head to his toes. His chest seemed to thrust out a bit all on its own.

Composing himself, Mr. Welch spoke again, this time with a soft and quivering voice. "We appreciate that you showed us enough respect to ask permission to wed our only daughter."

Alan wanted to smother them both with a hug but decided to give each of their shoulders a squeeze. "You're welcome. To be honest, my *madre* had the idea."

The Welches both chuckled out loud, but Maria jumped in with, "She's a wonderful woman. I knew I'd like her the moment I tasted her flan."

Mr. Welch gave Alan an obvious wink. "Oh, and if I were a betting man, I wouldn't like Veronica's odds of buying Rachel back to the hospital."

WITH THE MOST nerve-racking conversation Alan had ever endured completed, he made his way to the Trading Post. He didn't remember driving, just that he had arrived. He'd texted ahead the goal of his shopping spree (he wanted to look good, more like a local on New Year's Eve), and Bodie, in his usual organized manner, had a selection of possible ensembles in Alan's sizes ready for inspection.

"I will repeat to you the justification my female staff gave me when they made these choices," said Bodie, looking a bit uncomfortable. "I am not a man of fashion, as you know."

Alan tried on the outfit the ladies had recommended as the best look for him. He came out of the dressing room and stood in front of the three-way mirror.

Bodie cleared his throat. "The ladies said these jeans will be better at accentuating your posterior." He paused and looked at the floor. "Well, they used another word I'm choosing to not repeat."

Alan did an about-face and looked at the reflection of his backside. He shrugged with one eyebrow raised.

Bodie continued, "This dark green sweater with flecks of a golden yellow in it while being manly, will bring out the flecks of color from your hazel eyes." He was visibly uncomfortable. "Again, their words, not mine."

Alan stepped closer to the mirror. He was astonished, but the women who worked for Bodie were right. "I'll take it. Great work." He tried to stifle his snicker. "I appreciate you relaying the wisdom of your staff."

"They advise that you wash the jeans at least twice with fabric softener before wearing." With that statement, Bodie left, striding at a fast pace to get back to his position at the cash register. The first thing Alan did when he got home was to throw the new jeans in the washer.

Climbing into bed, he thought, *that's another thing checked off the list.*

CHAPTER 33

ON NEW YEAR'S EVE, Alan decided to leave his Jeep at the office. He walked to the community center alone. His new jeans had been washed three times and his sweater still smelled of fabric softener. His nerves were in disarray, but the air was crisp, and the Montana skies he had grown to love were clear. The clouds in Miami just didn't have the same effect on him as the variety in these parts. He couldn't explain it, but this patch of sky was special.

Bodie had picked up his mother in the sleigh, which was fine because making small talk until the trio arrived at the party was the last thing Alan wanted to do. He had rehearsed what he wanted to say to the woman he loved a thousand times.

Making a detour to the church across from the celebration, Alan looked up at the giant lit snowflakes and made his way around to view all four sides again. Maybe the third time would be the charm. He reminded the beaming light about the details of his wish. *I wished that Rachel could be with me for the rest of my life.* Like the first time he'd had the opportunity to experience the legend, the pastor came out to greet him.

"Alan. Hello, so nice to see you. Has your wish been granted yet? I try to document these things."

Alan flashed the pastor a smile and searched his pockets. Showing him the small square black velvet box, he whispered, "Can you keep a secret? I'm going to ask her tonight. If she says yes, then my wish will come true."

The pastor laughed out loud, then lowered his voice. "I'm certain Rachel will say yes." Looking up at the grand white lights of the snowflakes, he added, "Thank you." Then he bowed his head as he said a silent prayer.

"But I never said who I was going to ask. How did you know?"

"Ah, when Rachel came to ask me to help with your, um, rumor situation, the passion with which she spoke about your good character was a tell. Her feelings for you had to be more than respect. They were unconditional love." With great care, the pastor wrapped his stole around the delicate ring box, blessing it, and praying that the man holding it might find his true path that night.

Hearing these words warmed Alan's heart. As he stood basking in the glow of the lights, his nerves calmed and his courage soared. It had taken a storm in Miami to allow him to eventually find love for a lifetime in Montana.

GIVING the ribbon in her hair a final yank to affix it in place, Rachel looked at herself in the mirror. Flashy make-up and diva-dressing were not her thing, but for New Year's Eve, she'd try a bit harder. Usually, her getting-ready routine was designed to make her look awake and healthy. Tonight, she wanted to look her best. Pretty even, if she could manage it. She knew moving around the dance floor created heat. A sweater would be too much. So she wore a fitted blouse in pink and her most curve-hugging jeans. Her nursing scrubs or café apron hid her feminine wiles, but tonight she wanted them on display. Well, she wanted Alan to see she had them.

With growing excitement, Rachel looked forward to continuing to work with Alan and hoped beyond hope that the city council would stay out of her romantic life. She'd already politely told Veronica no thank you, so all of her nursing career eggs were in one basket. She wanted to live in Snowflake. Only one nursing job existed in town, and that was at the clinic, working with Alan.

How lucky she had been to be born a Welch and grow up with parents who loved her so much. She realized maybe she had misinterpreted people's actions after they found out she was a Welch. With another "wish, you were here" call to Sophie complete, she gathered her beloved family to ring in the New Year with the townspeople she loved.

A blast of country music hit her ears when she arrived, and Rachel was met at the door by a very pregnant, waddling Patsy. "The decorations looked better than I thought they could," shouted her friend over the twanging guitars. "This place is packed. The break in the weather brought everyone out to celebrate."

"Happy New Year!" Rachel hugged Pasty and wandered through the hall, enjoying the ambiance of the evening. Some of the Christmas decorations remained, like the big twinkling tree by the fire, but the mirror ball and silver streamers gave the room a dreamy look. People played with the noisemakers and popped confetti already dusted the floor. The popcorn machine was in high gear, and the buttery smell made the party atmosphere complete.

As part of her New Year's resolution, Rachel stayed away from the kitchen area, putting herself in vacation mode. This shindig was BYOB, and the snacks were Mrs. Jameson and Mrs. Wilson's concern. Free to enjoy herself, Rachel looked to see if Alan had arrived. She spied him giving Parrot a high five, which started a dainty flutter from the butterflies in her stomach. *Wow, he looks good. That must be a new outfit. Or maybe he'd dug deep into his closet tonight.*

Just as she was about to meander through the crowd to say hello, Irene and Heidi called out to her. *Oh geez, what now.* Making her way to the refreshment table, she reminded herself the night was young and these two loving ladies meant well. She shared the usual holiday pleasantries and sighed when the conversation turned to the latest gossip about town, concerning when the mill would open. Deep in her thoughts of how she could free herself from this conversation, Rachel didn't notice the music had changed to a slow dance.

A musky male scent mixed with the smell of popcorn approached, but she was too absorbed in trying to not cross her arms over her chest and squelching the blossoming scowl from her face to notice. Comfort and the sense of a perfect fit engulfed her fingers as someone clutched them. She knew in an instant, it was Alan. "May I have this dance?" *Alan saves me again.*

"Yes, please."

The dance floor was crowded, but all Rachel could see was Alan. With a commanding tug, he pulled her into his arms and led her in swaying to the beat. "You look amazing," he whispered in her ear. Then his palms fell to her waist. His strong fingers squeezed her. She heard a subtle moan escape his lips over the din. Willing herself not to blush, she looked up to meet his gaze. What she saw was confidence and heat. It made her smile. Content to enjoy being in his arms, she leaned in until the song ended, and was not surprised by how well their bodies fit together. A perfect match. Meant to be.

"Let's go outside." Alan escorted her to the coatroom. "I could use some air. I hear this is a dark sky area, and I want to see what it's like." Alan guided her to a northern-facing bench made from a natural tree, with bark on the underside, but smooth on the top for seating. He put his arm around her. She watched him take in the nighttime sky she'd known all her life.

"See the North Star, and you can follow your line of sight to the Big Dipper," she said.

"This is so beautiful, much better than what I could see from the inner city of Miami."

Glad that Alan seemed so, at ease, she continued the stargazing. "And if you look a little higher, you can see Cassiopeia and Pegasus."

He touched his cheek to hers, following her line of sight. She didn't dare move, but she managed to lean in, allowing as much of her to touch him as she could, her lips parting. This was heaven. Talk of jobs could wait. *Oh, kiss me. A kiss would be good about now.*

"Auntie Rach. Auntie Rach."

She'd heard that phrase often the past couple of days. She grinned as Parrot's footsteps came up behind her.

Rachel turned to greet her beloved nephew and had to chuckle at his timing. "Jacob, why did you come out without your coat?"

"Auntie Rach, play my game with me."

"Okay." *Where was this coming from?*

"Will you marry me?"

Rachel was confused as Jacob turned and ran toward the party. "Parrot, come back. Who said that?" She hadn't noticed that Alan had shifted. Out of the corner of her eye, she saw movement but settled back in her seat.

Startled by his new pose, she gasped. He was down on one knee, looking up at her with a joyous expression.

"Rachel Welch. Cupid shot my heart the day we met, and I've been falling in love with you ever since. I want us to be together as long as we both shall live. Wherever you are, I want to be. Whatever job you choose, we'll make it work together. I love you with all my heart. Will you marry me?"

Then he presented her with a small box. Through the mist welling up in her eyes, Rachel smiled seeing a sparkle coming from within. She gasped again—she couldn't help herself. She had dreamed of finding the perfect man who could complement her in every way. Now he was here in front of her, on bended knee.

"Yes! Oh, yes. Of course, yes." The answer flowed out of her.

Standing, tugging her into his arms, he kissed her, a deep, loving kiss that made her entire body tingle. Now she was quivering, not from the cold, but from sheer happiness and excitement. Fumbling for her left hand, he tried to put the engagement ring on her finger. She did her best to hold still but couldn't. Alan managed to glide the diamond into place. He kissed her again and joyous laughter escaped from both of them as their lips made their own music.

"It's my grandmother's. My maternal grandmother's ring. But if you want something modern, we can pick one out together." Alan stepped back to view her bejeweled hand.

Trembling no more, Rachel peered as the beauty of the setting pierced the haze caused by the eagerness. The ring was perfect, white gold with a large marquise-cut stone, complimented by two smaller emerald-cut diamonds.

"I love it." She kissed him again. "And I love you more." Wiping the tears from her face, she blurted out, "I told Veronica no thank you."

Alan got back down on one knee, looking serious, but grinning at the same time. "Will you be my partner in life and in healing?"

Hauling him up, Rachel unleashed a big laugh, jolly full-body laughter. She felt safe, respected, wanted and loved. This was the best day of her life. "I will."

They went back inside, and Rachel raised an eyebrow when she found all of her family and Teresa hovering by the entrance. Rachel flashed them a smile and flipped up her diamond-studded left hand. She was enfolded by a group hug that lingered for a good long while. Next, no surprise to Rachel, Mrs. Jameson and Mrs. Wilson swooped in to see what all the fuss was about. With much fanfare, Rachel got passed around the dance floor with Alan in tow, everyone asking for a look at her sparkling finger. The next song was another slow dance, and the good people of Snowflake went back to celebrating the coming of the New Year.

Afterward, Alan accompanied Rachel back outside. "Let's go to the church. I have one more thing I want to tell you." He walked her all the way around, gazing up at each of the four beautiful and blazing electric snowflakes without saying a word. Guiding her back to the front door of the church, Alan asked, "Have you heard about the legend of making a wish the first time you see the decorations lit?"

"Of course. Mrs. Jameson uses it to promote the town all the time." She turned to Alan with a puzzled look. "I was pretty young when I was old enough to make a wish."

"And did it come true?"

"Absolutely. I got a pony for my fifth birthday."

"I wished for you." He kissed her. "I mean, I wished that you would be a part of my life as long as we both shall live."

Rachel's shimmering left hand flew to her heart. "That's so sweet."

The tears flowed again. But through the soft sobs, she managed to say, "I love you so much."

As they were snuggling and kissing some more, the pastor came out. "I see another kind of celebration is in order tonight."

"She said yes!" shouted Alan. "The legend of the wish really does work."

"I'm so glad. The two of you belong together." And then with a cheeky grin, he showed them the camera he'd been hiding. "Can I take a picture?

"Of course," Rachel laughed.

Standing in a hug, with her engagement ring resting on Alan's shoulder for the camera to see, Rachel kissed her best doctor, best friend and best man.

- THE END -

EPILOGUE

Rachel and Alan got married the following June, and the snowflakes were put back up to honor the occasion. The wedding party consisted of Brett, Sophie, Monkey and Patsy, along with four of Alan's cousins. Jacob was the ring bearer and he did a good job of teaching Alan's niece how to be the flower girl. For a wedding in Snowflake, this bridal party was huge. But that paled in comparison to the wedding reception. The community center overflowed since a large Garcia contingent from Miami came to join in the celebrations.

At first, Alan moved in with Rachel into the apartment above the café, but the new Mr. and Mrs. Garcia saved up to buy land near the lake where they'd had their original date, set up by Mrs. Jameson and Mrs. Wilson. Monkey started asking Olga to join him for group activities to get to know her better. Sophie and Christina came back to Snowflake in good health. With the mill reopening, the businesses in the town flourished. The population of Snowflake soon topped 700.

Bodie added a welcoming center to the other services his Trading Post already offered. He bided his time waiting for Teresa to come around to the idea of a date. Mrs. Jameson used the engagement picture taken on New Year's Eve to make Snowflake into a destination wedding location. Brett received a commendation for his plow management plan that had saved Snowflake's and many other mountain towns' Christmas celebrations. Parrot earned the lead in his first-grade play, portraying a young George Washington. Of course, memorizing the lines was not a problem for the future movie star.

Alan encouraged Rachel to become a nurse practitioner. The two years, while she stayed in or commuted back and forth to Kalispell, weren't easy, but the medical clinic and the growing town benefited from her expanded education. Rachel ended up giving Alan a gift when she graduated—the news that he would soon be a father for the first time.

A new tradition was born in Snowflake. In early December the town hosted a festival of lights. People flocked from all fifty states to make a wish when the four brilliant, decorative snowflakes' on-switch was flipped. Thousands of wishes were made, and they really did come true.

ABOUT THE AUTHOR

Vickey Wollan caught the writing bug in elementary school, and her thirst for reading novels started in junior high. Although her career included journalistic and public relations writing, she recently jumped with both feet into writing romance stories.

She writes heartwarming, sweet, contemporary romances that tickle the funny-bone and wrap up with an always satisfying happily ever after.

Vickey lives in Central Florida, but her stories tend to be inspired from traveling. She likes the outdoors and sports so she creates heroines who are strong and multi-talented, but are still attracted to sexy modern men who appreciate the love of a capable woman.

With a background in wellness, she allows her creativity to emerge during a good workout. When not writing, she enjoys spending time reading and hiking through the beauty of nature or chilling-out with her husband.

She appreciates hearing from readers. Reach out to her at vickeywollanauthor@yahoo.com !

OTHER BOOKS BY VICKEY WOLLAN

A Snowflake Christmas is the first book in a three-book series. *A Snowflake Christmas – The Nutcracker* will be released in 2021.

Romancing the Holiday – A First Coast Romance Writers Anthology - Vickey Wollan was one of twelve authors who contributed a short story to this fundraising project. Proceeds from this novel benefit FCRW, a non-profit affiliate of Romance Writers of America®, that helps writers hone their craft and expand their knowledge of the publishing industry. A portion of the proceeds are also donated to FeedAmerica.org. More information about the anthology can be found at https://www.firstcoastromancewriters.com and at ebook retailers.

PLACES TO CONNECT WITH VICKEY WOLLAN

If you liked *A Snowflake Christmas*, she would greatly appreciate it if you left a review.

Here are her social media coordinates:

Website: https://vickeywollan.wordpress.com

Newsletter: https://mailchi.mp/dd2e4421315a/vickey-wollan-newsletter

Facebook author page: https://facebook.com/vickeywollanauthor

LinkedIn: https://linkedin.com/in/vickeywollan

Twitter: https://twitter.com/vickeywollan-author

Made in the USA
Monee, IL
18 November 2020